The Butcher and the Butterfly

Jim Antonini

Pump Fake Press—Morgantown, WV
Paperback ISBN: 979-8-218-53049-5
eBook ISBN: 979-8-218-53050-1
Library of Congress Control Number: 2024924358
Title: *The Butcher and the Butterfly*
Author: Jim Antonini
Digital distribution | 2024
Paperback | 2024

Published in the United States by New Book Authors Publishing

Dedication

I met the brilliant and eccentric painter Noel Rockmore in early 1990 at Johnny White's, a since-closed, infamous French Quarter dive bar, on my first visit to New Orleans. We watched a boxing match together there one evening. We had a great time. He was quite the boxing fan. He told me about his wonderful paintings, some of which hung on the walls of the bar. They were stained from years of exposure to cigarette smoke. I would meet with him again in the years before he passed. The last time I saw him we listened to Nirvana songs that he played on the jukebox repeatedly to the dismay of many of the bar regulars. He especially liked "Heart-Shaped Box." The story behind The Butcher and the Butterfly emerged from the smoky haze of those lazy afternoons spent there.

I also thank my friend Emmy Lowe for the brilliant cover artwork.

Book One

Introduction

Chapter One

The small arena was filled beyond capacity. Parked cars lined the clogged streets of the surrounding neighborhoods. Traffic was at a standstill. Over four-thousand tickets had been sold for the event, despite the venue having only three-thousand available seats. Hundreds of boxing fans milled about outside, still in search of tickets. The Baltimore County Fire Marshall and teams of local fire departments were on standby around the arena. So were the area news media. Bobby Raymond, the Baltimore Kid, was scheduled to fight in his hometown.

Despite it being a snowy December night, the arena was exceptionally hot and humid. The air conditioning hadn't been turned on in months. Building maintenance couldn't get it to work that evening on short notice after the indoor temperature soared due to the excessive number of bodies inside. The stuffy air was hazed with white smoke that hung heavy in the upper rafters of the antiquated arena.

Many in the crowd were drunk and raucous, having tailgated outside for most of the day as they roasted turkeys, grilled sausages and burgers, and drank copious amounts of beer and whiskey. The concession stands inside the arena were nearly sold out of beer. The pungent smell of cigars was everywhere, and the skunky aroma of marijuana lingered in the restrooms.

The overcapacity crowd stomped their feet and clapped in unison, imploring Bobby on to what was expected to be a certain victory. But the bout to that point was a toss-up as the ninth round ended—only one round left. It wasn't supposed to be that way. Bobby was heavily favored against the journeyman brawler, Alex Grainger. The fight against Grainger was supposed to be a tune-up for Bobby, one step closer to a top boxing ranking as well as a shot at the Light Heavyweight World Championship. But Grainger proved to be a formidable foe. He was experienced, but Raymond's camp believed Grainger didn't have the skillset to compete with Bobby. What they couldn't predict was Grainger's toughness and heart. No one had a bigger heart. And he had a powerful right hand. He punched hard.

The match was brutal. It was a bloodbath. A videotape of it could have been used as a more-than-convincing exhibit on the dangers of boxing and the need to outlaw it. The faces of both fighters were swollen. Blood, sweat, and spit covered the soiled canvas mat. Grainger's strategy was to pound Bobby's body—weaken him and drain his spirit. But he also knew he'd have to withstand the assault of Bobby's numerous hard right-hand crosses and uppercuts in the early rounds. Grainger's only chance to beat Bobby was to outlast him. His plan to that point had worked.

As the seconds ticked away in the ninth round, Grainger, his left eye swollen shut, had Bobby trapped in a corner, pounding at his ribs and kidney on the left side of his body. Bobby could hardly breathe as the bell rang, ending the round. The crowd, on their feet, cheered wildly. Bobby was in extreme pain as he awkwardly staggered like a drunk to his corner and pounced on the stool with a grimace.

"This is it!" his trainer screamed.

The cut men feverishly worked over him, pressing a piece of ice-cold metal against the swollen areas of his face as well as covering small cuts over his eyes and nose with a thick ointment.

"The last round! It's close, Bobby! You can't blow it now! You need to win this round!"

"Goddamn," Bobby muttered, nearly out breath. "He hits hard."

The trainer forced Bobby to drink water from an unlabeled plastic bottle. The cut men repeatedly splashed water in Bobby's face.

"You quit throwin' the right!" the trainer yelled. "Where's the right hand?"

"It's busted," Bobby mumbled, extending out his right arm, showing his cornermen the massive swelling around his right wrist and forearm. "It feels like a bag of broken rocks."

"You have to use it!" the trainer barked.

"I can't!"

"Use it! He can't see it!"

Bobby winced as he struggled to his feet, still gasping for air. The crowd chanted his name.

"Bobby! Bobby! Bobby!"

"Use the right!" the trainer shouted over the crowd as he reinserted the dripping mouthpiece into Bobby's mouth.

"There's nothing left."

"Don't quit," his trainer said while desperately shaking and rubbing

Bobby's fatigued and battered arms. "One more round! You never quit before, Bobby! Give me three more minutes! Throw the right hand! He can't see it! His left eye is closed shut!"

The bell rang to start the tenth and final round. Grainger charged. The crowd roared and continued to chant.

"Bobby! Bobby! Bobby!"

Grainger threw a hooking body punch that landed hard to Bobby's kidney. The crowd oohed then hissed, showering the ring with boos. Bobby's knees buckled as he doubled over and clutched onto Grainger, making it difficult for him to throw another punch.

"Come on, ref!" Bobby's trainer shouted. "The low blows!"

The referee separated the two sweaty fighters who were draped over each other in exhaustion and pain. Grainger charged again. Bobby chomped down on his mouthpiece and threw a wild right hook that caught Grainger squarely on the chin. The crowd exploded with excitement. Woozy, Grainger's legs buckle.

Bobby closed his eyes as the intense pain from the punch radiated from his broken right hand up his arm to the back of his shoulder. He then led with an overhand right to the middle of Grainger's face. The crowd roared louder.

As Grainger started to fall, Bobby nailed him with one last right cross to the side of the head. Grainger's mouthpiece flew out of the ring and into the third row of seats. Knocked unconscious, Grainger's limp body dropped to the canvas with a thud, shaking the entire ring. His trainer and cornermen as well as other medics in attendance dashed through the ropes to attend to him as the rowdy, cheering crowd filled the arena air with tossed cups of beer and soda and bags of popcorn and peanuts in celebration.

Bobby was too exhausted and beaten to even lift his arms in victory. He staggered to his stool in the corner and collapsed. A river of blood flowed uncontrollably from one of his nostrils. His broken right hand and puffy face were numb. It felt as if a knife had been stabbed into his left kidney.

He was nauseous and felt like vomiting. His heart raced. He struggled to catch his breath as numerous members of his corner and entourage converged and smothered him in excitement. The chants of *"Bobby! Bobby! Bobby!"* faintly echoed in his ringing ears as he struggled to stay awake, slipping in and out of consciousness.

Chapter Two

Holly, an aspiring ballerina, effortlessly twirled across the stage. She freely and easily floated among the other dancers as if she were connected to the music. She danced with a popular ballet company in New Orleans. They regularly performed in a theater in Louis Armstrong Park not far from the busy French Quarter nightlife district. She currently was the female lead in the famous ballet, *Giselle*.

It was nearing the end of the fall season. Every seat in the theater was sold out. Word had spread quickly around the area about the confident young dancer who had mesmerized audiences all season in the challenging role. Glowing reviews by local newspapers and entertainment critics were unanimous in their overwhelming approval of her charismatic stage presence and her emotive style of dancing.

She'd been training and taking ballet classes four to five nights a week for well over a decade. She had started when she was twelve years old after moving to New Orleans with her father, who went there in search of work. Her mother had unexpectedly died, and her father was looking for a fresh start. He recognized his daughter's sense of balance, athleticism, and almost unnatural flexibility at an early age. A co-worker suggested that he enroll her in dance classes. Her father also needed a babysitter. The nightly ballet classes kept her busy, focused, and constantly under adult supervision as he worked.

Because of Holly's recent success, the many injuries she endured through the years finally seemed worth it. She had them all—from back spasms to pinched nerves, slipped discs, two concussions, sprained ankles, shin splints, and blistered and broken feet. Her dream of dancing professionally was finally coming true.

As that night's performance of *Giselle* was nearing its solemn finale, Holly and the male lead were the only two dancers left on stage. As Giselle, she gracefully fluttered on point in a circle around the male lead. The hushed crowd was hypnotized. As the character, Albrecht, the male lead, desperately scrambled after her as she spun away from him, stopping at a tombstone with her name, Giselle, etched across it. He reached for her. She collapsed into his arms. They frantically searched each other's eyes. They longingly stared. She presented him a white rose and slowly slid away from him.

In a cloud of white smoke, she disappeared from the stage at the foot of the tombstone. Some in the audience audibly sighed; others cried. In despair, the male lead dramatically staggered to the front of the stage and buried his distraught face in his bended arm, letting the rose fall from his fingers. The stage lights suddenly went black, and the curtain dropped to thunderous applause from the crowd.

Chapter Three

Most of the hyped crowd in the cramped arena had gone home. Wearing only his blood-stained boxing shorts, Bobby sat alone in a puddle of sweat on a wobbly stool in an empty locker room. Several towels that had been soaked in cold water were draped over his back, shoulders, and head to cool his body. He was feverish. He couldn't stop perspiring. He still struggled to breathe.

The cuts over his eyes and on his cheeks burned, despite having been stitched immediately after the fight. He soaked his busted right-hand in a bucket of ice water. The bloody contents of his emptied stomach floated in a spit bucket behind him. In his left hand, he held a gold necklace. It was given to him when he was a young boy by his grandmother the night before she died. He would tape it to his ankle before fights for good luck. Squeezing the necklace more tightly, he started to sob. He couldn't stop the stream of tears that followed. Grainger had broken him.

Dropping his head forward, Bobby closed his eyes. He thought of his brother, Chuck, and one of the last times they spent together, vivid visions of the events that night. He wished he could go back in time and change them.

On that night as his boxing career was beginning to flourish, he and his brother were cruising the freeway on the outskirts of downtown Baltimore.

With a beer bottle between his legs, Bobby drove at a high rate of speed. He was twenty-one years old. Chuck was only eighteen. They were laughing and quite inebriated. Both felt invincible. Bobby glanced to Chuck who took a long drag of marijuana off a joint.

"Gimme some," Bobby said, reaching out.

Chuck held the joint out to him. As Bobby grasped it, he briefly glanced away from the road. The car suddenly veered to the left. Bobby quickly looked back to the roadway as the car careened into the median. Looks of fear had replaced their playful laughter. Chuck placed his hands on the dashboard, bracing for impact. Neither wore a seatbelt.

"Shit!" Bobby screamed as he tightly grabbed the steering wheel and slammed his foot on the brakes, losing control of the car.

The runaway car violently smashed into the back of a parked Maryland State Police car. The airbags in Bobby's car were initiated. The windshield exploded. Shards of glass, sparkling like diamonds under the bright freeway lights, flew everywhere. The car rolled over several times. Both Bobby and Chuck were ejected into the back seat. The smell of burning rubber and spilled gasoline filled the air. The night went black. With their bodies tangled together, both were briefly knocked unconscious.

The wooden door to the locker room swung open and banged against the wall, bringing Bobby back to reality. He lifted the towel off his head to see who it was. Tony Cannavaro, Bobby's agent, hurriedly entered. Grinning from ear to ear, he talked into one phone held against the side of his face and looked to the screen of another, before glancing to Bobby.

"You'll never believe this?" Tony excitedly called out, putting the phones away.

"Get me out of here," Bobby said as he wiped sweat from his head and back with the soaked and soiled towels.

"Do you know who I was just talking to?"

"Get me out of here, Tony. Now!"

"What?"

"The ringside doc wants to admit me to the city hospital tonight," he said, struggling to his feet. "I have to get out of here."

"You think that's a good idea? You got beat up pretty good."

"Get me out of here."

"Let 'em check you out. I need you healthy, buddy. We may have a big fight with a big payday in the coming months."

"Where's your car?" Bobby asked, pulling a hooded sweatshirt and track pants over his sweaty and bruised body.

"Can you even walk?"

"You may have to help me."

"Are you sure this is a good idea? You really should have the doctors check you out."

"Get me out of here."

Chapter Four

The sold-out crowd in the packed theater clapped and stomped their feet in unison. The group of tired but thrilled ballet dancers tried to catch their breath. They stood behind a heavy curtain that had dropped on *Giselle*, one of their final shows of the season. With her mascara running and her make-up smeared, Holly rested her outstretched arm on her male lead's shoulder. They both breathed heavily.

It had been a successful run of performances. With the fall season nearly over, the ballet had only one show left for the year. The group was to perform *The Nutcracker* during the coming Christmas holiday. Holly gushed as the other dancers gathered around and hugged her. The dancers looked like giddy grade school kids on the last day of school before summer break. The group's director wildly clapped in approval from the back of the stage.

The crowd continued to loudly cheer. Holly gestured the group of dancers to line up across the stage and hold hands. The director nodded to a pair of stagehands on each side of the curtain. They pulled on a set of ropes that lifted it. Everyone in the audience stood and cheered louder. The male lead nudged Holly forward. She looked at him and shook her head.

She was beaming.

He smiled and nodded. She stepped forward to the front of the stage. The crowd roared louder. Awkwardly, she waved and bowed. The crowd continued to applaud for many minutes. Continuing to wave, she scanned the packed theater several times, wiping at the tears that filled her sparkling emerald eyes.

Chapter Five

Wearing sunglasses to hide his damaged face, Bobby slowly limped through the night towards the small family-style Royal Tavern in the neighborhood in which he grew up. He needed a drink to dull the pain, and perhaps several shots of whiskey to help him sleep later. It usually took weeks for him to recover, both physically and mentally, after a tough fight.

Excited conversations from the small pub could be heard from blocks away as he approached the place. The large plate glass window in front was fogged over. He hesitated a moment before pulling the heavy oak door open with his left hand and shuffled inside with the collar of his coat pulled up over each side of his face in a futile attempt to not be recognized. His bandaged and broken right hand was buried deep in his leather jacket. He kept the sunglasses over his eyes.

The place was warm and cozy, but also was somewhat crowded. Although it was several weeks before Christmas, the bar was elaborately decorated. The house lights were dimmed. Multicolored Christmas lights and a large neon National Bohemian beer advertisement cast a festive glow over the small neighborhood pub.

There was a buzz in the air, obviously from Bobby's thrilling fight from earlier in the evening. The folks were there to celebrate. All the televisions were turned to a local sports highlight show that showed continual replays of the bout. Bobby was immediately recognized as a loud cheer rang out after he entered. Continually nodding to his adoring fans who patted him on the back and shook his left hand, he took a seat at an empty barstool at the end of the bar.

Charlie, the bartender, immediately greeted him with a bottle of Irish whiskey and two shot glasses. He poured the shots out, one for himself and one for Bobby who reached for it with his left hand.

"What a fight! What a fight!" Charlie called out unable to contain his enthusiasm as they knocked back the shots of whiskey. "You had us worried. But what a fight. What a win, Bobby. What a win!"

"Does this look like the face of a winner?" Bobby asked, lifting the sunglasses away from his blackened and swollen eyes and pushing the empty shot glass forward. "Gimme another."

Before pouring the next shot, Charlie studied Bobby's damaged face. Both eyes were bruised and bloodshot, swollen nearly shut. Small lines of stitches tracked over each eye and on one of his cheekbones. They appeared like tiny forgotten railroad tracks. A gaping purple and yellow cut oozed on the bridge of his puffy nose.

Charlie poured them each another shot. Bobby raised his glass. Charlie followed.

"And keep 'em coming. This is all I got to help me sleep tonight," Bobby said, before they drained the shots. "And get everyone in here a drink on me."

A loud cheer rang out after Charlie informed the patrons at the bar they had a free drink coming. As wild celebration swirled in the pub around him, Bobby pulled from the pocket of his jacket a photo of his brother, Chuck, and studied it a moment.

Chapter Six

The ballet dancers were crammed together in the tight confines of the theater's small dressing room. Several of the young ladies in the group were crying. It was the end of a demanding season for many of them. It would be the last time some of the ladies would ever see each other. Only a handful of them were performing in *The Nutcracker* later that month, and many wouldn't be continuing with the group in the spring.

Holly sat alone and stared into a lighted mirror. She had already changed clothes. Brushing at her blonde curly hair, she rushed to wipe the smudged mascara and make-up from her face. Gina, one of the younger dancers, approached her.

"Are you joining us for dinner?"

"I can't," Holly said, staring at herself in the mirror.

"Come on. We're celebrating. We're going for drinks after. Everyone is coming."

"I wish I could."

"It's closing night for many of us. Come celebrate."

"I really can't," Holly said, still trying to remove the make-up from her face.

"Do you have other plans?" Gina asked, but Holly didn't respond. "You always seem in a hurry to leave after the shows."

"I have to work."

"Every night?"

"Just about," Holly said, still not looking at Gina.

"Where?"

Holly turned towards the young lady, but she didn't answer.

"Can you meet us after then?" Gina asked.

"It'll be late."

"You were really great this week," Gina said as the two continued to stare. "Everyone loved you. The fans. The reporters. The other girls. I'm glad I got to meet you. You're going to be a big star."

Holly nodded with a polite smile.

"Are you coming back in the spring?" Holly asked.

"I think so."

"Good," Holly answered as she turned back to the mirror. "I think you're great as well."

"Thank you," Gina blushed. "Are you sure you can't change your plans and come to dinner with us?"

"Sorry," Holly said without any expression, studying herself in the mirror.

Chapter Seven

With a cigarette dangling from his lips and still wearing the sunglasses, Bobby stood over the filthy and stained urinal of the Royal Tavern's lone bathroom. He leaned forward and braced himself against the tiled wall behind the urinal with his bent left arm. He had a strong urge to piss but was struggling to get something to flow. Both sides of his lower back ached from the kidney punches he'd endured from Grainger. He strained for several minutes until he started to urinate. He cringed as the pain nearly took his breath away. He watched the urinal fill with the rusty, brown-colored urine that leaked from his body.

"Holy, motherfuck," he quietly muttered to himself. "Damn."

After he finished, he continued to lean against the wall for many more seconds. He took several deep quick breaths, hoping the pain in his sides would go away. He refused to look back into the urinal, afraid to see what had come out of his battered lower body. Finally, he zipped up and took several hard drags on the cigarette, before tossing the spent butt in the urinal.

He gingerly moved to the bathroom sink and washed up. After drying his hands, he took off the sunglasses and studied his badly beaten face in the clouded mirror above the sink. He lightly touched at his puffy eyes, nose, and lips. He barely looked human.

Disgusted at the reflection that glared back, he slammed his open left hand against the wall beside the mirror and closed his eyes. The vision of the car wreck with his brother Chuck returned.

Blue and red lights repeatedly flashed from several police cars. He and his brother moaned in pain as the local firemen and paramedics cut them out from their mangled car. He glanced to his brother, whose face was scratched and bloodied.

"You all right?" he asked him.

His brother nodded.

Safely out of the car, dazed and shaken, they were given water to drink and sat on the ground close to where Bobby's car impacted the back end of the totaled state police cruiser. Luckily, it had been an empty decoy along the highway to slow the speedy drivers. Empty beer bottles were scattered around the wreckage. The state policeman who filed the accident report approached them.

"Who was drivin'?"

The two brothers stared at each other a moment. After an initial hesitation, Bobby motioned to Chuck.

"Is that right, son?" the cop asked, looking to Chuck.

In near shock and disbelief, Chuck angrily glared at his brother.

"Is that right?" the cop asked again.

Bobby closed his eyes and turned away.

"I'm not askin' again," the cop said with a more serious tone, staring at Chuck. "Were you drivin' this vehicle?"

"Yes," Chuck mumbled, still glaring at his brother.

A knock at the bathroom door startled Bobby back to the present. He turned on the faucet again and wetted his burning face before taking one long last look at himself in the mirror. It would be many days before he could look at himself again.

Chapter Eight

Neon lit the night as Holly rushed through the growing crowd that clogged the narrow Bourbon Street. She avoided eye contact as the crush of strangers buzzed by her, staring only at the uneven brick sidewalks. This had been her routine just about every evening for the past several years. She stopped at the front of Russell's, one of the most popular gentlemen's clubs in the area. Blinking white light bulbs brightly illuminated the club's entrance. Like most nights, she took a deep breath before entering.

The busy club was rowdy. Its patrons were drunk and horny. It smelled of spilled beer, sweat, and cheap cologne. Desperation hovered in the air. Multiple young ladies stripped under large spotlights on different stages throughout the dark club. Confrontation lurked in the shadows. Bouncers were stationed everywhere. Holly raced to a room in back.

Russell, the club's owner, sat behind a massive nineteenth century antique wooden desk, smoking a cigar and sipping high-end bourbon. He was in his mid-fifties and slightly built. He had a silver front tooth, sported greased hair dyed black, and wore several rings made of gold and diamonds. He counted tall stacks of cash that were piled in front him.

Holly entered the backroom and passed through his smoke-filled office into a dressing room where other young ladies were changing into skimpy outfits. She hurriedly pulled off her coat, exposing a tight negligee underneath. She quickly glanced into a mirror and checked her freshly applied make-up before heading for a door that led back into the club.

"Wait," Russell snapped.

Holly stopped at the door but didn't turn to him. Russell got up from his cushioned seat behind the desk and approached her.

"You're late again."

"There's more to me than this place," she said, turning. "You know that."

"You're my best girl." He stepped forward and leaned his face so close she could smell his sour breath. "I can't have my best girl show up late."

"I'm here every night for you."

"And I pay you good. Not because I'm your father," he paused as they glared at each other, "but because you're my best dancer."

She turned away from him. Before she could leave the room, he violently slammed his fist against the door beside her head. She flinched and closed her eyes. He leaned forward and put his lips against her ear.

"Now shake that pretty little ass of yours," he whispered, "and make your big papa proud."

He eased the door open for her and motioned to the pulsating dance music that reverberated from the club's booming sound system. She hesitated a moment before stepping into the chaos of the crowded strip club.

Chapter Nine

It was late. The Royal Tavern had emptied some. Bobby had knocked back several shots of whiskey in hopes of easing his pain. It was still there. He especially felt it when he rotated his body, even slightly, on the barstool. But as the night slipped away, he didn't think about it as much.

He threw three hundred-dollar bills onto the bar and slipped the photo of his brother into his pocket. He motioned to Charlie that he was done. A bar regular named Ray stared at him.

"All alone tonight, Bobby?" Ray called out.

Bobby didn't respond as Charlie approached.

"Keep it," Bobby said, referring to the change.

"Hold on." Charlie retrieved two more shot glasses and filled them with whiskey. "Congrats again on the big win, buddy!"

"Where's Mary?" Ray shouted to Bobby, who ignored him.

"Rest up," Charlie said, pushing one of the shots of whiskey to Bobby.

"Where's Mary?" Ray yelled again.

Bobby didn't respond as Charlie flashed Ray a dirty look and motioned to the shots.

"Our great boxing hero left out in the cold," Ray teased. "No license. No car. No way home."

"Cut it out, Ray," Charlie grumbled.

Bobby and Charlie threw back the shots, not looking at the heckler.

"Hey, Bobby?" Ray called out again as Bobby finally glanced over. "You know where Mary is, don't you? Everybody knows."

"Knock it off, Ray," Charlie warned.

"She's busy suckin' Frank Miller's dick. That's where she's at. Suckin' Frank Miller's dick!"

In a flash, Bobby left his barstool, ripped Ray from his, and slammed his thin, bony body on the floor.

"Bobby!" Charlie called out. "Bobby, don't!"

Bobby grabbed the collar of Ray's shirt with his good left hand, lifted him up, and bounced his skinny body several times against the wall.

"Bobby, please," Charlie pleaded. "You can't get in trouble again!"

Bobby continued to bang Ray's limp body against the wall. The jukebox suddenly stopped; the bar lights brightened. Charlie rushed from behind the bar. Bobby pressed his hand against Ray's throat. Gagging, Ray closed his eyes; his face reddened.

"I'll break you in half, motherfucker."

"Bobby, stop," Charlie continued to yell, tugging at Bobby's shoulders. "Stop! He's not worth it!"

Bobby pressed Ray harder into the wall before letting him drop to the floor. Gasping for air and looking stunned, Ray rubbed at his scratched and bruised throat.

"This isn't over!" Ray called out. "I know who you are! You can't hide from this! I'll sue your ass, you fuckin' animal!"

Bobby looked to Charlie who shrugged, before disappearing out the bar with a slam of the door.

Chapter Ten

Wearing only a bikini top and thong, Holly danced on a table to the '70s Heart song "Barracuda" for a group of drunken Louisiana State frat boys from Baton Rouge. She spun away from them as they groped and pawed at her. Frustrated, she continually gazed to the many bouncers working the club, trying to get their attention. But the bouncers mostly ignored her.

"How much?" one of the young guys called out, holding a twenty-dollar bill over his head.

"For what?" she asked, letting the kid stick the bill in the waistband of her thong. She spun away from him after his hand wandered a little too close to her private area.

"To take us all on," he yelled out, grinning, "all at once."

"Y'all have neither the cash nor the stamina," she shouted over the blaring music.

As she twirled her body back towards the group, the biggest, meatiest kid held up a hundred-dollar bill. She pulled one side of the thong from her waist and approached the kid as he slid the money in.

"You meatheads are just paying my rent," she teased, but the big kid reached for the thong and started to pull it down off her waist.

"These need to come off," he roared in laughter, tugging at her thong.

She frantically scanned the club, looking for help from one of the bouncers. They still ignored her as she tried to twist and pull away from the muscle-bound college student. She glanced to a VIP balcony. Russell watched her. She glared at him. He turned his back and disappeared behind a curtain.

As the kid yanked at the thong, she wheeled around and violently shoved him in the chest with her spiked heel shoe. He fell awkwardly back into his seat that flipped over on him. Like a turtle stuck on its back, he drunkenly struggled to get out from under the toppled chair as his buddies laughed hysterically.

Furious, Holly again glanced to a bouncer who shrugged. Kneeling, she grabbed at the piles of cash that had been strewn all over the stage and gathered the parts of her outfit she had removed during the act, before stomping away to the dressing room in back.

Chapter Eleven

A DJ spun hip-hop records on the elevated stage of a nightclub near Fells Point in Baltimore. The hypnotic music was excessively loud. Bobby dragged hard on a cigarette. He was alone. He held a vodka and soda that shook in his hand. Bright strobe lights flashed around him. He really wasn't into the club scene but wanted another drink. He didn't have too many other places to go. It was one of the few bars still open in the city.

A group of attractive young ladies stared at him and whispered among themselves. He pretended not to notice, stubbing out the cigarette and downing the rest of his drink. One of the ladies confidently approached as he dug another cigarette from its pack.

"Why's a local celebrity like yourself drinking all alone?"

"Celebrity?"

"I saw your fight tonight."

"I didn't think pretty young ladies watched boxing matches."

"Are you celebrating?" she asked as a waitress delivered him another vodka drink.

He shook his head. "More like medicating."

"Where's all your fans?"

"Fans?" He looked around. "You might be it. Can I get you a drink?"

"Do you want to go for a drive?"

"Let's have a drink first."

"I'm Beth," she introduced herself.

Chapter Twelve

Russell had returned to his office. From the VIP balcony, he'd taken a set of secret stairs used only by employees. He was seated at his desk when Holly busted through the door. Without hesitating, she angrily threw the large stack of cash she had earned in his face.

"Thanks for back-up!" she yelled as the bills scattered across his desk and on the floor. "I'm leaving!"

Holly stomped by him into the dressing room and aggressively heaved her shoes and the pieces of her outfit into her locker. She hastily dressed and stormed by Russell who was on his hands and knees scooping up the money off the floor.

"Don't forget," he called out before she could leave the office. "You work a double tomorrow. I need you here by five. Don't be late."

She left the office with a slam of the door and disappeared into the mayhem of the lively club. Russell smirked as he counted the exceptionally large sum of money she had earned for him that night.

Chapter Thirteen

Without a valid driver's license, Bobby drove Beth's brand new, sporty red Honda Civic at a high rate of speed on a dark rural road on the eastern side of Baltimore County. His license had been suspended for years because of numerous speeding tickets and reckless driving incidents.

Staring at him, Beth smiled from behind the straw of a cocktail. As he drove, he constantly touched at the burning cuts and bruises on his face. She kicked off her shoes and nestled her bare feet into his lap. He sat up straight as she dug her feet deeper between his legs. He soon pulled into a dark, vacant lot of a closed shopping plaza.

With their bodies locked together, Bobby and Beth fervidly made out in the front seat. Both of his hands were under her satiny blouse. On top of him, she rubbed at the crotch of his pants with her knee, but he felt nothing. Like the rest of his body, his groin area was numb. She dug her knee deeper into his crotch. Still, there was no response. Discouraged, he tried to push her away, but she wouldn't let go.

"Get off," he mumbled, his face buried in her chest as she continued to grind her knee into his crotch. "Get off of me."

She didn't move. Frustrated, he pushed at her. She still didn't move off him.

"Get the fuck off me!" he groaned, pushing her lithe body more forcefully.

"Jesus," she moaned, rolling away from him as he sat up. They stared a moment, before he looked away.

"Get out."

"Huh?"

"Get out of the car."

"It's my car."

"Get out!" he yelled, reaching for the door handle on the passenger side.

"I just wanted to have some fun."

"I won't be any good for that," he said, nudging her out of the car.

"It's okay, really."

"Get out!"

Her feet bare, her coat and purse in her hands, she awkwardly stepped onto the icy pavement, frantically readjusted her bra and buttoned her shirt. Before she could say another word, Bobby put the car in gear and peeled away with passenger side door flapping open. He sped around the parking lot until he glanced over and picked up one of her shoes on the seat beside him. He slammed the brakes and wheeled the car back, pounding at the steering wheel.

He quickly returned to the spot where they were parked. Beth hadn't moved. Her arms were crossed against her chest. He pulled the Honda next to her and pushed the passenger door open.

"What is wrong with you?"

"I'm sorry," he said.

"You're crazy!"

"Let's get a coffee somewhere."

"Take me home."

"Let me get you a coffee or a bite to eat," he said again. "I could use some company."

"Take me home."

"Are you sure?"

"Take me home!"

Chapter Fourteen

It was late. Holly sat alone in a 24-hour dive bar in the French Quarter of New Orleans named Tommy Black's. The place was dark and nearly empty. She smoked a cigarette and drank cheap draught beer from a plastic cup at one end of a long wooden bar. She looked exhausted. The only light came from a set of coolers behind the bar, a popular jukebox in the back corner, and a small hallway light outside the bathrooms. The gray-haired bartender, Butchie, approached her.

"You all right?" he asked, looking concerned.

"Just tired."

"Your body language tells me there's somethin' more." He grabbed a bottle of Irish whiskey and a pair of shot glasses. "Shouldn't you be at work?"

"Yes."

"You wanna talk about it?" he asked, filling the two shot glasses.

"You've heard it before."

They picked up the whiskeys and nodded to each other, before swallowing them down. Butchie cringed and shook his head. Holly didn't react. She threw a crumbled hundred-dollar bill on the bar. He pushed it back to her with a shake of his head.

"These are on me."

"Thanks, Butchie."

"You need a vacation."

"I need something more than this."

"Get out of town. Take a week off."

"You know I can't."

"Take a long weekend. Go to the beaches in Mississippi. Get away. I'll get you a key to my cousin's beach house in Biloxi."

"I wish," she said, finishing the beer and pushing the empty cup forward. "Can I get another one?"

"Two beers, huh?" he said, filling the cup. "What's the occasion?"

"I don't think I can move from this stool."

"You need a break. This life's killin' you."

"I may not be able to walk home tonight. My legs and both feet, they're shot."

"I'll get you a cab, when you're ready."

"Thanks, Butchie, but right now, this beer is all I need. I feel like getting drunk."

Chapter Fifteen

It was near daybreak. The sun had yet to rise. Mary Riley had spent most of the evening with her new boyfriend, Frank Miller. He was a lawyer, a very successful one. With a puzzled look, she pulled into the driveway of her house and saw a light on in the living room. She cautiously entered to a soft snoring sound and peeked around a wall. Beaten up, Bobby awkwardly slept in a recliner. She could smell him from across the room. He reeked of cigarettes, alcohol, and antiseptic. It had been months since she had kicked him out of the house.

"Bobby?"

He awoke and glanced around, appearing confused. He recognized Mary's lipstick-stained cigarette butts in the ashtray on the table beside him. His head pounded. His jaw was nearly swollen shut. She stared at him from across the room. He still loved her and suspected she still loved him as well. But he knew their relationship was over and had been for a very long time. He also knew it was all his fault.

"What are you doing here? We've discussed this."

"Where've you been all night?"

"You better go."

"Mary?"

"Just go. Please."

"Let me stay here a day or two. I'm really beat up this time. I don't have anywhere else to go."

"Frank will be here soon."

"I won last night."

"I heard," she said, setting her purse down and walking into the kitchen.

"Did you watch it?"

"No," she said as she prepared a pot of coffee.

"You used to like coming to my fights."

"I need my key back," she said, entering the room.

They stared a moment, before he pulled the key out of his pocket and placed it on a table.

"You have to go."

"Give me another chance."

"Please." She walked to the front door, before opening it.

The first floor of the house quickly filled with the pleasant, caramel-like aroma of freshly brewed coffee.

"You have to leave."

After some hesitation, he finally lifted himself up from the chair. Wincing, he slowly limped to the door.

"Can I get a cup of coffee first?"

"Don't come here again, please," she said, reaching for a stack of unopened mail on a small table by the door.

"I love you, Mary."

"Take these. Your bank keeps calling."

He reached for the mail and paused at the door before leaving.

"My dad's dying," he said before she could close the door on him.

"I heard," she nodded. "I'm sorry, Bobby."

"And here," he said, pulling a handful of hundred-dollar bills from his jacket pocket and reaching the money to her.

"What's this?"

"It's not everything I owe you."

"You don't have to giv—"

"I'll get you the rest later," he interrupted. "Take it. It was part of my advance for the fight."

"I can't take your money."

"Please. Take it. It's okay. I'll get paid the rest for the fight later this morning."

"You know I still worry about you," she said, reluctantly taking the money.

A new silver BMW suddenly pulled into the driveway before he could respond. It was Frank Miller. Both Bobby and Mary glanced to the car. Frank shut off the engine and waited in the car to allow Bobby to leave.

"You have to go, Bobby."

They briefly stared at each other. She looked away as he hesitated at the front before finally limping away.

Chapter Sixteen

It was a gray December morning. Wanting to get paid, Bobby had called his manager Tony to pick him up not far from where Mary lived. Tony was young, in his late twenties. Bobby was his top client. He drove a new white Mercedes sedan to where Bobby was waiting. He seemed to change cars as often as he did clothes, leasing a different one every few months. Tony always wore expensive designer suits, gold watches, and diamond rings. No matter what the weather or time of day, he always had a pair of sunglasses on top of his head.

Grimacing, Bobby gingerly crawled into the passenger seat. He stared out the car window and wouldn't look at Tony. He felt horrible. He didn't know if it was the hangover or if the painkilling effects of the alcohol had worn off. He couldn't feel his face from the fight, and he could barely unlock his jaw to open his mouth. His head continued to pound, and it hurt to take a breath. He needed rest.

"Last night's win will get you in the top five, my man," Tony barked with enthusiasm. "What a beautiful win. What a gutsy last round. You have heart, Bobby! And toughness! All promoters love heart and toughness!"

Bobby continued to stare out the side window, fumbling with a cigarette he pulled from his jacket pocket.

"I had nine phone messages after the bout," Tony ranted as Bobby lit the cigarette that dangled from his lips. "I may get you on the under card of a championship fight this spring."

Tony reached over, took the cigarette from Bobby's lips, and flicked it out the window.

"What'd I tell you? No smoking."

"You got the check?" Bobby asked bluntly, not sharing Tony's excitement.

"You have to be busting, man! Goddamn, this is exciting!"

"Do you got my check?"

"Yeah, yeah," Tony pulled a check from his shirt pocket as Bobby grabbed it. "We're on our way, man."

"There's something wrong here," Bobby said, studying the check. "Forty-three thousand? I thought I was getting eighty-five."

"We did, but after I took my cut and my expenses, and other expenses, and we paid your trainer."

"I filled that fucking place for them. We should've gotten more than eighty-five thousand."

"We didn't negotiate a percent of the gate. I thought eighty-five was a good deal. That's almost more than twice we ever made before. Next time, we'll know to get some of the gate, especially if we fight in town here again."

"There won't be a next time," Bobby said, staring out the car window.

"What do you mean, 'won't be a next time'?"

"I'm done."

"Huh?"

"I'm done."

"Done with what?" Tony asked, glancing back and forth from the road to Bobby.

"Fighting. It's over."

Looking concerned, Tony pulled the Mercedes into a parking spot on a downtown street.

"Bobby, Bobby, come on now."

"My body can't take it anymore."

Bobby put a cigarette to his lips and took a long hard drag before Tony could take it and toss it out the window.

"I know you're hurting this morning, but rest for a few days, and you'll be ready to jump back into the ring."

"Not this time."

"You can't quit now."

"I'm done. I mean it."

"Two more wins, and we may be fighting for the world championship, man. Just two more wins, goddammit!"

"I have nothing left."

"You're still young. You haven't even hit your prime yet."

"My right hand, it's busted real bad. It may take a long time to heal, if ever."

"Everyone has dreams," Tony broke in, "but you're lucky. Your dreams are right there in front of you. You can't quit now, man. Not now!"

Bobby pulled another cigarette from his jacket and awkwardly strained to get out of the car.

"It's over, Tony."

As Bobby lit the cigarette and walked away, Tony slammed both hands on the steering wheel.

Chapter Seventeen

Wiping at his nose that continued to run and spot blood, Bobby waited in line at the bank and flipped through the stack of old mail that Mary had given him. As he stepped to the teller's window, he tossed all the mail into a nearby trash can. He handed the check for forty-three-thousand dollars to the teller. He touched at the cuts on his face as blood continued to trickle from his nose.

"Cash," Bobby said.

The teller studied the check. He stared at Bobby a moment before looking to the computer screen in front of him.

"I was at the fight," the teller said as he studied Bobby's account. "Seems your checking account is overdrawn, Mr. Raymond."

"How much?"

"Eight-thousand, seven-hundred, forty-four dollars."

"What does that mean?"

"We'll have to take it out of your check."

"Okay."

"And another twelve hundred in daily fees for the overdraft."

"Okay."

"Cash, right?"

Bobby nodded as the teller counted out large stacks of hundred-dollar bills.

"That was one hell of a thrilling fight," the teller said, pushing the cash to Bobby. "You really had to earn this."

"It wasn't worth it," Bobby mumbled, stuffing the money into his leather coat pocket.

Chapter Eighteen

With a heavy sigh and a pained grimace, Holly strained to roll her aching body over onto her back. From the couch of her cramped four-hundred-square foot apartment, she scanned the darkened room for a clock. Her apartment was nothing more than three small rooms—bedroom and bathroom that were separated only by a beaded curtain, and a combined room that was both a kitchenette and living area. Her apartment was one of four in a seventeenth century two-story Creole cottage enclosed by a half-acre of silver-painted wrought iron fencing.

There was a lush courtyard in the back she had access to but never used. Her place was by far the smallest of the others. It was on the ground floor, and the front door faced Esplanade Avenue. It could get loud at night from the steady parade of late-night revelers trekking back and forth between the popular Frenchmen Street in the Marigny neighborhood where her place was located and the even livelier streets of the nearby French Quarter.

As she squinted in the dark for the clock that hung on the wall next to the door, her hungry belly growled. She wore the same clothes she had on when she stormed out of her father's club the previous evening. Somewhat hungover, she was nearly paralytic. She could barely bend her sore knees and elbows. Her head pounded from too many cheap beers and whiskey shots she shared with Butchie at Tommy Black's late into the morning.

Her hamstrings and calf muscles were cramped from all the dancing she'd done in the club and with the ballet the previous days, weeks, and months. She was dehydrated. Both of her Achilles tendons burned. Her feet were swollen and covered in red, oozing blisters. Heavy blankets covered all the windows of her apartment to block the sunlight so she could sleep. Seeing that it was nearly four in the afternoon, she groaned in disappointment. She had to be back at her father's all-night gentlemen's club in an hour where she'd have to perform two back-to-back grueling shifts—the first from five to eleven, the second from midnight to six.

She pulled her lone cover, a frayed Afghan blanket her mother had knitted for her before she passed, over her head and loudly screamed into the solitude of her empty apartment. She needed a change, a new way of living. She was wasting the best years of her life. Her current situation was killing her—both her body and her spirit. She wanted to run away. But she had neither the resources nor the courage. Fortunately, she had ballet. It was the only thing saving her.

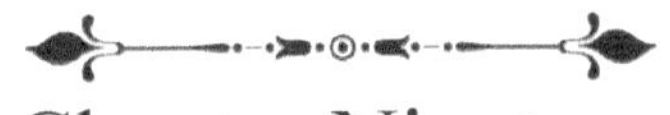

Chapter Nineteen

Bobby limped into a dingy boxing gym near downtown Baltimore. After he entered, the workouts stopped, and a loud cheer rang out. Like a hero returning home, he raised his bandaged right hand. The boxers working out applauded as he slowly walked to an office in the back of the damp and musty-smelling gym.

He knocked on the office door and entered. The face of the wrinkled black man who owned the gym lit up. He immediately came out from behind his cluttered desk and enthusiastically hugged Bobby.

His name was Willie Strickler. He was called The Mule from his long-ago boxing days. He never got knocked out in over fifty-five professional fights, and he never seemed to tire. He was a workhorse in the ring. Willie was Bobby's first trainer in boxing. Bobby was Willie's most celebrated fighter.

"Bobby!" Willie grinned, embracing his former pupil. "Oh, my goodness. Beautiful. Beautiful. Just how I taught you."

Willie motioned for Bobby to sit.

"How you doin' this mornin'? Looked like you got worked over pretty good."

"Grainger beat the hell out of me."

"You left yourself too exposed. You were too wild with your punches in the early rounds. But you hung in there. And won because you wanted it more."

"It sure doesn't feel like a win. I think he broke me."

"You need to take some time off. Heal up."

"I miss you, Willie. I wish you were still handling me."

"I took you as far as I could."

"I may be done. I don't know if I can get back in the ring."

"All fighters know when they've reached the end. And nearly all 'em end up fightin' past it."

"I don't want to be like that."

"A fighter goes crazy when they don't got nothin' to do."

"I stopped here to give you this," Bobby said, tossing a large stack of cash on Willie's desk.

"What's this?" he asked, glancing back and forth from Bobby to the money. "What'd you go and do, Bobby?"

"Last time I saw you, you said you needed thirty-thousand dollars to pay this place off," he said as Willie reached for the cash. "After all these years, this place can finally be yours."

"I can't take this. It's too much."

"I owe you everything. I made some good money last night. Please take it. You saved me, Willie. I'd likely be dead if it wasn't for you."

Chapter Twenty

Bobby returned to the house he had shared with Mary. It was late. He had been wandering the downtown streets of Baltimore most of the evening. He pounded on the front door.

"Mary, open up," he called out, continuing to pound on the door until the porch light came on. "Mary!"

Frank Miller pulled the door open.

"Let me talk to Mary."

"She doesn't want to see you."

"Bullshit. Let me talk to her."

"It's late, Bobby. She's asleep."

"I need to talk with her." He leaned his head in the door and called out. "Mary!"

"Shut the fuck up, man," Frank whispered, blocking the door. "You'll wake the neighbors."

"Mary!" Bobby called again.

Wiping sleep from her eyes and yawning, Mary suddenly appeared at the door. She had pulled on a robe over a slinky nightgown.

"Bobby," Mary whispered but in a stern tone. "Quiet."

"I need to talk to you."

"Find someone new. I'm done picking up the pieces when you fall apart."

"Please, Mary."

"Get the fuck out of here," Frank grumbled, taking a step towards Bobby who leaned towards him.

"Frank, go inside," she said, stepping between them.

Frank glared at Bobby before backing inside as Mary stepped forward and closed the door behind her.

"Leave, Bobby, please."

"Let's go out on the town tonight. Like old times."

"You have to go."

They studied each other.

"You look nice, Mary."

"Go, Bobby," she said, sounding frustrated. "I mean it."

"Come on. I'm leaving town soon."

"Leaving town?"

"Tomorrow."

"Tomorrow? Where?"

"New Orleans."

"New Orleans?"

"I need to find my brother."

"Chuck? No one's seen him in years. You know he doesn't want you to come look for him. He made that very clear when he left town."

"I want to bring him home for Christmas. It might be my dad's last."

"When are you leaving?"

"In the morning. So come on, let's go out one last time. I may never see you again."

"You have to leave."

They stared at each other a moment before she opened the door and glanced behind her. Frank stood in the shadows close by.

"I love you, Mary," he said, glancing at Frank.

She didn't respond.

"I'm sorry for everything."

She didn't initially react, stepping back into the house. But before he could walk away, she called: "Be safe, Bobby. Please be safe."

Chapter Twenty-One

It was a wintry December night. Scattered snow flurries fell from a black sky. Bobby sat alone on a mostly empty Greyhound bus. Shivering a little, he huddled up against a frosty window. He had no blanket and few belongings. He wore only denim jeans and his black leather jacket over a collared shirt. He had pulled his arms in tight against his chest, trying to keep warm. He constantly touched at his running nose and the itchy, stitched cuts over his eyes and cheek.

As the bus drove away from Baltimore, he thought of the last time he spoke to his brother, Chuck.

He and Chuck were seated in a guarded visitation area in a police station. They were divided by a glass window. Chuck was wearing an orange prison jumpsuit. Bobby struggled to make eye contact.

"I really don't want to see you," Chuck said, glaring at Bobby.

"I'm here to bail you out."

"I don't want your help."

"You need to get out of here," Bobby said, still avoiding eye contact.

"Dad kicked me out of the house."

"What?" Bobby asked, glancing up and staring directly into his brother's eyes.

"I have nowhere to go."

"You can stay with me."

"No fucking way, man!"

"I'm serious."

"That's the last place I want to be."

"Chuck. . ." Bobby mumbled, looking away.

"Because, as you see it—and dad and mom, too—my life is meaningless."

"Don't, Chuck," Bobby said, looking back.

"And I'm not the hero of the neighborhood."

"Stop it."

"Or the shining star of the family. . ."

"Chuck. . ."

"I'm not the chosen one," he said, before briefly pausing. "I'm nobody."

They stared a moment.

"Let me get you out of here."

"This is where I belong," he said, standing. "So long, Bobby. . ."

In the back seat of an empty Greyhound parked on Loyola Avenue at the bus station in New Orleans, the bus driver tapped Bobby on the shoulder, but he didn't respond.

"Buddy," the driver said, leaning close to Bobby's ear. "Hey, Buddy!"

Bobby slowly opened his eyes and glared back at the driver with a distant stare. His eyes were bloodshot and glassy. His hair was a matted mess. He needed to shower and shave. He had slept through most of the entire forty-hour trip.

"You need to get off here," the driver said as Bobby rubbed his blackened eyes, sitting up and stretching his cramped body. "This is the last stop."

"Where are we?" Bobby mumbled, squinting out the dirty windows of the bus.

"Welcome to New Orleans."

Book Two

Everyone Needs an Angel

Chapter Twenty-Two

A swift but warm breeze blew directly into Bobby's face. The morning sky was bright. He wondered if it was always this hot in New Orleans in December. Thick gray rain clouds, however, hung high in the sky away in the distance. It appeared as if it would storm later. He was advised by a local at the bus depot to begin his search for Chuck in the popular French Quarter area.

He caught a cab that dropped him on Canal Street after a short ride. He walked a block down the deserted Royal Street and took a left onto Conti before turning right onto the red brick sidewalk of Bourbon. Some of the bars were still open, but the morning streets were relatively empty. Plastic cups and empty food containers littered the street, trampled flat the previous night. He couldn't escape the awful stench. New Orleans smelled like no other place he had ever been. All odors—spoiled seafood scraps, rotting vegetables, stale beer, ammonia cleaning detergent, vomit, urine as well as horse and dog feces—blended into one overwhelming stink. And the heat certainly didn't help.

Looking for a busier area, he cut down St. Peter Street before looping back towards Royal. He passed a dive bar, Tommy Black's, and looked inside. The place was dark and raucous. He couldn't believe it was that busy at such an early hour. One of the crazy characters at the bar stared out to him. Bobby briefly considered going in for a beer, but he knew it was best to move on.

Most of the other businesses, souvenir shops and restaurants, were still closed. He came upon two grungy fellows on the sidewalk in front of a Rouse's grocery store, sharing smokes and counting their change. Bobby leaned down and showed them the picture of Chuck.

"Have you seen this guy?"

They shook their heads and shrugged, holding out their dirty hands, looking for a donation. Bobby handed them each a dollar and walked towards the Mississippi River into the lush green lawn of Jackson Square at the end of St. Peter. He stopped for a moment to admire an impressive white stone church, which he later found out to be St. Louis Cathedral. The Square was quiet. Nothing stirred except for a homeless man sifting through a garbage can at the foot of the cathedral.

"Where are you, Chuck?" Bobby muttered to himself, studying the photo of his brother.

Chapter Twenty-Three

Chuck was alive and well and indeed still in New Orleans. He'd been there for over three years, trying his best to support himself. His life was rather simple but grueling. He worked over sixty hours a week as a bartender at a 24-hour dive in Mid-City called Delia's, living above the bar in a cramped, two-room apartment.

He owned little—a coffee pot, a radio, and a couple drawers of well-worn clothes. He slept on the floor, using a sleeping bag for a bed. He survived on a daily diet of rum and diet Cokes, black coffee, seafood gumbo, and cigarettes, lots of cigarettes.

He made good money in tips but saved none of it. He didn't have a bank account or credit card. He was broke every night by the time he went to bed or passed out, whichever came first. His family and old friends from Baltimore likely wouldn't have recognized him. It was as if he disguised himself. He'd put on over thirty pounds and had grown his dirty, blonde hair significantly longer since arriving. He was a pleasant and funny young man, though, who was well-liked by the regulars who hung out at the bar he worked. But he was troubled. He never talked about his past or where he came from. He had become someone else.

It was early afternoon. Delia's was relatively slow. Chuck worked the bar and easily laughed with the customers. The jukebox roared. James Brown songs played. It seemed that the place was busy only when Chuck worked. He would start each of his shifts playing all twenty songs in order from the James Brown Greatest Hits compact disc on the jukebox. Chuck learned right away that nothing could change the sometimes-dreary mood of a lifeless bar more quickly than a rousing James Brown song. The happy patrons of a lively bar drank more, spent more, and left bigger tips.

A petite young woman at the bar named Elizabeth stared at him. She often came into Delia's when he worked. She was friendly and easygoing, with an infectious giggle. She laughed at everything, especially at the things he said and did. She never called him Boozer, a nickname he was embarrassed by. Even if it was sort of accurate. She wasn't the prettiest of the young ladies who came in there regularly, but she may have been the most appealing with her warm and engaging manner.

Chuck had a serious crush on her, constantly bumming cigarettes off her and buying her shots of whiskey. She lived down the street and was a server at a nearby upscale restaurant. She'd started coming into the bar several months before with co-workers after her evening shifts. Chuck would flirt with her and tell her jokes.

She liked the attention. He liked that she laughed at his awful jokes and didn't find him as repulsive as most other women did. She could see beyond his gruff appearance. But to that point, she had resisted his advances and many requests to meet her outside of the Delia's when he wasn't working.

"Hey, Elizabeth!" Chuck yelled from across the bar as he stood near the cash register. "What's the difference between a Corvette and a hard-on?"

She glanced to the ceiling and thought for a moment before asking, "I don't know, Chuck. Tell me. What is the difference between a Corvette and a hard-on?"

"I don't currently have a Corvette." He laughed as the guys around the bar giggled.

"Another round!" one of the bar regulars shouted as Chuck grabbed a bottle of Irish whiskey and filled shot glasses.

"No, no, my turn," Chuck said, reaching into his tip jar that overflowed with money and stuffing three $20 bills into the cash register drawer.

"Gross," Elizabeth grinned at the punch line to the joke, shaking her head as Chuck looked to her with a wink and a grin.

"I told that joke to another young lady last night," he said, approaching to fill her empty shot glass.

"How'd she respond?"

"She walked away, like they all do," he said, before raising his shot of whiskey. "Salute, everybody!"

Everyone loudly cheered before knocking back the whiskey as the James Brown song, "Think," blared from the jukebox.

"Like they all do, really?" Elizabeth asked, continuing her conversation with Chuck.

"Well, all of 'em except you."

"Do you ever think about getting out of here?" she asked.

"Yeah, I'm off in a few hours."

"No. Get out of this bar and get out of New Orleans. For good."

"Every single day."

"What keeps you here?"

"So many things."

"Like what?"

"For one, I needed somewhere to disappear. This seemed like a good place for that. My life is easy here."

"Disappear? Who are you hiding from?"

"A past life I'm trying to forget."

"What happened?"

"I was betrayed by the person I loved the most."

"An old girlfriend?"

"My brother. He ruined me. I can't even talk to my family."

"What happened?"

"He jus' better not come looking for me. You don't even want to know what I might do to him."

"What did he do? It must've been awful. You don't seem the fighting type."

"You working tonight?" he asked, changing the subject as he grew angry thinking of Bobby.

"Not tonight," she said after a short pause, waiting to see if he'd answer her.

"What are you doing later then?"

"Probably coming here."

"You like food?"

"Do I like food?" She grinned, puzzled by his odd question. "Yes, I like food."

"I get off at six. You want to grab a bite somewhere for dinner? I know all the best gumbo joints in town."

"I'd like to but. . ." Her voice trailed off.

"That's okay," he said quickly so she didn't have to make up an excuse. "Another time, maybe?"

"Sure, another time," she said, sensing his disappointment.

Chapter Twenty-Four

Bobby continued his search for Chuck. He had no idea where he was headed, cutting down an empty street near the French Market Place. He quickly discovered how most of the streets in the Quarter looked similar. Two-story houses and buildings painted in a variety of bright colors lined the narrow streets.

Their balconies were decorated by jungles of fern plants and terra cotta pots with pink and purple flowers he didn't know the names of. Colorful flags of different countries and plastic beads from forgotten Mardi Gras hung from cast iron railings of porches and balconies. The shuttered windows of the apartments were closed. It didn't appear as if anyone anywhere was home. He found the afternoon to be unusually quiet—almost too quiet.

As he pressed on, the clouds had rolled over the city, turning the day gray but cooler. He continued his search for hours, not really knowing if he was looking in the right parts of town. He glanced to the downtown area. A part of New Orleans he hadn't been to yet. Many tall buildings and hotels loomed in the distance. He felt alone, nearly helpless. He quickly realized what a difficult task finding his brother would be. New Orleans seemed to have lots of places to hide. And he wondered, like Mary, if Chuck was even there.

Bobby continued, though, exploring the residential portion of the Lower Quarter and the Marigny neighborhood, getting lost in the maze of Decatur and Frenchmen, up and down Barracks and Esplanade, and into Washington Square. The area was filled with colorfully painted wooden houses and cottages with courtyards encased in brick walls and iron fences.

He was struck by how green everything looked, even in December, which wasn't the case in Baltimore when he left. He didn't see a soul until stopping in a small corner store called Cajun Quick Stop for a bottle of orange juice. He showed the cashier the picture of Chuck. The cashier briefly glanced at the picture out of courtesy and shook his head.

After circling through the Marigny a few times, he traveled in the direction away from the Mississippi River and crossed North Rampart. Unlike the other neighborhoods, this one was a little livelier. Many young school children wearing backpacks walked the streets away from the school bus stop. Washed sheets and blankets, blowing in the wind, hung on tangled plastic lines that connected some of the houses. Overflowing trashcans and rusty automobiles lined the cluttered streets. He was startled by the big bark of an angry pit bull behind the fence of a courtyard. But he kept walking, studying anything or anyone that moved.

Cutting across North Villere, he passed through Louis Armstrong Park. He walked over a renovated walking bridge that spanned a pond with an active fountain. The park was mostly deserted except for two guys passed out in the shade under a tree. Empty bottles of Thunderbird wine lay emptied on the ground by their heads. They wore wide, contented smiles as they slept. Careful not to disturb them, Bobby quietly stepped by, cutting back down North Rampart.

He studied the face of a homeless man who loudly snored on an unfolded cardboard box. The man used a newspaper and plastic trash bags as blankets. Bobby followed an energetic teenager who dribbled a basketball past a busy dry cleaner and small diner with a crowded and lively food counter. When the boy stopped, Bobby showed the picture of his brother.

"No, sir." The boy shook his head and shrugged.

Leaving the teenager behind, Bobby turned onto Burgundy and headed towards downtown New Orleans. For nearly an hour, he walked up and down Canal on both sides of the street, passing numerous discount electronic and luggage stores and t-shirt shops that blasted the music of Clifton Chenier, Kermit Ruffins, and Buckwheat Zydeco. He walked into several of the stores. It seemed that many of them were selling the same things at the same prices.

Each street corner was busy with young children jumping out of school buses and men in three-piece suits on their way home from work. The diners, chicken and po-boy joints, and biscuit shops were full. Noisy city buses, spitting black diesel smoke, zoomed by. He flashed Chuck's picture to several strangers milling in front of a local coffee shop. They shook their heads. He showed the photo to a group waiting for a streetcar at the intersection of St. Charles and Canal. They took quick courtesy glances at the picture. No one seemed to have seen Chuck, and no one seemed to care.

Chapter Twenty-Five

It was a little after seven o'clock in the evening. Chuck had been sitting on the other side of Delia's bar for a few hours after his long morning-and-afternoon bartending shift had ended. He was quite intoxicated. Along with the numerous whiskey shots he drank during his work shift, he had since consumed several double rum and diet Cokes.

A commercial for a drug for erectile dysfunction loudly came on the wide screen television that hung on the wall behind the bar. The spokesman for drug on the commercial warned that an erection lasting more than four hours would need immediate medical help.

"If I had an erection for that long," Chuck joked out loud, "I wouldn't be the one needing medical help."

In addition to the alcohol, Chuck already had smoked over two packs of cigarettes that day. He got most of his cigarettes from an old 1970s style, four-legged cigarette vending machine at the back of Delia's, spending nearly fifteen dollars per pack. It had to be the last of its type in all New Orleans. Because of the outrageously overpriced cigarette packs in it, it was thought that Chuck was the only person who ever used the machine. It was mostly just taking up space.

As Chuck laughed with the regulars to his ongoing, joking commentary to the television broadcasts and commercials, three burly fellows from a local vending company were trying to lift the dated and weighty cigarette machine and carry it out the bar. The owner of Delia's was tired of spending money on its repairs. It was always breaking down and cost too much to get it fixed. The three men strained for many minutes, finally pushing the hefty machine across the cement floor of Delia's. The ugly grinding noise was deafening. The men humped the bulky machine towards the door of the bar and neared the stool where Chuck was sitting.

"Stop!" Chuck screamed out in horror over the commotion. "Stop! What are you doing? Stop!"

The guys moving the cigarette machine immediately stopped and let go of it, frantically looking around as if they dragged the heavy machine over someone's foot. The bar went silent, and everyone glanced at Chuck.

"Where are going with my girlfriend?" he said, pointing to the machine that supplied his daily fix of nicotine.

Everyone in the bar including the three men moving the machine laughed. One guy at the bar even spit out the beer he'd been drinking at Chuck's comment.

After the bar settled down, the front door to the place suddenly opened. A large group of people entered. They scattered out of the way as the three movers maneuvered the cigarette machine out the door. Chuck glanced to the long mirror behind the bar and watched the reflection of Elizabeth as she entered with some of her co-workers. She spotted him and approached.

"How long are you going to be here?" she asked, gently easing her body against him.

"Until I sober up," he said, hunched over his drink and not turning to her, "which could be years."

"Do you want to join us?" She motioned to her friends, tapping his shoulder.

"I got a 10-pound bag of brown rice, four ounces of weed, and a half-gallon of rum in my apartment," he said, turning on his barstool and staring into her eyes with a serious gaze. "The world may end tonight. You want to come upstairs and hang out?"

She giggled as he continued to stare at her with the most serious look.

"You're joking, right?"

"No." He shook his head. "Not at all. Let's hang out."

"I'm here with friends, and…" She again motioned toward her co-workers who were sitting at another table.

"Come on, let's get out of here. Let's shut this town down. Let's show it what we got. You and me. We'll be the king and queen of the night."

"I can't." She grimaced, crushing his spirits. "I'm here with friends. Do you work tomorrow?"

"I work in the morning, but I'll back be here around six."

"I'll see then. I'm off tomorrow."

He half-grinned and politely nodded as Elizabeth walked away. After watching her take a seat at a table with her friends and co-workers, he tossed a twenty-dollar bill on the bar and pointed to his empty pint glass and the three regulars sitting around him. Ned,

Delia's owner and occasional bartender, filled Chuck's glass with ice, plenty of rum and just a splash of diet Coke, before pouring whiskey shots for the others. Standing, Chuck swallowed his entire drink in one quick chug.

"Where you headed?" Ned asked.

"I'm closing this town down tonight."

"It can't be done. Many have tried, and they've all failed."

"I'll give it my best shot," he said, turning for the door.

"Chuck?" Ned called out. "You, okay?"

"Yeah, why?" Chuck asked, turning to him.

"Are you in need of money or havin' any problems or in trouble?"

"No, why?"

"You can come to me for anything. You know that, right?"

"Yeah, yeah, of course."

"You sure there's nothin' you need to tell me?"

"No, nothing."

"Be careful, Chuck. Please. You're about the best bartender I got. You helped me bring this place back to life. I'm worried about you. Maybe back off the drinkin' a little."

Chuck nodded but stopped at the door to take one last glance at Elizabeth before leaving.

After Chuck had left, Arthur, Delia's manager, approached Ned.

"Well?" he asked Arthur with a shrug.

"His cash drawer was short again."

"How much?"

"The same, just like every day the past few weeks."

"Three-hundred dollars?"

"Yeah. Three-hundred dollars."

"You think he's stealin' it? I can't picture that."

"I don't like him. He's an asshole. He's not careful. He's a terrible drunk. I'll have Ben from the kitchen keep an eye on him."

"Come on, he's a good kid, and you have to admit he's a fun bartender. Maybe workin' in a bar isn't the best place for him."

"You finally have this place hummin' again," Arthur said. "You don't want to fall back into that hole of a few years ago. We almost lost this place. You don't want to lose it because of some out-of-control kid bartender."

"But he packs this place."

"But at what cost?"

Chapter Twenty-Six

Night had fallen on Bobby's first day in New Orleans. He was even more determined to find Chuck, so he kept searching through the night. He found himself near the Superdome among a grouping of hotels and a couple of hospitals, one of which appeared to be abandoned.

The area was surrounded by blocks and blocks of empty brick buildings and parking lots. Spooked by the quiet of the area, he walked toward the light of the Superdome. Intrigued by the familiar and massive structure, he circled it and even tried to get inside. He was immediately intercepted by a security guard. Bobby showed him the picture of Chuck. The security guard wouldn't look at it.

Leaving the Superdome area, Bobby discovered Poydras Street and followed it for several blocks. He weaved his way back onto Canal Street, before eventually reaching the banks of the Mississippi River. On his way, he passed a casino and studied a line of red and white riverboats docked on the river's bank. He found a shopping mall that ran beside the river for several blocks. Sweating and tired, he ducked into the lobby of a luxury hotel to use the restroom.

Beyond the shopping mall stood an expansive convention center. A flow of aging conventioneers in outdated business suits hurriedly descended upon the convention center like a swarm of ants to a drop of honey. Most of them proudly displayed their names and corporate affiliation on tags pinned to their chests.

Bobby passed the convention center and trudged down the dark and mostly empty streets of the warehouse district. Some of the old buildings there, formerly owned by companies that appeared to be closed for years, were refurbished with new masonry work and fresh coats of paint. He passed a hotel; several buildings that housed apartments, townhouses, and condominiums; a few jewelry shops and art galleries; and a few bars.

Not really seeing anyone, he turned back and walked along the river towards the Quarter. He'd finally had enough. His knees and sides sore from his last fight were hurting, and he was exhausted. He needed a cold drink and thought of the dive named Tommy Black's he'd studied with curiosity on St. Peter. After a full day of searching, he seriously wondered what he was doing. Finding Chuck seemed unlikely. Stopping along the banks of the Mississippi, he rested on a bench of a lit walkway not far from the city's aquarium. The swollen river was busy with tankers and tugs, gliding over the dirty water, aimed for the open mouth of the Gulf. The bell from a passing riverfront streetcar clanged behind him as he pulled out the photo of his brother.

"Where are you, man?"

While Bobby was lost in thought, a skinny, middle-aged black man in tight faded jeans and a clean white t-shirt had wandered over to him. Bobby studied him a moment.

"I don't mean to disturb you, sir," the man said as Bobby nodded and cautiously checked over his shoulder.

The man held a spiral notebook rolled up in his hand. He politely bowed and then showed Bobby a nervous but sincere grin. His front teeth, top and bottom, were completely gone. His tiny hands were cracked and wrinkled. Bobby nodded again as the man opened the notebook to a handwritten list of song titles on the first page.

"Uh, sir," he said in a rough, baritone voice, "I'm supportin' a wife and three lil ones. I got me a job, and we get by all right. To make some extra monies, I go around singin' these songs of gospel to folks interested in hearin' 'em. You don't have to pay a thing. But I gladly take a quarter, dollar, whatever."

"What songs are on the list?" Bobby asked.

"I got it all—Mahalia Jackson, Louie Armstrong, Queen Aretha, and these two on the bottom. They're mine."

"Let me hear one of those," Bobby said, pointing to the song on the bottom of the list called, "You Can't Get Away, You Just Get By."

"Good choice." He grinned. "I wrote that one six-seven years back. I apologize beforehand. My voice is little rough, been singin' for folks all day up and down this here riverbank."

He started snapping his fingers and swaying his body back and forth. Looking skyward, he closed his eyes and started to wail with the deepest but sweetest of voices. Bobby listened closely to the words.

You can't get away
No matter what you say

Too much work, you slave
Not enough time, you go all day
Knocked out, worn down 'til you die
You can't get away
No, no, no, you can't get away
You jus' can't get away
But you jus' might get by.

He opened his eyes and looked at Bobby who nodded and smiled. The man cleared his throat and started into the next verse.

You can't get away
Your hungry children say
Britches to buy, lil mouths to feed
Never too much, always jus' enough
Knocked out, worn down 'til you die
You can't get away
No, no, no, you can't get away
You jus' can't get away
But you jus' might get by.

"I'm sorry, sir," the man apologized, opening his eyes.

"Nah," Bobby smiled, shaking his head, "sounds great."

"It could be better," the man shook his head. "My voice jus' ain't right. Been a busy mornin'. That's for sure. Been doin' a lot of singin' this week. Okay, now, one last verse."

Now you can get away
To all, let me say
Gigglin' girls to meet, card sharks you beat
Crawdad high, whiskey bottle dry
Knocked down, passed out you smile
I'll be singing 'til the day I die
You can't get away
No, no, no, you can't get away
But you just might get by
Yeah, you will, you will get by.

The little man finished his song with a bow. Bobby quietly clapped then reached into his pocket and pulled out a hundred-dollar bill.

"Take the rest of the night off, man," he smiled, holding out the money.

"Thank you, sir. Yessir. God bless you, sir," the man continually nodded, taking the money. "Thank you, sir."

"That's a tough way to make a living," Bobby said, touching at the cuts and scabs on his own face.

"I will sing all day long." He beamed. "Nothin' tough about that. I'll do another for free if you want?"

"Save your voice."

"God bless you, sir."

Chapter Twenty-Seven

Chuck had just finished an early morning bartending shift at Delia's. He sat at the bar, sipping a post-shift rum and diet Coke. Loud, retching sounds could be heard from the men's bathroom. The vomiting was so loud, it could be heard over the song on the jukebox.

"Who's in there?" Chuck asked. "Julius Caesar? Jesus, man! Sounds like the feast went well."

All the heads in the bar turned to the bathroom. A smallish man finally exited. His face was white as a sheet. He rubbed his round beer-belly as he headed for a stool at the end of the bar. Chuck pointed at him.

"I'll have what he had."

"I've always wanted to go to an all-you-can-eat buffet when it opened and try to stay and eat all day until it closed," one of the regulars at the bar said. "It's on my bucket list."

"Sounds like a stupid bucket list to me," another regular said.

"Your mom's on my bucket list," the first regular said.

"What'd you say?" the second regular asked, standing with his fists clenched.

"Cut it out," Chuck groaned, throwing a wet bar rag between them. "It's too early in the day, and I'm too tired to break up a fight."

After the angry regular returned to his barstool, Chuck glanced outside and noticed Elizabeth smoking a cigarette by the front door of the bar. He got her attention and waved for her to come inside. She waved back, wanting him to come outside.

But before he could go outside, a filthy young man in his early twenties with long dreadlocks and a heavy pack on his back wandered into the bar. His small dog wearing a bandana around its neck followed.

"What'd I tell you?" Chuck called to the kid. "You're allowed in here but not the dog. Not my rule. The health department's rule."

The young fellow led the dog back outside and looked to Elizabeth, who grabbed its chain leash to watch it for a moment. The kid went back inside and pulled from his backpack two billiard balls, one a cue ball and the other an eight ball. The kid handed them to Chuck.

"You brought me one of each this time, huh?" Chuck said, studying the two shiny balls. "What do you want for them?"

"Five each," the kid said.

Chuck pulled a twenty-dollar bill from the stack of money on the bar in front of him and handed it to the kid.

"Keep it, man."

The kid quickly grabbed the money and grinned. "I'll bring you more."

"Sure," Chuck nodded as the kid rushed outside and retrieved his dog.

Chuck reached the two balls to Arthur who was bartending.

"Put these in the drawer with the rest."

"We don't need no more," Arthur said, opening a drawer behind the bar filled with numerous different numbered billiard balls. "We only got one pool table. Where do all these come from?"

"He steals them from other bars."

"And you keep givin' him money?"

"I guess I'm a sucker," Chuck said, pushing his stack of money in front of him to Arthur to pay his tab and glancing to the others around the bar. "See you guys around."

Chuck stepped out of the bar and joined Elizabeth.

"Can I get one of those?" he asked, pointing to the cigarette she held.

"What are you doing now?" she asked, pulling a cigarette from the box and lighting it for him.

"Why didn't you come inside?"

"I was waiting for you out here."

"I'm headed to another bar. You want to go?"

"Any interest in stopping at my place first?" she asked, her eyes locked on his.

"What for? Music?" he asked.

"Sure, I got music."

"Food. You got any food. I haven't eaten all day."

"Yeah, I got some food. I have plenty of leftovers from the restaurant."

"Movies?"

"I'm not in the mood to watch a movie," she said, taking his hand and trying to lead him towards her apartment.

"What are we doing?" he asked, stopping before they walked too far down the street.

"Going to my apartment."

"I know," he asked as she pulled on his arm, "but why?"

"You heard me. Let's go."

"Why now?" he asked, not budging from the spot where they stood. "And not the two hundred times I asked you to go somewhere with me before?"

"I was standing outside the bar just thinking about everything going on in my little world here," she said, yanking at his arm until he started to follow her. "My crummy job. My shitty apartment. My lack of money. This tiresome city. None of it good. I glanced in the bar and saw you. Not only did I laugh, I laughed out loud."

"Because I'm the clown in your world."

"No," she shook her head. "You make my world tolerable. You're the light. I feel better when I'm around you."

"So, we're not going to watch a movie?" he asked again, stopping as they neared her apartment.

"Come on," she said, tugging his arm.

"I may need more cigarettes."

"More cigarettes?"

"I smoke more when I'm nervous."

"Nervous? You don't seem the nervous type."

"And Viagra?"

"You need that stuff?"

"I don't want to let you down."

"Just be yourself. You won't let me down."

Chapter Twenty-Eight

Not having anywhere to sleep and not wanting to blow what money he had left on a room, Bobby returned to the bus station. He spent a restless night on a stiff metal bench. Later that morning, he found himself back in the grid of narrow streets of the French Quarter. The late morning sun had burned away the heavy clouds that lingered overhead. He pulled off his leather jacket and flipped it over his shoulder.

Bourbon street was crowded with tourists on foot, and many of the bars and restaurants started to open. Taxi cabs, horse-drawn carriages, and beer delivery trucks lined the street. The balcony seats of the cafes above the street were full for brunch. Everyone seemed in high spirits. Strolling through the Quarter and continually glancing up to the bright blue sky, Bobby couldn't help but feel better himself. There wasn't a cloud in the sky.

He needed something to eat and wanted a beer, but he had to freshen up first. He was quite hot and sweaty from a long trek from the bus station. He hadn't showered since Baltimore. He remembered a large chain hotel at one end of Royal Street. He returned and walked through the revolving front door as if he was staying there. He scanned the vast lobby and noted several glass pitchers of ice water with lemon and orange slices near the registration desk. He casually approached and gulped down several cups of the icy citrus water.

As he guzzled the water, he spotted the lobby's public men's room. He hurried in, hung his sweaty leather coat on a coat rack, and lathered his hands with soap. He scrubbed his face, hair, and under his arms with soapy hands. For several minutes, he tried his best to rinse the soap from his hair by placing his head under the running water of a sink faucet.

The door to the restroom opened. He glanced to the mirror. Luckily, it wasn't a member of the hotel staff but an older gentleman, who disappeared behind the door of a bathroom stall. Bobby lifted his head from the sink and rushed to dry his dripping hair with wads of paper towels. He studied his ragged appearance in the mirror and ran his fingers through his wet shaggy hair like a brush, trying his best to straighten it. As always, he touched at his swollen eyes and the burning cuts on his face.

Out of the bathroom, he spotted what the hotel called a business center. He slipped into the room and sat at a lone computer that was primarily used by guests to check flights and print airplane boarding passes. He typed in the search terms 'Charles Anthony Raymond' and 'New Orleans.' One listing appeared in the e-yellow pages for New Orleans. Bobby hurriedly jotted down the address and phone number for the listing on a scrap of paper.

"This may be nothing," he mumbled, "but it's a start."

He stuffed the piece of paper into his pocket and left the hotel. With soap still in his hair and behind his ears but feeling somewhat refreshed, he walked Royal Street towards St. Peter. He planned to finally stop for a beer in the dive called Tommy Black's that piqued his interest the day before.

Royal was closed to traffic and as festive as ever. Numerous performers filled the popular street. Reaching St. Peter, he stood beside Rouse's grocery, where he had had held out the photo of Chuck for the two grungy fellows the day before. This time he watched a brass band playing old ragtime favorites. The young lady playing clarinet was exceptionally good.

A crowd of tourists had gathered around them. They snapped photographs or videotaped the band with their phones, filling the tip jar after each song. A tall black man on stilts dressed as Uncle Sam entertained for tips as well, standing high above the crowd, dancing stiffly and awkwardly to the band's jumping tunes. Bobby closely studied the crowd and didn't see a single person who wasn't smiling.

After the brief break, he turned up St. Peter and headed towards Tommy Black's. A pretty blonde standing across the street caught his attention. He watched her. She glanced down the street in his direction, about to cross the intersection. She caught him staring at her. He immediately looked away. Just before she entered Tommy Black's, a scarf dropped from the leather satchel that hung from her shoulder. She disappeared into the bar as Bobby scrambled towards the scarf.

A gust of wind lifted the scarf into the air and blew it half of a block down the street, but he quickly gave chase. As he grabbed for it, a short but stocky black man who leaned on crutches called out. He was missing his lower leg and foot below his right knee. Deep and prominent wrinkles covered his face. His teeth were stained and partially rotten. His eyes were tinted yellow. He noticed Bobby was carrying a photo.

"Hey, boy! Who you lookin' for?"

"Huh?" Bobby grunted, picking the scarf off the sidewalk.

"Who you lookin' for?" the man asked again, pointing to Chuck's picture with crooked fingers.

"My brother," Bobby said, showing him the picture.

The guy stared at the picture and shook his head.

"Ain't never seen him."

"No?"

"Oh, I would know," he grinned. "I gots a good memory. Yessir."

Bobby glanced to Tommy Black's.

"Thanks, but I need to. . ." Bobby started to say, motioning to the bar.

"What's your name?" the man asked him.

"What?"

"Your name?"

"Bobby."

"Nice to meet you, Bobby," he grinned. "You gots anything to spare?"

Bobby stared back at him, before digging through his pocket and pulling out a crumbled five-dollar bill.

"Aw right, now!" he said, his easy grin grew wider. "That contribution is a tax DEE-duction, seeing that I'm a non-profit entity, even though I never 'tended it to be that way. Shit."

"Take care," Bobby nodded as the man reached out his large, calloused right hand.

"Eddie Doomes," he proudly announced as Bobby shook his hand before walking away. "That's 'D-O-O-M-E-S'. Don't forget the 'E'. People's always forgettin' the 'E'."

Carrying the scarf, Bobby finally entered Tommy Black's and studied the place. Although it was a sunny day with a bright clear sky, the bar was dark and dreary and smelled of stale beer and disinfectant. The classic rock tune "Major Tom," by David Bowie, blared from the jukebox.

He quickly scanned the dive, searching for the young lady who dropped the scarf. The place wasn't very busy. A handful of older gentlemen were scattered about the long wooden bar. A couple groups of young tourists were sitting in the back, pounding drafts of Guinness stout and shots of whiskey.

"What's in the cup, Jack?" Butchie, the bartender, asked one of the regulars, pointing to a Styrofoam coffee cup the guy fiddled with.

"Huh?"

"The cup? What's in the cup?"

"Blood."

"Blood?" Butchie asked with a shake of his head. "Whose blood?"

"This gal I've been seein'. We were getting kind of intimate, you know. She bit me."

"Whose blood, Jack?"

"My blood."

"Bit you?"

"Yeah, bit me."

"Where?"

"Over on Dauphine."

"No. Where on your body?"

"The goddamn thing leaks now when I piss," Jack said, glancing to his lap.

"Why'd you bring the blood here?"

"Evidence. I may file assault changes."

"Gimme the cup, Jack."

"I scraped this off the floor. . ."

"The cup!"

"But she may have rabies," Jack said as he reluctantly handed the cup to Butchie. "I've been nauseous and itchy all morning."

Butchie took the filthy cup and tossed it in the trash as he noticed Bobby at the end of the bar.

"Did a young woman with blonde hair come in here?" Bobby asked him.

"She just left," Butchie answered.

"She dropped this outside," Bobby said, holding up the scarf.

"I can take it," Butchie said. "Holly's in here nearly every day at this time."

"Holly?"

"Or come back tomorrow. Give it to her yourself."

Bobby started to hand the scarf to Butchie but stopped.

"I'll come back tomorrow."

"Can I get you something?"

"How about a High Life and a shot of whiskey?" Bobby said, noting the bar's daily five-dollar beer-and-shot special.

Butchie returned with the drinks and placed them in front of Bobby, who reached out the photograph of Chuck.

"Have you seen this guy?"

Butchie slid the reading glasses that had been propped on his forehead over his eyes and studied the photo.

"I could have," he shrugged. "Every young fellow that comes in here looks like this to me. Sorry. I don't know. Maybe."

Chapter Twenty-Nine

Chuck was scheduled for a morning shift at Delia's. He awoke in an unfamiliar bed in a dark apartment just before ten o'clock in the morning. Smacking his chapped lips, he glanced around like most mornings trying to figure out where he was and how he had ended up there. His mouth was dry from drinking too much rum, and his throat was sore from smoking too many cigarettes. He rolled over and bumped into a warm, sleeping body beside him under the covers.

Still half-asleep, Elizabeth snuggled more of her warm naked body into his. The biggest of smiles stretched across his face as memories of the previous night flooded his racing mind. Suddenly, it felt as if a swarm of somersaulting butterflies filled his belly. He glanced down to her sleeping contented face and stared. He had just a few minutes to get to work without being late. He wished he was off that day. There was nowhere else in the entire world he wanted to be other than in that little apartment with Elizabeth.

Knowing he couldn't be late, he tried to ease his heavy body from hers and slide out of bed without waking her. She opened her eyes as he dressed in the dark and watched him. She didn't say anything. He turned toward her and noticed she was looking at him.

"You okay?" he asked, cautiously hoping she had as a good of time as he did.

"Yes," she answered, still studying him.

"I had fun last night."

"It was the best," she whispered.

"I have to go to work, or I'd stay…" he shrugged as his voice trailed off.

"I'll meet you after, if that's okay."

"Yes, of course. That's okay."

"We could get dinner. I'm off tonight."

"Yes, yes." He nodded excitedly. He checked the clock again. He didn't know whether to lean down and kiss her or run away.

"Go, go," she said, sensing the awkwardness. "You don't want to be late."

Chapter Thirty

Chuck sprinted to Delia's. It didn't feel as if his feet were touching the ground. His stomach was in knots but in a good way. As he raced down the street to work, people stared at him. He wildly waved both arms the entire way like propellers of an airplane. He was on top of the world.

He dashed into the bar, anxious to tell someone about his night. He abruptly stopped and his excitement faded a bit as Arthur, Delia's manager who he didn't care for, appeared to be tending the bar. Ned, the owner, also was there and seemed to be waiting for him.

"You'll never believe this!" Chuck beamed, bouncing onto the barstool next to Ned. "You know Elizabeth who comes in here?"

"Elizabeth?" Ned shrugged and motioned to Arthur to pour a couple of whiskey shots.

"Yeah, Elizabeth. The small, dark-haired young lady who comes in here," Chuck said as Ned shook his head and continued to shrug. "She works at Ace Seafood. She's always in here late. You know her."

"We need to talk, Chuck," Ned said, sounding serious and pointing to the whiskeys.

"Elizabeth invited me to her place last night! Can you believe that?" Chuck gushed, reaching for the whiskey shot. "We had the greatest time! I think she likes me! I can't believe it! She may really like me!"

"We have a problem," Ned said. They knocked back the whiskey.

"We're going to dinner tonight! Me and Elizabeth!" Chuck exclaimed, not paying attention to Ned. "I haven't been this excited about anything for a long time!"

"Listen to me, Chuck," Ned solemnly said. "Your cash register drawer. . ."

"Yeah, what about it?"

"Your cash register drawer has been short."

"Short? Bullshit!"

"It's been short three-hundred dollars for over fifteen straight shifts."

"Bullshit, Ned! Sometimes I throw most of my tips into it to cover the drinks I buy for everyone in here. Short, my ass!"

"Have you counted it?"

"No, I let Arthur. . ." Chuck paused, turning and looking for Arthur who had conveniently slipped into the back and out of sight. "He counts it."

"I've lost nearly five-thousand dollars."

"I didn't take your money," Chuck shook his head, craning his neck as he looked for Arthur in the back.

"I finally have this place turnin' a profit after nearly losin' it."

"You know me! What would I do with it? You see how I live!"

"I want to believe you, Chuck. I do. You're a great kid and have really helped me get this place back to where it used to be. But. . ."

"But, what?"

"I have to believe Arthur. He's been with me here for nearly twenty years now. We've been through a lot together. He's very protective of this place."

"Fuck Arthur!"

"I also had Ben from the kitchen keep an eye on things here as well."

"So, Ben was spying on me."

"You do drink a lot in here. Maybe workin' in a bar isn't the best thing for you."

"Fuck Ben! Fuck Arthur!"

"Don't lie to me, Chuck. You spend a lot of money on booze every day."

"I didn't take your fuckin' money! This job's all I got! I'm telling you the truth! You know that!"

"I'm sorry, Chuck. I think it's best for all parties involved that I let you go."

"So, I'm fired?" Chuck yelled, slamming his fist on the bar. "Fuck you!"

"You can still hang out here," Ned said, handing him an envelope of cash, "but we're worried about you. Here's the backpay from your last few shifts."

"You want money?" Chuck screamed, pulling the stack of twenty-dollar bills from the envelope and waving it in Ned's face. "Here you go, asshole! Take your money! Fuck off!"

Chuck angrily tossed the entire envelope of money into Ned's face and stormed out of the bar.

Chapter Thirty-One

Inside Tommy Black's, Bobby stood at the bar and sipped at an ice-cold High Life beer. A cigarette burned in the ashtray in front of him, surrounded by several empty shot glasses. The place was mostly empty, and the jukebox was extremely loud. The Nirvana song, "Heart-Shaped Box," played. Holly walked in as Butchie poured her a draft of light beer in a plastic to-go cup. She pulled out a cigarette. But before she could light it, Bobby snapped out a flame. She leaned towards him and took a long drag off the lit cigarette.

"Thanks," she said, blowing a puff of smoke into the air from the side of her mouth.

"Is this yours?" Bobby asked, holding up her scarf.

"Oh, my goodness!" she exclaimed with an excited grin. "Where d'you find it? I've been looking all over for it."

"You dropped it on the street yesterday. By the time I got in here, you were already gone."

"This was my mother's," she said, taking the scarf as she intently studied his scarred and bruised face.

"Your mother must've been a beautiful lady."

"Hey, Butchie, I want to buy. . ." she called out motioning to Bobby but not responding to his comment.

"Bobby."

"I want to buy Bobby here a drink."

Pulling a bottle of High Life from a tub of ice, Butchie popped the cap and slid it over to him as Holly started for the door.

"Hey, wait," Bobby called. "What's your name?"

Holly left Tommy Black's without answering or even turning to him. Taking a sip of the icy bottle of beer, Bobby wheeled around on his barstool and glanced to the jukebox. An older, disheveled guy in a paint-stained black shirt and pants with graying black hair and thick wispy eyebrows again played the same Nirvana song, "Heart-Shaped Box." The song obviously agitated the wiry, bald bar regular named Jack.

"Jesus Christ, Broadmore!" Jack moaned over the noise. "Not that fuckin' song again! How many fuckin' more times do we have to listen to that shit?"

"It's the only good song that's been written in the last twenty years! You son of a bitch, Jack!"

"You have no taste, Broadmore!" Jack shouted, before chugging the rest of his draft beer and turning to Butchie.

"I'm gone, Butchie! I can't take it here anymore. Back in the day, this used to be a classy joint."

Jack stormed out of the bar.

"Good! And don't come back!" Broadmore yelled, before looking to Butchie. "Could you turn this up a little bit more?"

"It's as loud as it goes, Broadmore."

Chapter Thirty-Two

Later that day, as fate would have it, Chuck entered Tommy Black's, the same bar where his brother spent most of the afternoon. The place was crowded and loud, but Bobby had already left, hours before. The jukebox blared the Beastie Boys song, "Girls." Flushed and shit-faced, Chuck badgered a young lady at the bar. He'd been drinking hard with the last of his tip money from his last shift at Delia's ever since he got the news that he'd been fired.

Thoughts of Elizabeth and their happy encounter the night before was long gone. He kept reaching over and pinching the young woman's ass at the bar. Annoyed, she continually slapped at his probing hands.

"Cut it out!" she barked at him as he slowly reached for her ass again. "Cut it out, I said!"

"Excuse me," the young woman called to Butchie, who was still bartending. "What's your name?"

"Huh?"

"What's your name?"

"Me?" Butchie pointed to himself.

"Yeah, what's your name?"

"Butch."

"What's his name?" she asked, pointing to Chuck.

"You mean Boozer?"

"Butch, can you please tell Boozer to quit grabbing my ass?"

"It's time to go, Boozer," Butchie ordered.

"But I still got a drink to finish."

"You have to leave," Butchie said, taking his drink. "Come back tomorrow after you've sobered up."

They stared a moment, before Butchie walked away to wait on another customer. Chuck awkwardly slid himself off the barstool and struggled to stand straight. He glanced around the busy bar, before extending his arm to pinch the young lady's ass one last time. She wheeled around and slapped him across the face, nearly knocking him off his unsteady feet.

"That's it!" Butchie hollered, stomping towards Chuck who teetered on drunken legs. "You're outta here! For good this time! I don't want to see your fuckin' face ever again! You're out!"

"I'm banned?"

"You're fuckin' banned!"

"But I love this place," he said, reaching for a half-filled, unattended cocktail on the bar and chugging it.

"Get out!" Butchie yelled, ripping the glass from his hand. "Get out now!"

Chuck clumsily stumbled towards the door. On his way out as he started to lose his balance, he reached for the bar for support and accidently swiped his arm across the top of it, knocking over several glasses that crashed to the floor. As he fell towards the door, he tumbled into the street and landed face-first onto the pavement out front.

Chapter Thirty-Three

obby had returned to the business center in the large chain hotel at the end of Royal Street. He pulled from his pocket the scrap of paper where he had written the phone number and address for the only Charles Anthony Raymond listed in the New Orleans area. He punched in the number of a courtesy phone in the room. The phone on the other end rang several times before an automated voicemail answered. Bobby took a deep breath and spoke into the phone after the buzz on the other line.

"I'm trying to reach Chuck Raymond," he paused, not knowing what to say next and having no return number to leave. "It is concerning an important matter."

He hesitated a moment before hanging up. He decided not to leave his name. If it was Chuck's number, he didn't want to spook him by letting him know his family was searching for him. He was certain Chuck was content to be hiding, or he likely would have called home sometime since he left Baltimore years before. He also was worried about how Chuck may react, knowing Bobby was in town looking for him.

Before Bobby could leave the business center, a hotel employee entered the room. Bobby studied the scrap of paper and looked up.

"Excuse me," Bobby said, looking to the slip of paper, "do you know where Banks Street is?"

"Yeah, in Mid-City."

"Can I walk there from here?"

"You could, but it may take a while."

Chapter Thirty-Four

As he continued his day of binge drinking, Chuck had limped into a dark dive bar on Dauphine. The bar was full and lively. The air in there was stale and thick with cigarette smoke. The jukebox blared the Dwight Yoakam version of the song "Suspicious Minds." Chuck sat between a passed-out, tattoo-covered old biker and a skanky blonde whose tight denim top and shorts barely covered her flabby tits and pasty white thighs.

The biker wore a black leather vest with an orange bandana on his head and was massive, weighing well over three hundred pounds. His loud snoring could be heard in the breaks between songs on the jukebox.

Slovenly and tanked, Chuck dragged on a cigarette with one hand, while playfully running his other hand under the blonde's short skirt.

"You're great!" he blurted. "You're really, really great!"

She squirmed on her barstool as he dug his hand deeper into her chunky thighs. Chuck stubbed out his cigarette, finished his drink, tossed several twenty-dollar bills onto the bar, and ordered shots for everyone.

The biker beside him opened his sleepy eyes and lifted his head. As Chuck leaned forward to gather his drink, the blonde edged over and whispered in the biker's ear.

"What the hell?" the biker shrugged, noticing Chuck's hand under the blonde's skirt.

Grinning, Chuck leaned back and held his glass of whiskey up to the blonde. Then he turned to the biker, who angrily slapped the shot glass from his hand, knocking it across the bar.

Chapter Thirty-Five

With fists clenched and arms cocked, the biker slowly circled a wobbly Chuck on Dauphine Street in front of the bar as a dozen people looked on. With his open hands held out in front of him, Chuck pleaded for forgiveness.

"I didn't know she was your old lady!"

The biker threw a wild punch at Chuck who ducked.

"She's great and all," Chuck stuttered, "but, but not my type! I like 'em younger, a lot younger. And thinner."

"Hey!" the blonde woman yelled.

"But not too young!" Chuck said, ducking from another wild right hand punch from the biker. "Or too thin!"

After missing with the right, the biker countered with a violent left cross that caught Chuck right between the eyes. Chuck dropped to the pavement like a ton of bricks, knocked out loaded. The crowd of onlookers audibly groaned at the sight of Chuck's limp body hitting the ground. Before returning inside the bar, the biker delivered a hard kick to Chuck's ribs and spit on his motionless body.

Chapter Thirty-Six

After his short, unintentional nap, Chuck staggered with the help of a stranger across the street to a fire hydrant with a steady drip. Battered, he filled his cupped hands with water several times and wiped his bloody face. A young family on vacation stared at him, before a teenager in the group snapped a picture. Slowly standing, Chuck raised his arms above his head like a monster in an old horror movie.

"Grrrrrrrr!" he growled at them, causing them to run away. "I'm not an animal! I'm fuckin' human being."

Before limping away, he grimaced from the pain in his ribs and caught a glimpse of his distorted image in the window of a closed storefront. He stared at himself a moment, studying the bruises and oozing cuts on his face.

Chapter Thirty-Seven

Night had fallen. Unsteady on his feet, Chuck stumbled up Dauphine and turned onto St. Peter. He wanted another drink and maybe some friendly conversation or to see a familiar face. The pain in his ribs burned, making it hard for him to breathe. He had a deep gash on the back of his head that wouldn't stop bleeding. After several blocks, he was back in front of Tommy Black's.

Using the door frame as support, he lifted himself up the one step and gracelessly entered. Butchie glared at him from behind the bar and immediately shook his head as he motioned outside.

"Out, Boozer!" Butchie yelled. "Get out!"

"Come on, man," Chuck pleaded. "This is my favorite place."

"I told you not to come back here! Get out!"

"I have a lot of friends here," Chuck said, glancing around the empty bar.

"Out!" Butchie ordered. "Get out! I'm not tellin' you again!"

Chapter Thirty-Eight

Bobby stood on Banks Street in front of a moderate home painted dark blue with gray trim. Two flags hung from poles on the front porch. One was a New Orleans Saints flag, and the other was for the Chicago Cubs. As he studied the place and re-checked the number on the scrap a paper, a young woman in her middle to late twenties stepped out of the house onto the porch.

"Can I help you?"

"I'm looking for someone named Chuck Raymond. Does he live here?"

"What do you want with him?"

"I'm his brother."

The young lady opened the door and called inside, "Chuck, you better come out here."

As Bobby waited, it felt as if his heart dropped into his gut. After a few anxious minutes, the man who lived at the house stepped outside. The man had blonde hair and was athletically built, standing over six feet, five inches tall. It wasn't his brother.

Chapter Thirty-Nine

A skinny, 20-year-old stripper danced for Chuck, who was sitting alone at a table in a sleazy strip club on Iberville. Besides a few dancers, the bartender, one doorman, and only three other men were there. They sat at the bar separated by multiple barstools.

The young stripper who danced for Chuck had an elaborate red, orange, and yellow flame tattoo that extended from her chest around her breasts down between her legs and up over her entire back. After the dance, Chuck waved a thick handful of twenty-dollar bills at her. Her eyes lit up as she took the money.

"You'll never believe this!" Chuck excitedly yelled over the loud music to her.

"What?"

"I just can't believe it!" he continued to yell, shaking his head.

"What?"

"I can't fuckin' believe it!"

"What?" she yelled back in an excited tone, shaking her arms.

"I have the exact same tattoo!" he joked, pointing to her intricate tattoo.

"No way!" she stared back at him with a puzzled but excited look, not getting the joke.

"Way!"

Chapter Forty

Elizabeth appeared in the doorway of Delia's. She was anxious to see Chuck. Her hands were shaking. She had never felt that way before. She knew then the feelings she had for him were real. She also was excited about going to dinner with him that night. She cheerily pounced onto an empty barstool but immediately sensed something was wrong. The jukebox was quiet. No one in the place would make eye contact with her. Arthur, Delia's manager, appeared behind the bar from the back. It seemed odd to her that he would be bartending. She scanned the place, searching for Chuck.

"Where's Chuck?" she asked as Arthur approached.

"What do you see in that guy anyway?" Arthur asked. He had always been jealous of how popular Chuck was at the bar. "He's a mess."

"Yes, a mess. But a glorious mess to me. Where is he?"

"What are you drinking?" Arthur asked, ignoring her question.

"A vodka and soda," she said, studying Arthur. She glanced to the man next to her. "Where's Chuck?"

The man didn't respond until Arthur walked away to make her drink.

"He got fired," the man whispered.

"Fired? What happened?"

Arthur returned and set the drink in front of her.

"Rumor has it," the man next to her said, waiting again for Arthur to walk away, "that Chuck's been stealing from the cash register every night."

"Stealing? Chuck? He wouldn't steal. It's not in him to steal. He has all he needs."

"Chuck thinks he was framed."

"Oh, no. Where is he now?"

"No one knows."

"How'd he take it?"

"Not good."

"Shit, I better go look for him."

"You better hurry. Someone saw him a few hours ago. Seems he was on quite a bender."

"Jesus Christ, Chuck," she mumbled to herself. "Please don't do anything stupid."

"Ned's out lookin' for him now. I guess he feels terrible about the whole thing. He knows he overreacted. He's so damn worried about losin' this crummy bar."

Chapter Forty-One

In her search for Chuck, Elizabeth caught a bus from Mid-City to the French Quarter and hustled to Tommy Black's. Chuck always talked about how much he liked that place. He also asked her almost nightly if she wanted to meet him there. She thought if he was anywhere, he'd likely be there.

She rushed inside. The bar was loud and lively. Butchie immediately approached her.

"I'm looking for someone," she said. "I know he likes to come here."

"What's his name?" Butchie asked.

"Chuck."

"The funny kid? A little chunky, longish hair? You mean Boozer?"

"Yeah, that's him. Was he here?"

"Yeah, I had to kick him out. Twice!"

"Twice?"

"He's never been a problem before. I've seen him drunk plenty of times but not like today."

"Do you happen to know where he is?"

"No, sorry."

"When did you see him last?"

"About an hour or two ago."

"Do you know of any other places around here he may hang out?"

"Is he in some kind of trouble?" Butchie asked, suddenly looking concerned.

"I need to find him."

"I'll keep an eye out for him. Who knows? He may stumble back in here later."

"I pray that he does."

Chapter Forty-Two

Filthy and still bleeding, Chuck sat alone on large, jagged rocks along the banks of the Mississippi River at the end of Canal Street. Giant rats scurried about him. He drank hard from a bottle of Ten High whiskey hidden in a brown paper sack. Staring into the black water, he wadded up twenty-dollar bills and tossed them, one at a time, into the flowing river.

Chapter Forty-Three

85

Chuck staggered alongside the streetcar tracks that ran parallel with the Mississippi River. A whistle from an approaching streetcar howled. Chuck stopped and turned to the oncoming streetcar. The car sped by him, generating a stream of air that tossed his long shaggy hair over his face.

Pushing the hair from his eyes, he continued his trek with no destination in mind. He walked between the tracks for another fifteen minutes or so, nearly falling a few times. Another streetcar neared. It sounded its whistle several times. He stepped away from the track and stared at the streetcar that rumbled towards him.

Chapter Forty-Four

Holding a drink, Bobby sat on a barstool by the opened doorway of Tommy Black's and watched the passing crowds of tourists. Like the day before, several empty shot glasses were on the bar in front of him. He had spent many hours that morning searching for Chuck. A Frank Sinatra song loudly played on the jukebox. A white-haired man, Harry-O, slept with his head on the bar a few stools away as Jack fidgeted at the other end. Harry-O always slept on the bar. He struggled to keep himself awake as he suffered from narcolepsy.

Broadmore wobbled in at the exact time he did every day and went directly to the jukebox. Like always, he was in his all-black shirt and pants. They were stained with different colors of fresh oil paint. Before he could put money in the jukebox, Jack stood and aimed a pistol he pulled from his coat at Broadmore. Everyone in the bar immediately ducked.

"Don't you dare, Broadmore!" Jack shouted. "You're not playin' that fuckin' shitty song by that fuckin' shitty band today!"

With a startled look, Broadmore put his arms in the air and slowly backed out of the bar, before dashing down the street.

"It's nothing but Frank today, all day and all night," Jack squawked.

"Put the gun down, Jack," Butchie warned in a calm voice with his arms outstretched in front of him. "Put it down."

With a mischievous grin, Jack pointed the gun at the sleeping Harry-O and pulled the trigger. Water squirted from the realistic-looking handgun and wetted his hair, waking him up. Harry-O looked confused.

"Jesus Christ. What the—" he mumbled, patting at his hair and glancing to the ceiling. "There's a leak in here, Butchie! You have a leak!"

As Harry-O continued to study the ceiling and around him, he started to yawn and began to lay his head back down on the bar. Once he closed his eyes, Jack squirted him again. Harry-O's head shot up like a rocket as he touched at his wet hair.

"Cut it out, Jack," Butchie said as Harry-O took a drink of beer and glanced around the bar.

Lighting a cigarette, Holly stepped out of the sunlight of the beautiful day and into Tommy Black's. She walked towards Bobby as Butchie poured her a beer in a plastic cup.

"You're still here?" she asked Bobby, dragging on the cigarette and reaching for the beer.

"Leaving so soon?" he asked.

"Are you going to be in here every day at this time?"

"It gives me something to look forward to."

She glanced outside and hesitated a moment before taking a seat next to him at the bar. She motioned to the empty shot glasses.

"Bad day?" she asked.

"A bad week, month, year. Pick one."

"You from around here?" she asked, curiously staring at his blackened eyes as he shook his head. "What are you doing in New Orleans?"

"Looking for my brother."

"You won't find him sitting in here."

"I've been all over this city for two days. I'm spent."

"What happens when you find him?" she asked, draining nearly half of her beer in one gulp.

"Pray he doesn't kill me."

"What'd you do to him?"

"I'm bringing him home for Christmas."

"Where's home?"

"Baltimore."

"You don't have much time."

"I'll find him."

"What happened to your face and hands?" she asked as Bobby glanced to his scarred hands.

"Long story."

"Make it quick," she said, finishing her beer and motioning to Butchie that she wanted another. "I need to go."

"I was a professional boxer."

"I've never met a real boxer before. I've known a lot of guys who thought they were."

"I fought my last fight a week ago."

"How did it go?"

"What do they say? You should've seen the other guy."

"Why'd you quit?"

"My job was to hit some of the baddest dudes around repeatedly as hard and as vicious as I could before they did the same to me. I can't do that anymore."

She stood and put out her cigarette.

"How 'bout you?"

"There's nothing to tell."

"Yeah, right? An attractive young woman comes in this old man bar for a beer and cigarette every afternoon."

She searched through her bag, not looking at him.

"Nobody bothers me here. I'd like to keep it that way."

"Stay a little longer. I'm feeling alone here. You know, new town."

"Go look for your brother."

Holly lit a cigarette as a hulking bouncer from the strip club named Todd entered the bar.

"Come on," he called to her.

"Hang out some more," Bobby said to Holly, not much louder than a whisper. "One more beer."

"You don't even know me," she said as Todd approached.

"Come on," the bouncer called out again. "Russell needs you. Now."

"I'll get there."

"Now!"

Todd stepped closer to Holly as Bobby stood.

"She said she'd get there," Bobby snapped as he stepped between Holly and the bouncer.

She studied Bobby as the bouncer flashed a look to her, then glared at Bobby before leaving.

"Who's Russell?"

"Now that you're done fighting," she said, not answering him. "Are you looking for a way to make some money?"

"I'm just here to find my brother."

"Will you be here tomorrow?" she asked.

"This is all I got."

She stood and gathered her things before tossing a twenty-dollar bill on the bar. She turned from Bobby without saying a word.

"What's your name?" he called.

She stopped at the door and briefly hesitated.

"Holly," she answered. "But you knew that, right?"

"I wanted you to tell me."

Chapter Forty-Five

Elizabeth repeatedly canvassed the French Quarter streets and desperately checked many of the Mid-City bars near Delia's long into the night in her search for Chuck. Exhausted, she returned home and spent a restless night in the same bed she'd shared with him the night before, tossing and turning until daybreak. She finally fell asleep sometime around nine o'clock in the morning.

Waking in the early afternoon, she quickly dressed and rushed to Delia's, hoping he had somehow showed up. She was sick to her stomach. It all seemed like a horrible nightmare. Reaching the bar, she hesitated before pulling the door open. She feared the worst.

She stepped inside. The place was quiet. Ned glanced to her from behind the bar. He looked worried. The television was tuned to a local news station. The jukebox was powered off. She glanced to the few other regulars who were gathered at the bar. They blankly looked at the television or stared into their drinks. The place felt like a morgue.

Not in the mood for a drink, she turned for the door. She stopped before leaving and scanned the inside of the place one more time and walked out. She went back to her apartment, crawled back into bed, and waited.

Chapter Forty-Six

Tommy Black's was rowdy. The Billy Joel song, "Only the Good Die Young," blared from the jukebox. Bobby was somewhat inebriated. He had been at the bar most of the afternoon. He sat with Jack, Harry-O, and Lucas, a tall wild-looking character with tattoo-covered arms and long brown hair. He appeared to be in his late twenties. Lucas didn't come to Tommy Black's much, but the dreary bar would light up whenever he entered.

"Butchie," Bobby called, holding several twenty-dollar bills and motioning to the guys at the bar. "Another round."

"Can't?" clucked Harry-O. "Who says I can't? Just tell me how many days until the New Year? I got me some lofty plans. You shall never see me here ever again. Tell me when and I will begin the countdown! Can't? Can't never did anything."

"New Year?" Jack mumbled. "Hell, I don't want this one to end. It's been a plenty good year for me. I had only one heart attack and no divorces."

"What's happenin' New Year's, Harry?" Butchie asked, distributing drinks and shots to the group.

Harry-O scanned the bar a few times while wiping at his sleepy eyes. He couldn't help but let his head nod forward. Within seconds, he was snoring like an out-of-control locomotive chugging down the tracks. Butchie shook him and asked again.

"Harry, what's happenin' New Year's?"

"I'm flying to Mexico City to make a pick-up," he said with a pause as he wiped at his sleepy eyes. "There'll be a car. Hundreds of pounds of hash, smack, coke. If I make it back, I get sixty-thousand dollars in unmarked bills, which is just exactly enough to let me live like a king until I die."

"Which may happen before you leave, Harry," Butchie mumbled while pouring a draft of beer.

"And if I get busted, the United States of America will take me off the streets, clean me up, get me sober, and feed me three well-rounded meals a day all at their expense. And that doesn't sound too bad either."

"You'll never make it, Harry," Jack called out. "You'll fall asleep and miss the flight to Mexico, if there really is a flight to Mexico."

"Butchie?" Harry-O asked in a whisper, leaning forward and ignoring Jack's comments. "Can I get a High Life? One on the house."

Butchie shook his head but grabbed Harry-O a bottle of beer, twisting the cap off for him.

"Let the countdown begin!" Harry-O shouted again in his hoarse voice, hoisting the bottle high in the air as beer foamed out the top.

After his proclamation, he took a small sip with a shaking hand and was soon asleep again, his white head hidden in his folded arms.

Suddenly, Broadmore rushed into the bar. He carried a pair of large hedge clippers. The 24-inch blades were opened wide. He walked directly to the jukebox. Without hesitating, he positioned the power cord of the jukebox between the blades and slammed the handles of the clippers closed. A shower of sparks exploded around him as he cut the cord in half. The power in the bar blinked several times before going completely out.

"Hey!" Butchie screamed. "What in the hell are you doing, Broadmore?"

"I can't fuckin' stand Billy Joel!" he yelled back before storming out the darkened bar.

"Get out, Broadmore!" Butchie hollered. "And stay out!"

"Someone needs to do something about him," Jack moaned. "He's a menace to this bar! He's a madman! He's nuts!"

"Relax, Jack," Butchie grumbled, moving to a utility box in the hallway near the bathrooms.

He flipped the breaker, and the power flickered a few times before coming back on. Harry-O lifted his head a moment before resting it again on the bar. Lucas moved a beer bottle away from him as Harry-O stretched his arms out on the bar and nearly knocked it over. Butchie pulled the cut but live cord from the wall socket and placed an out-of-order sign on the jukebox. The socket and the wall above it were charred.

"The fix is in at the Fairgrounds on Saturday," Lucas whispered to Butchie as he returned behind the bar. "You still game?"

"Yeah, I'm still game," Butchie said, thumbing through a small black book and searching for the jukebox service phone number. "I need a big payday. I have to get the hell out of this goddamn place for good.”

Lucas took a sip of his drink and glanced to Bobby who knocked back his whiskey shot.

“I’m headin’ to a party—a baaall for aaaall, where no one’s outta place. Not in this town, man. It’ll be a blast. Come with me.”

Butchie pushed another shot of whiskey to Bobby.

“Everyone who’s anyone will be there. The socialites and money class,” Lucas went on. “The politicos and police chiefs. Drag queens, sex queens, drug lords, slum lords—you name it.”

“Sounds like trouble,” Bobby said, swallowing hard on the whiskey as two attractive young ladies approached Lucas. One was a sexy, leggy brunette named Rachel, and the other was a curvy redhead, Miranda.

“Speakin’ of trouble,” Lucas broadly grinned.

With squinting eyes, Bobby stared at Rachel who wore an oversized black leather coat over a short, slinky dress. He thought about his brother, but his eyes kept dragging back to Rachel’s legs.

“That’s Rachel,” Lucas whispered to Bobby from the side of his mouth.

“Are they going?” Bobby asked, still staring at Rachel as he finished his beer.

“Absolutely,” Lucas smiled, wrapping his arms around the waists of the two pretty women. “Come with us, man.”

“I got to piss,” Bobby grumbled, slowly sliding off the barstool. “Let me think about it.”

“Come on. No fun ever happens when you have to think about anything.”

Chapter Forty-Seven

Bobby urinated into a stained trough filled with ice. Apparently, the ice was used to help hide the bathroom's overwhelming stench. After a minute or so, the urine reluctantly began to flow from him. He clenched his teeth in pain.

"Oh mother," he groaned to himself in the empty restroom.

The urine was still a rusty brown color. The kidney pain in his lower back had nearly become unbearable. When he was done, he zipped up and lingered at the trough a moment, trying to catch his breath. After regrouping, he slowly staggered out of the bathroom. He thought of his brother, his parents, Mary: home. He noticed a pay phone that hung from the wall near the restroom door. He lifted the receiver and listened for the tone. It was live. It had to be one of the last active pay phones in the city. He quickly dialed a number. Mary answered on the other end after accepting the charges.

"Bobby? Where are you?"

"New Orleans. I made it."

"Where are you calling from?"

"Some dive in the French Quarter. Tommy Black's."

"Why are you calling me?"

"I needed to hear a familiar voice," he said. "And I'm not doing so well. I need to see a doctor."

"Come back to Baltimore."

"I can't. Not yet."

"Then don't call here. Please."

"Because of Frank?"

"No. Because of me. It's over, Bobby. You know that. It's best you not call here again."

"But Mary—"

"I don't know if you heard," she said, interrupting. "Your dad has taken a turn for the worst. You need to come home. That's why I answered."

"Not until I find Chuck."

"How's the search?"

Maybe if he found a map, his search would be more focused, he thought, but before he could respond, Rachel tugged at his jacket.

"Are you coming to the party with us?" she asked as he put his hand over the phone's receiver. "I want you to come with us."

Bobby looked away from Rachel and spoke into the phone, "I have to go, Mary."

"Frank and I are getting married. I thought you should know."

There was a long pause as Bobby looked back to Rachel who smiled and held her hands together in front of her like she was praying.

"Hey," Bobby said into the phone with a cheerful but insincere tone. "How 'bout that? I'll send a wedding gift."

"Come home, Bobby. Your mother needs you."

"So long, Mary," he said after a short pause. "Send my best wishes to Frank."

His voice drifted as Mary started to say something. He hung up the phone and gently tapped the receiver a couple of times before turning to Rachel.

"You, okay?" she asked.

"I'll be all right," he said, trying to smile.

"I'm Rachel," she introduced herself, reaching out her hand.

"Yeah, I know," he said, taking her hand in his and shaking it. "Bobby."

"What happened to your hands?" she asked, caressing the knuckles of his bruised and swollen hands before looking up. "And your face?"

"Bad career choice."

"You need a friend, Bobby?"

"God, you smell nice," he said as she dragged him away from the pay phone and back to the bar.

"Are you coming to the party with us?"

"So many questions."

"What are you doing in New Orleans?" she asked before they reached the others.

"Searching for someone."

"We all are."

Chapter Forty-Eight

It was a warm December evening. A full moon hung large over a palatial, four-story mansion in the city's Garden District. Several giant, 100-year-old oak trees lined a long driveway that divided a perfectly manicured lawn. Bright lights, set on the ground five feet apart, illuminated each side of the driveway. Loud laughter and music from inside the house filled the night. Rachel and Miranda playfully sprinted through the damp grass for the front door. Several feet behind them, Lucas and Bobby drunkenly gave chase.

The ladies entered the house first. Lucas and Bobby followed. Hundreds of bodies were tightly packed together in the expansive living room, dancing at a frenetic pace to the synthesized beat of electronic music. A young DJ and his sound system perched in the middle of the room on a small, make-shift stage. The DJ was nearly hidden behind stacks of vinyl, shelves of turntables and microphones, and a tall bank of speakers.

The enormous room was dark except for the rapid, repetitive flash of colored strobe lights. Giggling, Rachel pulled Bobby into the throng of bodies that bounced with the vibrating beat of the music. He tried to hold fast to his resolve to find his brother, but Rachel began to sway on the dance floor. As if from a distance, he grew aware they were dancing, wildly, their bodies locked together. Rachel ran her hands all over him. Her short, flimsy dress under her leather jacket clung to her sweaty body. She leaned her face forward into his neck before moving to his lips. She kissed him long, and she kissed him hard. Breathing heavy, he tried to pull away. She wouldn't let him.

"You got to keep up," she whispered, pressing her lips and tongue against his ear, the last of his resolve blew away.

He nearly melted as she blew her warmth breath into his ear. She reached for his hand. He opened it. She placed a pill in his palm. He tried to look at it but couldn't tell what it was in the flashing light. Without hesitating, he threw the pill into his mouth and swallowed it.

Chapter Forty-Nine

The kitchen was crowded, and everything was a blur. Bobby was there with Lucas. He had lost Rachel somewhere on the dance floor. He was unsteady on his feet, fidgeting by a door that led outside to the back yard. Lucas yelled over the loud chatter of conversation, talking to the owner of the house and the party's host, Sidney Dorgenois. Sidney was an obese gay man who owned numerous successful businesses in the New Orleans area, including restaurants, night clubs, seafood wholesalers, liquor stores, and smoke shops. He also was heavily involved in the local city government.

"Lucas, love!" Sidney greeted him as they enthusiastically shook hands.

"Sidney! Good to see you, my brother!"

"Lucas, hon, you look fabulous!" he said before pointing to the six-foot, eight-inch transvestite standing behind him. "Y'all remember Kitty Kitty Meow, don't you?"

Kitty reached his meaty right hand out as Lucas shook it. Bobby studied Kitty with squinty eyes. It had been thirty minutes since he had taken the pill that Rachel had given him, and he didn't know if what he was seeing was real or not. His body seemed an empty shell. His hands tingled. His mouth was dry. Both his heart and cluttered mind raced. He felt as if his body was anchored to the floor, but his insides were slowly drifting away to the kitchen ceiling above—like his soul was leaving him.

He had an overwhelming urge to reach up and pull what was left of his soul back. Instead, he wildly flailed his arms into the open air around his body. He must've been a sight to the others there. Heavily perspiring, he continually shot glances to the door behind him, thinking someone was there. He needed air. He wanted to leave. But suddenly he couldn't move.

"Lucas, babe," Sidney's voice boomed as he pointed towards Bobby. "Who's this damaged young thing over there?"

"That's Bobby. He's looking for his brother," Lucas said, motioning to Sidney. "Bobby, this is Sidney. Nobody throws a better party. Nobody."

"Yeah, you right about that," Sidney grinned, approaching Bobby. "What happened to your face?"

With a sneaky wink, Sidney reached out his fleshy arm to Bobby. Uncomfortable with his advance, Bobby awkwardly backed into the door behind him before being smothered in Sidney's sweaty embrace. The cologne Sidney wore to try and hide the heavy stink of his body odor nearly caused Bobby to hurl the content of his unsettled guts.

Chapter Fifty

A high-stakes game of poker took place in a crowded recreation room. The gymnasium-sized space was filled with partiers playing numerous vintage video arcade games, like Pac-Man, Donkey Kong, Frogger, and Space Invaders. A few people shot hoops at an indoor basketball court at one end of the room. There also were multiple ping-pong tables that weren't being used and a regulation-sized bowling alley. Several large, muted televisions hung from the walls and rafters of the room. Some were tuned to 24-hour sports channels. Others showed popular movie classics.

Thousands of dollars and scores of colored plastic chips were scattered over the green felt of a large poker table. Several people sat around the circular table. Sidney had dragged Lucas, Kitty Kitty, and Bobby there for a few expensive hands of cards. That is where Bobby reunited with Rachel. They played together as one team. She smiled over her cards and squirmed in his lap. She continued to glance back to him, digging and wiggling herself deeper between his legs.

Before Bobby could check the cards they were dealt, Rachel made a call as he choked down a glass of beer, trying to put out the volcanoes he perceived in his head. After losing the hand, she tossed the cards to the table with a pouty face, trying to appear angry but laughing at the same time. Bobby finally checked to see what cards she held.

"You didn't have anything," he said, studying the five cards. "Not even a pair."

"I was bluffing," she giggled.

"Bluffing? We just lost five-hundred dollars."

"How do we win your money back?"

"We don't. That's it. I'm broke."

Chapter Fifty-One

Bobby and Rachel explored all four floors of the house. She excitedly dragged him up multiple flights of stairs and through different bedrooms, a study, and even a library, periodically stopping at times for short but steamy make-out sessions. He tried his best to keep pace with her as well as not lose his mind. The drug she gave him was hitting him harder. It had affected his ability to walk as he clumsily chased after her.

His legs were jelly, and it didn't feel as if his feet and legs were attached. Each new flight of stairs seemed a mountain, and he was nauseous. The drug wasn't sitting well. His heart and mind still raced. He couldn't focus. His hands shook.

They found the room Rachel was searching for, the master bedroom. She checked over her shoulder before slowly opening the closed door and pulling Bobby in with her. She rushed for the double king-size bed but was too late. It was occupied and being used by two young and beautiful couples, who appeared to be sharing partners. They were so into themselves and their naughty activity that they didn't notice Bobby and Rachel watching.

Bobby stared at the couples until Rachel yanked him into a walk-in closet the size of most French Quarter apartments. They followed a dark hallway beyond the closet and entered a small storage area. It was filled with hundreds of Mardi Gras costumes hanging on racks positioned throughout the room. Many elaborate and colorful masks hung from the walls of the room. Some of them were humorous, and others were frightening. Many were cartoon-like, funny faces of celebrities or well-known characters from movies and TV shows. Some were papier mâché replicas of Greek gods and goddesses that many of the Mardi Gras parades were inspired by. Some of the masks were of animal heads, like a fox, a bull, a monkey, or a donkey.

Rachel reached for the dusty bull mask and roughly plopped it on Bobby's head, nearly knocking him down. He staggered around the room in a circle, trying to regain his balance. The mask was five times larger than his head; the horns on top spanned four feet from the tips of each one. She then pulled a white mask of a rabbit head from the wall and slipped it on. Bobby dropped his head backwards, trying to see from under the bottom of the mask what Rachel was doing. She forcefully pushed him onto the floor on his back and crawled on top of him. She sat on his waist with her legs pressed tight against his bruised sides and roughly unbuttoned his shirt, grinding her bottom into his groin.

"Your heart?" she said, positioning her hands on top of Bobby's pounding naked chest.

"Yeah, it's ready to explode."

"Because of me?" she playfully asked, grinding her body into him.

"And other things." He tried to nod. "What will you tell the paramedics when they come for my body?"

She sat heavy on his groin. He lifted the awkwardly large mask slightly and could see her face from under it. She had removed the rabbit mask. He couldn't look away as she pressed her tailbone deeper into him. Like most of his body, that area was numb. He didn't feel a thing. It was dead as always.

Trying to get more of a response from him, she hiked her dress up a bit around her waist and pulled the bottom of her panties to the side. She slid more of her body towards his chest and rocked it back and forth. He could feel the moist, bare skin under her dress on his exposed belly. She reached back and dug her hand deep between his legs.

"You gave me the wrong kind of pill," he mumbled under his breath, not feeling much of her touch.

"I can fix you," she whispered, squeezing his groin more tightly.

"You're too late."

"You don't know me," she groaned, rocking her body deeper and harder into him and tightening the grip of her legs against his sore ribs.

His heart raced faster. He tried to catch his breath. He felt as if he were about to pass out. He needed air. He tugged at the mask that was nearly suffocating him. Despite his lack of arousal, she rode him harder and faster. She sighed louder. She grabbed for his chest with both hands, digging her nails into his skin. She yelled out his name before collapsing into him. He wrapped his arms around her heaving body. She sighed and continued to pant. He tightened his grip around her and gently caressed the back of her head. After a deep breath, she sat up. They stared at each other.

“Tell me,” she quietly said, softly running her warm, slender fingers over the red and bruised knots and stitched cuts on his face. “What happened to you?”

“Don’t look at me like that. I’m a nightmare.”

“Not to me.”

Chapter Fifty-Two

Bobby and Lucas were crammed together in a small half-bathroom that was situated next to the arcade room. Bobby had lost Rachel again. She had left him on the floor of the closet and rejoined the party, again disappearing into the crowd of dancers in the living room. It had taken Bobby many minutes after their encounter to gather himself before he could stand and leave the closet.

Staring into the bathroom mirror, Lucas lightly brushed at his wild, long hair with a wetted hand as if in a trance. In his other hand, he held a lit cigarette. The long and growing ash at the cigarette's end perilously dangled over an expensive imported Persian rug. Bobby sat on the floor, hugging a gold toilet. Taking several deep breaths, he wiped at his mouth after having vomited and dry heaved for many minutes.

"You could be a rich man come Saturday," Lucas said, talking to his reflection. "The fix is in on the tenth race at the Fairgrounds."

"How rich?" Bobby groaned from the floor.

"How much do you need?"

"Is it a sure thing?"

"I'm best friends with the jockey and trainer of the horse who's supposed to win. Can't get any surer that that. It'll be like an ATM."

Chapter Fifty-Three

After regaining his composure and cleaning himself up, Bobby left the bathroom alone in search of Rachel. He walked into the living room. The music was louder, the beat faster. The strobe lights seemed to be flashing more quickly. He stared into the crowd. The bodies moved together with the beat like the waves on a stormy, agitated ocean. After several minutes, he finally spotted her. She seductively danced with a handsome young stranger.

She noticed Bobby watching them. She grinned as the stranger slipped his hand under her skirt. She dropped her head back and sighed before leaning into him. She playfully whispered in his ear and kissed him. Bobby studied them a moment before walking out.

He returned to the rec room in search of Lucas. Bobby was ready to leave the party. He scanned the busy arcade. A blur of people shared cocaine divided in lines on the consoles of the different video games. Others lounged on plush couches and love seats behind thick clouds of white, skunky-smelling smoke, smoking weed or making out. He checked the bathroom they had shared earlier. It was empty. He hurried through all the areas of the game room. Lucas was gone. He found a stocked refrigerator and pulled out a bottle of local beer. He drained it in two large swigs, while staring at one of the muted televisions showing sports replays. A boxing highlight came on; he watched it a moment before turning away. He grabbed for the remote control and quickly changed the channel.

Bobby found a door, searching for a way out of the house. It led to a multicar garage that was filled with seven parked luxury vehicles. He turned sideways and slid between a black Cadillac Escalade and a spotless Land Rover then slipped by a Lexus SUV and what looked to be a brand-new Bentley. He discovered a red button on the wall and pushed it. The heavy steel and wooden garage door quietly hummed to life and slowly but smoothly lifted off the ground. Bobby kneeled and ducked under it before it was fully opened. He rushed into the driveway. Unexpectedly, Rachel called from the front door of the house.

"Bobby?"

He initially kept walking, pretending not to hear her.

"Bobby?" she called again, trotting after him and pulling on her leather coat. "Wait!"

He stopped and turned as she hurried towards him.

"You were leaving without me?"

"I have to find my brother."

"Where are you going?"

"I need to get back to the Quarter."

"Can I go with you?"

He stared at her and didn't respond, knowing he should leave alone.

"I'll get us a cab," she said, digging for a phone in her purse.

Chapter Fifty-Four

The popular local radio station WWOZ softly played as a ceiling fan spun awkwardly out of balance. Rays of the setting sun slipped through the shuttered windows of Rachel's apartment on St. Ann Street. She and Bobby hadn't made it there until sometime after daybreak. They had barhopped their way through the Quarter after leaving the party. They passed out together soon after getting there and slept the day away.

Shirtless, exposing his bruised sides, Bobby slumped on the edge of the bed, staring at Rachel who peacefully slept, the chaos of the previous night long over. The debilitating effects of the drug she had given him had worn off. He expected to feel much worse. Instead, he felt nothing.

He glanced to her. Rachel's tanned back shined in the darkened room. He knew the simplest thing would be to crawl back into bed and curl up to her warm bare body. He dragged hard on a cigarette, waking her. He reached for a mostly full bottle of flat beer that sat on the floor at the foot of the bed. She rolled over. She studied him. Her hair was messed. The mascara she wore was smeared. Lips that were once painted ruby red were bare. She appeared much younger than when he first met her.

"Come back to bed," she sighed, knowing that he was leaving. "Get some sleep. You need it."

"I have to go."

"Where?"

"I'm here to find my brother," he said. "Not for the party."

"You don't have to leave now. You can stay here while you look for him."

He slowly stood and grimaced in pain.

"You can have anyone you want," he said as they continued to study each other. "Why me?"

"Come back to bed, Bobby."

"Goodbye, Rachel," he said, pulling on his shirt and limping to the door.

"See you Saturday?" she said, sitting up.

"Saturday?" he asked, not turning to her.

"The horseraces," she reminded him as he turned. "Day after tomorrow."

"Saturday seems like a long time from now."

Holding the bottle of stale beer, he stepped outside and gently closed the door behind him. Rachel threw herself back onto the bed and buried herself under the blankets before slamming her fist into a pillow. He dug out the last cigarette from a pack he pulled from his shirt pocket and took a seat in the small entranceway at the front door of Rachel's apartment.

Lighting the cigarette, he checked his watch. He knew he was late. He took a sip of the warm beer and glanced up. The sky in the distance was fiery orange from the setting sun. As he quietly enjoyed the smoke, he closely studied each of the faces in the long line of people who streamed into the French Quarter via St. Ann. He searched the faces for Chuck, wishing he had more cigarettes and something stronger to drink.

Chapter Fifty-Five

Holly sat alone at the bar of Tommy Black's. She'd been waiting several hours for Bobby. She fingered the rim of a plastic cup half-filled with beer. A couple of empty shot glasses and a pile of one- and five-dollar bills were in front of her. She checked her watch and thought about getting another beer. She glanced to the door every time someone walked in.

She looked to Butchie. He quietly chatted with a regular at the other end of the long bar. She swallowed the last gulp of beer in the cup and pushed the stack of money in front of her, leaving it as a tip. She glanced to the bar's front door one last time and stood. She slung her leather satchel over her shoulder and walked out.

A few minutes later, Bobby approached the bar. He looked like a wreck. His clothes were wrinkled and stained. He didn't have his leather coat. He thought he had lost it, not knowing he had left it at Tommy Black's the previous night. His hair was a matted, wild mess. He was exhausted. He was supposed to have met Holly but knew he was late. Because of that, he almost didn't return to the bar. He figured he'd blown any chance he had with her.

As he neared Tommy Black's, he saw a familiar face. With his back against the brick wall of the building next to the bar, Eddie Doomes leaned forward on his crutches, a cigarette dangling. He called to Bobby.

"Hey, kid, you find that brother of yours?"

"Huh?" Bobby mumbled, turning to the voice.

"You lookin' for your brother, right?" Eddie asked, bouncing off the wall and hopping out of the darkness towards Bobby. "You find him?"

"Not yet."

"He don't want you to find him."

"What?"

"I know, kid," Eddie said. "I've been gone a long time. Folks used to search for me. I didn't want 'em to find me, so they didn't. When you're gone, you're gone. Your brother is long gone."

"If he's here, I'll find him."

"Maybe so," Eddie shrugged. "Look all you want. But you need to know where to look. You need help. I know these streets. Nobody knows these streets better than me. If anyone can find your brother, I can."

"You can help me?"

"Gimme that picture of him. I'll look for you."

"Why do you want to help me?"

"I been lost a long time," Eddie answered. "And no one's lookin' for me now."

Bobby reluctantly handed the photo of Chuck to Eddie who studied it for a moment. He then looked up to Bobby with his easy grin.

"If he's here, I'll find him."

"Don't lose that," Bobby said, pointing to the picture. "That's the only one I have."

"I ain't lost nothin' in twenty-five years."

"I'll be back here at this bar on Saturday morning. Meet me then."

"Yessir, you right. If he's here, I'll have somethin' by then," Eddie nodded as Bobby slapped a twenty-dollar bill in his hand. "Aw right now! This here night has started off just right!"

Bobby watched Eddie hop away on his crutches, wondering if he had made a mistake. He then stepped into Tommy Black's and scanned the bar before checking his watch. The bar was mostly empty. Holly was no longer there. Butchie approached Bobby. He knew Bobby was there to meet Holly.

"You just missed her," Butchie said, pouring Bobby a shot. "She was here all afternoon and most of the evening. She's never stayed that long."

"Do you know where she went?"

"I think she got called into work."

"Where does she work?"

"She'll likely be back here tomorrow."

Chapter Fifty-Six

Appearing uneasy, Holly picked at a plate of food in a famous steakhouse on the corner of Bourbon and Iberville in the French Quarter. She looked stunning in a sparkling silver evening gown. As a favor to her father in return for a much-needed day off, she agreed on short notice to entertain a well-connected and rich regular client of her father's club.

The man was from Mississippi and called Big Country because of his obscene wealth and imposing physical presence. He was morbidly obese, weighing over four-hundred pounds and standing over six feet, three inches tall. His name was Louis Jordano, and he always got what he wanted. His affinity for beautiful women was only matched by his unsatiated appetite for gourmet food and top-shelf liquor.

Their table was covered with assorted appetizers and several of the restaurant's signature dishes. There were plates of raw and flame-grilled oysters and shrimp cocktail. Salads and main courses of thick-cut ribeyes, crawfish etouffee, and loaded baked potatoes were scattered in front of them. Louis shoveled large bites of bloody pieces of steak into his mouth and washed it down with gulps of expensive cabernet. Reaching across the table, he emptied one bottle of the red wine into Holly's glass. He refilled his glass.

"Eat, baby," he said, chewing the food with his mouth partially open. "Eat."

She glanced up from the plate of food she barely touched as he awkwardly stared at her. Uncomfortable in his gaze, she checked her watch, wishing she was somewhere else.

"More wine," he grumbled between bites, searching for a server. "We need more wine!"

Holly took a small sip as he scanned the crowded eatery. She glanced to the window that faced Iberville Street. To her surprise, Bobby watched, his face inches from the glass windowpane. She quickly looked away and fidgeted in her seat as the server returned with another bottle of pricey red wine. She glanced back to the window, but Bobby had disappeared.

Louis filled his glass with more cabernet and stabbed at the last piece of steak on his plate. He studied Holly who stared at the empty window.

"What's a matter, baby? You don't seem to be enjoyin' yourself."

Holly returned her attention to Louis.

"Food not good?" he asked. "I know that ain't it. You can't get a better plate of food than this place anywhere in town."

"I'm not that hungry."

"Come on and smile for Big Louie."

She politely smiled.

"That's better," he grinned, deeply staring into her bright green eyes and causing her to look away. "Damn, girl. How'd Russell get so lucky with you? You sure are a fine one."

Suddenly, there was a commotion at the entrance of the restaurant as Bobby barged into the place. The manager and the host were struggling to hold him back. Holly and Louis looked to the disturbance. Seeing Bobby, Holly glanced away and slid down low in her seat. She pretended not to know him.

"I told you to get the hell out of here!" the manager yelled as Bobby fought to free himself.

"I just want to talk with my friend!" he hollered. "Holly! Holly!"

"Is he here for you?" Louis asked as Holly shrugged.

"Holly!"

Two other restaurant employees joined the manager and host and forcefully pushed him towards the front door.

"Holly!" he called one last time before being kicked out of the place.

"I'm not your only admirer tonight, I guess," Louis said, chugging a nearly full glass of wine. "Looks like I have some competition."

After several minutes, Holly finally looked to the front entrance of the restaurant. Bobby was gone. She quickly glanced to the window where he was before. No one was there.

Chapter Fifty-Seven

olly had never worked as an escort for her father before, but Louis was a special client. She assumed she was hired only as an escort for the night and would be able to leave after dinner and some drinks. After dinner, they shared cocktails at a carousel bar in a swanky hotel on Royal Street. The circular bar gradually moved, almost unnoticed, in a circle like the slowest of kiddie rides at a carnival. The bar was popular with tourists.

She tried to be polite as her inebriated companion droned on about his childhood in Mississippi, his family, his struggles, and how he accumulated his great wealth over the years. He was a prospective new client for her father and a potential investor in New Orleans real estate. Because of his wealth, Russell was pressing him to purchase an exclusive and very expensive yearly VIP package to his club that included all the booze, food, and women Big Country and his buddies could handle. So, Russell chose Holly, his best girl, to seal the deal.

But the carousel bar was the last place she wanted to be, and Louis was the last person she wanted to spend the evening with. She needed to rush out of there and search for Bobby. She had yet to process why she wanted to be with him after having only met him a few times. But she felt a comfort she had never known before when he was close to her. She thought he was the safety net her life needed.

Now excessively drunk, Louis struggled to maintain eye contact with Holly. She was uncomfortable in his awkward stares. His wandering eyes were too fixated on her long perfect legs tightly crossed at the barstool beside him. He would reach over and briefly touch them. She pushed his hand away after every attempt. He seemed hypnotized at times, losing his train of thought as he studied the revealing, low-cut evening gown.

After finishing up at the bar and stepping into the lobby of the hotel, it was time for Louis to pay the escort fee and hopefully the exclusive membership to Russell's club. At least, that's what Holly thought.

"My checkbook's up in the room," he said, placing his hand on the bare skin of the small of her back and trying to direct her to the elevator. "I believe I will take your father's offer. We must go upstairs for the check."

Holly knew it was a mistake, but she reluctantly followed him up to his suite. She had to decide what was worse, trusting him in a hotel room or facing her father empty-handed after blowing the big deal. Louis had booked an executive suite on the top floor of the hotel for the week. He pawed at Holly, continually stroked her hair, and leaned into her for the entire ride up the elevator. Her plan was to get the check and get out of the room as fast as possible.

They entered the immaculate room. It was three times the size of her apartment. The suite had multiple bedrooms and two bathrooms. A serving table had been set up and covered with different trays of fruits and vegetables and meats and cheeses. A tub of ice also had been placed on the table and filled with bottles of champagne and different imported beers.

Holly lingered near the room's main entrance as Louis staggered to a set of shuttered doors, opening them to a balcony and a spectacular nighttime view of the French Quarter. St. Louis Cathedral, Jackson Square, and the Mississippi River glowed in the distance. A pleasant breeze blew, quickly filling the room with warm but comfortable air. Louis stepped onto the balcony and leaned on the iron railing. He studied the scenery a moment before turning to Holly.

"Come out," he called. "The view is breathtaking."

"I thought we came up for the check."

"We did, but what's the rush?" he asked, motioning to the serving table. "Get a drink. Have a snack."

"I'm much too full, thank you," she said, not moving much from the front door of the suite. "It's been a long night."

"Come on, come on," he said, stepping into the room from the balcony. "I won't bite."

He reached for one of the bottles of champagne and two glasses. He popped the cork and quickly filled them.

"Come here," he said, holding out the two glasses. "We'll have a celebratory toast and drink, then I'll get you the check."

With some hesitation, she stepped towards him. Sensing her uneasiness, he opened a desk drawer and pulled out a checkbook.

"See," he said, pulling out a signed check written to her father and setting it on the nightstand several feet away from her. "The check's right here."

Holly slowly approached him as he extended one of the champagnes to her. She took it. He held his glass in the air. She lightly tapped her glass to his.

"To a long and beautiful relationship with your father's company," he said, throwing back the champagne in one large gulp. "And perhaps another date with you, my most beautiful escort."

She took a small sip, still not trusting him.

"Here, here," he said, moving closer to her and easing his arm around her waist. He took the glass of champagne from her hand and placed it on the serving table. She tried to back away from him as he eased his nose into her neck.

"Goddamn, you're beautiful," he mumbled, herding her towards a wall by the balcony door.

He quickly had her cornered between the serving table and the wall, pressing his thick, heavy body against her. She tried to push him away, feeling the sweat under the pits of his arms that had leaked through and stained his sports coat. For the first time, he was close enough in which she could smell his rotten breath. He clumsily thrust his rough, stubbled cheek along her neck and awkwardly slobbered in her ear. She was repulsed. She had never been so disgusted in her life. She turned her head away from him as he played with the straps of her dress and tugged at her gown.

It wasn't long until his stubby but active fingers found their way under her short dress. She pulled her legs together to limit what he could touch. He worked to kiss her. She moved her head from side to side, trying to avoid him.

"Come on, baby," he said, half belching. "Where's the sugar?"

Not cooperating, she squirmed and struggled in his arms. He pressed more of his large body forward, pinning her against the wall. He yanked both straps of the dress off her shoulders.

"Your daddy guaranteed me a good time. He says I get whatever I want."

As he dug in his pocket for a phone, she turned to face him. They stared a moment.

"Damn, bitch, you're the finest whore I've ever seen."

"Please let me go. I need that check."

"I paid your daddy a lot of money," he groaned, pulling the phone from his pocket to his ear. "I'll see what he says. I expect more than dinner and a pretty face."

"Please, can you step back?"

Ignoring her, he continued to nearly smother her, pressing her more forcefully against the wall as he glanced to the phone to dial it. After the phone started to ring, he looked back to her and smirked. Pieces of half-chewed food were stuck in between the front of his teeth.

Hearing a voice come on the other line, Holly unexpectedly and aggressively smacked the phone from his hand. His face immediately reddened as the phone bounced off the serving table and fell to the floor. He reached for her throat and cupped it with his right hand, trying bend over and reach for the phone near his feet.

"You little slut!"

Slapping and kicking at him as he tightened the grip around her throat, she noticed a fork on one of the trays of hors d'oeuvres on the nearby serving table. As his attention was focused on his phone on the floor, she grabbed the fork from a plate of fruit and vegetables. He squeezed her throat tighter, pulling her down with him as he kneeled for the phone.

"You're mine tonight, bitch! I paid for you!"

As he reached for the phone on the floor, she violently plunged the fork into his fleshy hand, causing him to instantly release her. He wailed like a sick and starving baby, as she raced about the room, gathering her purse, jacket, and the check.

"You whore!" he screamed, fumbling with the phone as blood flowed from the stab wound. "You goddamn whore!"

She hurried out of the room, slamming the door behind her. She sprinted down the hotel hallway and quickly slipped through the closing door into an empty elevator. She frantically and repetitively pounded the elevator button to the lobby. Within seconds, the elevator descended. Once the door opened, she dashed through the lobby and into the street, nearly knocking over an elderly couple who were entering the hotel.

Chapter Fifty-Eight

Russell joked at the elegant bar inside his club with some regulars and a few of his bouncers. He wore a tuxedo. A beautiful young woman in her twenties dressed in a formal evening gown hung on his right arm and continually whispered in his ear. He couldn't wipe the half-sneer, half-grin from his flushed face. The place was packed and rowdy as always.

The money just flowed in. A long line waited outside. He stared toward the set of turn-of-the-century crystal chandeliers that hung over the bar as his young lady friend blew her warm breath into his ear. The hair on his arms and the back of his neck stood up. He ordered the busy bartender to get his group a round of whiskey shots.

As he reached for his whiskey, the phone in his pocket began to ring. He motioned to the group to drink up as he checked the number on his phone. Recognizing the number, the smile on his face immediately vanished. He pulled away from his lady friend. The angry voice of Louis yelled on the other end. Russell profusely apologized, turned off the phone, and stared at his untouched whiskey. Finally, he put his phone back into his pocket and glared at his bouncers.

"What is it, boss?" Todd, his main henchmen, asked.

"It's Holly," Russell moaned in disappointment. "You know what to do."

"Where is she?"

"How the hell would I know?" Russell barked, grabbing the shot of whiskey. "Just find her!"

Todd looked to the other two bouncers at the bar and nodded. They hopped off their barstools and headed for the club's entrance.

"And don't touch her face!" Russell called out. He swallowed the whiskey. "Please don't mess with her face."

Chapter Fifty-Nine

With spiked heel shoes in her hand, Holly walked quickly down the darkened but busy Chartres Street. She constantly checked over her shoulder. She was four blocks from Esplanade Avenue, heading in the direction of her apartment. She knew she had to get there before her father or his thugs did.

Nearly out of breath, she peeked over her shoulder again. A black Cadillac limousine suddenly appeared. It felt as if her heart skipped a beat as she started to trot. She was two blocks from Esplanade. She felt sick to her stomach. She crossed to the other side of Chartres and again glanced behind her. The Cadillac slowly followed. She was frightened. As she trotted, the Cadillac passed her. She pretended not to notice, but it stopped ahead of her.

Todd climbed out of the back seat and stood tall before her. He motioned to the open door to the back seat. Panicked, Holly slowed her pace and glanced around as if searching for an escape route.

"Don't make this difficult," he calmly said. "You won't get away."

She closed her eyes in defeat with a deep sigh as he directed her into the Cadillac with the palm of his hand in the middle of her back and followed her in.

"You can have another day off," he said. He slammed the back door so hard she winced. "A gift from your father."

"No, thanks," she said, sounding defiant but looking frightened.

She glanced to the front seat where the two other bouncers watched. "I'll be there tomorrow for my shift. Like always."

"Your ever-loving dad does have a message for you," Todd said, taking her left hand and gently caressing it. "Just like baseball, your dad has given you three strikes."

As Holly watched him play with her hand, her eyes widened, and her heart raced. The pace of her breathing quickened as he gripped different fingers on her left hand. He stopped at her pinky. Holly tensed.

"You fuck him once," he said, suddenly increasing the pressure of the tight squeeze he had on her left pinky finger. "It's strike one."

She took a deep breath, closed her eyes, and clenched her teeth. With little warning, he snapped her finger with his thick strong hand like a pretzel rod. The pain was unbearable. She nearly passed out. She wanted to cry, and she needed to scream.

She tried not to let him see her suffer. But her teary eyes and pained expression told the real story. She couldn't hide the excruciating pain. Biting her lower lip, she glared at Todd as he continued to play with her broken finger then stared at the other two bouncers.

"You fuck him three times," Todd said. "You're out! And I mean all the way out!"

He aggressively squeezed and yanked at her bent finger one last time. Holly managed not to make a sound as he opened the back door of the limousine and pushed her into the street. She awkwardly stumbled to the pavement, bracing her tumbling body with her uninjured right hand. The back window of the Cadillac opened, and Todd tossed her shoes to the ground beside her. She grabbed them and slid herself over out of the street and onto the curb.

She sat there alone for many minutes, trying to regain her composure. It didn't take long before the pain took over her whole being. She was lightheaded and felt like she was about to vomit. As she struggled to stand, tears flooded her eyes. But she didn't scream as she quickly jogged to Esplanade and crossed the street. Afraid they would come back, or her father would be waiting at her apartment, she checked over her shoulder to see if anyone was following and scurried to the next-door neighbor's house.

Chapter Sixty

The neighbor's place belonged to Emma Delore. Emma was a tall and elegant black woman in her eighties. Despite her age, she had a clear mind and was still quite active in the New Orleans community. She lived on the top floor of a freshly painted, two-story white house with tall green pillars beside the apartment complex where Holly lived.

Holly followed the stone walkway to a large wooden porch that wrapped itself around the front of the house. Continually checking over her shoulder, she tiptoed up a set of stairs on the side which led to Emma's front door on the second floor. Emma had been a good friend and mother-figure to Holly for years. Holly had even lived with her for a short period of time.

Holly cupped her hand and peeked inside. Emma's place was dark. Holly repeatedly tapped on the door and checked the empty street below her. After a few minutes, the porch light finally came on. Wearing a robe and slightly hunched over, Emma appeared, rubbing her sleepy eyes with one hand and teasing her kinky gray hair with the other.

"Girl?" she yawned, studying Holly. "Do you know what time it is?"

Emma stared at Holly's eyes, which were red from crying. Holly cradled her injured left hand gently across her chest. Emma noticed the crooked pinky finger.

"What'd you go and do now, baby?" Emma asked. "Come on in here. Let's fix that up."

"Can I stay here?" Holly asked, following Emma inside.

"Girl, you can stay here anytime you like," Emma said, shuffling into a bathroom as Holly dropped onto the couch.

"I can't take it anymore."

"Then don't!" Emma said, returning with bandages, tape, and a bottle of bourbon with two glasses. "A glass of this for your pain? Looks like you need it."

"He needs to be gone!" Holly moaned, reaching for the bourbon-filled glass.

"Who needs to be gone?"

"You know who," she said, before pausing to swallow the full glass of bourbon. "He needs to be gone, or I do. I can't go on like this. Something needs to be done. And I think I know what."

"Hush, hush, girl," Emma said, before taking a small sip of her bourbon. "Don't be stupid. You got too much going for yourself."

"I won't have peace until he's completely gone from my life. I may have found someone to help me."

"Don't talk crazy," Emma said, pouring Holly another bourbon.

"I'm sorry. I'm sorry," she softly sobbed and repeatedly shook her. "I don't know what to do. I'm at the end."

"Now, now," Emma slid beside her on the couch and hugged her. "Stay here for a day or two. This will pass. I promise. I'll help you."

Holly tried to smile, taking a sip of the bourbon, her hands trembling. Emma lightly brushed at the blonde curls that had fallen over Holly's face and wiped at the tears in her eyes.

"I think that too, Emma. I think that too. This will pass. I want to look forward, I do. But I know I must return to that awful club tomorrow, then the next day, and the day after that. I have nowhere to hide."

Chapter Sixty-One

It was the Saturday morning of the supposedly 'fixed' horse race. Bobby sat at the somewhat quiet Tommy Black's bar, drinking from a bottle of beer. He had searched the Quarter and parts of the downtown area for his brother for a couple of hours before going to the bar. He even checked a homeless shelter and a drug and alcohol rehab center. He worried that Chuck's love for the party scene may be too hard to resist. New Orleans and its extended nightlife were filled with temptation. And Bobby also worried about himself.

He waited at the bar for Lucas to go to the Fairgrounds and bet on the day's tenth race. As he waited, Eddie and a friend walked into the bar. His friend, Sleepy Boy Turner, was a filthy little black man with sad and droopy yellow eyes. They hopped onto barstools next to Bobby. Butchie, who was bartending, hurried over to where the three were sitting.

"Out!" he yelled at Eddie. "What have I've told you? No money, no entry! Out! Get out!"

"It's all right, Butchie," Bobby spoke up. "They're with me. I'll get their drinks."

"He's trouble," Butchie said, pointing to Eddie.

"It's all right," Bobby repeated as he turned to the two. "What are you guys drinking?"

"A Jack Daniels whiskey with a splash of Coca-Cola, just a splash," Eddie said and motioned to his friend. "And don't forget about Sleepy Boy here."

"Jack Daniels whiskey," Sleepy Boy grinned. "But no coke."

Butchie poured the drinks and placed them in front of Eddie and Sleepy Boy. Bobby tossed a twenty-dollar bill onto the bar and motioned for Butchie to keep the change.

"You got anything about my brother?" Bobby asked Eddie.

"Bobby, Bobby," Eddie grinned. "Before we get into business, let me introduce you to my good friend here, Sleepy Boy Turner."

Bobby nodded as both Eddie and Sleepy Boy sucked the drinks empty through straws from the small plastic cups.

"It's a hot mornin' out there, Bobby. Me and Sleepy Boy had a long walk to get all the way over here. We's both quite dry," Eddie said. "Ain't that right, Sleepy Boy?"

"Yeah, you right," Sleepy Boy nodded.

Bobby tossed another twenty-dollar bill on the bar, and Butchie refilled the drinks.

"What do you have?" Bobby asked Eddie. "Any leads about Chuck?"

Eddie reached his open hand towards Bobby as if asking for a handout.

"I gots all the news," Eddie smiled, keeping his hand extended to Bobby. "I gots bad news. I gots good news. And I gots no news."

Bobby placed a ten-dollar bill in his hand.

"I don't gots a job," Eddie said, not moving his hand with the bill on it. "This here is hard work, lookin' for some damn lost fool. It ain't so easy bein' a regular James Bond with little resources. Shit!"

Bobby slapped another five-dollar bill into Eddie's hand. Eddie quickly stuffed the money into his shirt pocket.

"What'd you want first?" Eddie asked. "The bad, the good, the—"

"Gimme the bad first," Bobby interrupted.

"Of all the folks I've talked to, and it's been a lot, no one's seen your brother."

"What's the good news?"

Eddie smiled and delicately held a slip of paper out in front of him.

"I gots a name. That's right, Bobby. I gots a name." Bobby took the scrap of paper and studied the name on it. "I hear that's his lady friend. If I's placin' bets, I'd say he's with her right now."

"What's this name? Tammany? Do you have an address?"

"That's the news I ain't got," Eddie shook his head. "But I's workin' on it."

"You like the horses?" Bobby asked.

"Horses?"

"Horse races."

Eddie's grin widened, and his face lit up as he glanced to Sleepy Boy.

"Do we like the horse races?"

"Yessir," Sleepy Boy nodded. "Yeah, you right."

"I'm headed to the Fairgrounds with some people in a little while," Bobby said. "I'll take you if you promise to get me that address."

"Sleepy Boy, too?"

"Yeah, Sleepy Boy, too."

"Well, now," Eddie laughed. "Since I suddenly have a little more incentive, I'll see what I can do."

As Eddie and Sleepy Boy enjoyed their drinks, Lucas enthusiastically strutted into the bar. Rachel followed close behind. She looked exceptionally attractive in a very short skirt and tight tank top. She scanned the place as if looking for someone. She smiled upon seeing Bobby. Butchie popped the caps off the tops of two bottles of beer and slid them to Lucas and Rachel.

"The tenth still lookin' good?" Butchie asked Lucas.

"Lookin' damn good," Lucas nodded. "You comin' with us?"

"I wish. I couldn't find anyone to cover my shift today," Butchie shook his head, slapping five $100 bills on the bar in front of Lucas. "All of it on your horse in the tenth."

"All of it?"

"Yeah, all of it."

"Hey, Bobby," Rachel grinned from behind the icy bottle of beer in her hand. "Are you coming to the races?"

"Do you have room for a couple more?" Bobby asked, motioning to Eddie and Sleepy Boy.

"I think we can squeeze 'em in." She glanced at Lucas. "Isn't that right, Lucas?"

"Squeeze what in?" he asked, staring at Eddie and Sleepy Boy with a shake of his head. "Who, them?"

Chapter Sixty-Two

The five were packed into a vintage 1974 gold Lincoln Continental that Lucas had restored. Bobby, Eddie, and Sleepy Boy were in the back seat. Eddie's crutches were laid flat across their laps. Lucas and Rachel were in the front. She flirted with Bobby in the back by spying on him from the rear-view mirror glued to the sun visor above her head.

Appearing agitated, Lucas turned the key in the ignition, and the 215-horsepower V-8 engine fired to life with a roar as he pumped the gas pedal a few times. He glanced back to Eddie and Sleepy Boy. Sensing Lucas's uneasiness, Eddie leaned forward and extended his hand.

"I hadn't the chance to introduce myself," Eddie said, holding his open hand over Lucas's shoulder. "Eddie Doomes. That's Doomes, 'D-O-O-M-E-S'. People always forgettin' the E."

"Jus' sit back, boy, and mind your own business," Lucas grumbled, ignoring Eddie's invitation to shake hands. "It's not often I let a crippled sewer rat ride in my car."

Eddie shook his head and pulled his hand away.

"I'm not here to do no one no harm. I's just tryin' to be friendly. That's all," he said. "Now, there's no harm in that, right, Sleepy Boy?

"Nope. No harm in that. No sir."

Eddie, who was sitting in the middle in the back seat, leaned into Bobby next to him and whispered, "Now, me and Sleepy Boy won't have much fun at the track, seein' that we're nothin' but a couple poor fools, broke as broke can be."

"All I got left to my name are these six twenties," Bobby said, pulling out the cash from his front shirt pocket.

"One will just about do it," Eddie grinned, delicately pulling the top bill off the pile with his crooked, calloused fingers.

Chapter Sixty-Three

Bobby sat with Eddie and Sleepy Boy in a row of bleachers behind Lucas who sat alone at the New Orleans Fairgrounds. Rachel was snuggled up against Bobby. It was a gorgeous day. The afternoon air was warm and dry. The bright sky was a pleasant blue. There wasn't a cloud in sight. The crowd cheered as the pack of horses in the day's first race jockeyed for position around the first turn of the red dirt track.

"I do have that address," Eddie mumbled to Bobby, elbowing him in the side and reaching out a small slip of paper.

"What?"

"I didn't think you'd be so kind to me and Sleepy Boy. Buyin' us drinks and takin' us to the track, you know."

"What's this?" Bobby asked, studying an address scribbled on the paper.

"That's where your brother's gal is supposed to live."

"You don't say," Bobby mumbled, before drifting into thought.

"Hmmm. Chuck had a girlfriend? Maybe coming to New Orleans had been right for him. Maybe everything was coming up roses for Chuck. Maybe I can finally let go of this nearly suffocating guilt I can't shake."

"Down the stretch they come!" the public announcer's voice boomed through several speakers arranged in different places around the track, causing Bobby and Eddie to look to the racing horses.

Most of the crowd rose to their feet as the tight pack of horses pounded towards the finish. Grinning, Lucas turned and nodded to Bobby. Eddie squirmed in his seat as the horse he bet on pulled to the front.

"Gitty up! Gitty up!" Eddie yelled, leaning on his crutches to stand. "Come on, baby! Gitty up! Gitty up! Hang on, goddammit! Hang on!"

The crowd wildly cheered, stomping their feet and clapping their hands. Eddie let out a victory scream as his horse held on for the win. Disappointed and shaking his head, Lucas ripped up his bet ticket and tossed the pieces into the air.

"Now, that's how it's done!" Eddie boasted, loud enough for Lucas to hear who glared back at him. "I can't think of any better way to start the day. Can you, Sleepy Boy?"

"No, sir," Sleepy Boy shook his head. "No better way to start. Yeah, you right."

"Now, go get me my damn money," Eddie said to Sleepy Boy, handing him the winning ticket.

Chapter Sixty-Four

Holly sat alone at the empty bar at Tommy Black's. She wore dark sunglasses to hide her red, swollen eyes. She lit a cigarette. Butchie stared at her bandaged finger.

"Shouldn't you be at work?" he asked, taking the empty plastic cup in front of her and refilling it with cheap beer.

"I have the day off."

"Good for you," Butchie said, setting the beer in front of her.

"But I may go in anyway." She took a drink of beer.

"Don't do that. Don't do that to yourself. Stay here. Keep me company," he said. "I'll order us some take-out. Anything sound good? Country Flame? Johnny's Po-Boy?"

"I'm not hungry."

"What's with the sunglasses?"

"A long night." She took another drink of beer.

"Like I said, my cousin's beach house on the Mississippi coast is available. You need a vacation."

She didn't respond, finishing the drink and stubbing out the smoldering cigarette in the ashtray.

"What happened to your finger?" he asked as she stood without answering, setting a couple of twenty-dollar bills on the bar for him.

"Come on, tell me. How'd you hurt your finger?"

"Apparently, it's part of my workplace compensation plan," she said, throwing her bag over her shoulder.

"Be careful, Holly," he called out as she stepped out of the bar.

Chapter Sixty-Five

Tall shadows had crept over the grandstands at the Fairgrounds. Sleepy Boy deliberately counted out loud a stack of money he held with both hands. Eddie studied the race program. Rachel and Bobby sipped beers beside them. She giggled, massaging his back. Standing, Lucas emptied his wallet of all the money he had left after an unsuccessful day of betting. The horses were being led to the starting gate for the day's last race. It was the supposed 'fixed' race Lucas had been waiting on all afternoon.

"How much we up?" Eddie asked Sleepy Boy.

"Ninety-eight bucks."

"I say we bet it all, an exacta on the two favorites, Blue Stocking and Gandy Dancer," Eddie said.

"No Gravedigger's Luck?" Bobby asked Eddie about the 60-1 longshot Lucas was guaranteeing to win.

"Shit, Bobby!" Eddie shook his head. "Long shots like that, they only win in fiction books and Disney shows."

Holding a handful of cash, a discouraged-looking Lucas leaned towards Bobby.

"No luck today, huh?" Bobby asked him.

"I'm down a grand, but we still have our one race to go," he said. "You still in on Gravedigger's Luck? I'm playin' him a thousand to win. I was hoping to have a little more than that to put on him."

"Throwin' your money away," Eddie barked as Bobby handed Lucas most of the money he had left.

"Gravedigger's Luck, all the way," Bobby said, trying to sound confident. "This is my last hundred dollars. I'll play it all to win."

Lucas took Bobby's money and sneered at Eddie as he walked away to place the bets.

"If I lose," Bobby said, turning to Eddie, "will you buy me a beer later?"

"Shit, Bobby! After I win, I'll buy you a 36-ounce prime rib soaked in whiskey."

Chapter Sixty-Six

Still wearing dark sunglasses, Holly entered her father's office in the club on her way to the dressing room. He glanced up from his desk as she coolly walked by him. She didn't acknowledge or look at him. He stared at her from the time she entered his office until she took a seat in front of a locker in the dressing room in back. He watched as she undressed and changed into a bright red, leather bikini.

"You don't have to be here," he called out as she stood and checked her appearance in a long thin mirror that hung from the locker door. "I gave you the night off."

"I didn't ask for it off," she said, removing the sunglasses and staring at her reflection.

"I have enough girls tonight, if you want to go home."

Ignoring him, she methodically applied eyeliner, and patted at her thick, blonde curls. She puckered her bright red lips a few times as she continued to stare at herself. She then eased the locker door closed and headed for the door of Russell's office that led into the club. He stepped in front of her, blocking her way. She grimaced as he reached for her wounded hand. He studied the bandaged pinky.

"It's only business. You know that."

Chapter Sixty-Seven

The crowd roared as Blue Stocking and Gandy Dancer, the two race favorites, sped to the finish line well ahead of the rest of the horses. Eddie hopped on one leg, holding both of his crutches with his outstretched arms high in the air. Lucas kicked the bleachers in disappointment and dropped into his seat to stare at the ground. Bobby could only shake his head. Gravedigger's Luck finished the race in eighth place out of ten horses, well out of the money.

"I can't believe it!" Eddie celebrated, continuing to hop on one leg. "I just don't believe it. No sir. Shit!"

"You did it, buddy!" Bobby congratulated him. "You did it!"

"How much we win, Sleepy Boy? How much?"

"Just about two grand," Sleepy Boy said.

"Two thousand in dollars?" Eddie yipped. "That's a lot of damn money! Ain't that right, Sleepy Boy?"

"Yeah, you right."

"Wowee!" Eddie crowed, falling back into his seat on the bleacher. "What am I gonna do with all that? Shit! I never expected that. No sir! Shit, almighty!"

"You did it, Eddie!" Bobby cheered. "You did it, you crazy son-of-a-bitch!"

Lucas angrily turned as Sleepy Boy and Eddie embraced.

"I's sorry about your loss, Bobby," Eddie teased. "But that sure was a lot of damn money to lay down on an untested long shot. Wasn't it, Sleepy Boy?"

"Yeah, you right," Sleepy Boy nodded. "A lot of damn money."

Lucas stepped over the row of bleachers behind him towards Eddie, who stood.

"Listen here, Flavor Flav!" he said, leaning his face inches from Eddie's face. "Gutter trash like you shouldn't be fuckin' allowed in a place like this."

"I know," Eddie said calmly as his easy grin widened. "I win too much. I's bad for their business."

"Fuck you," Lucas growled. He shoved Eddie hard onto the bleachers behind him.

Bobby immediately stepped in between Lucas and Eddie, both fists clenched.

"Cut it out, man!"

"Find your own fuckin' way back!" Lucas grabbed Rachel's arm. "You're coming with me."

"But I want to stay with them," she said, struggling as Lucas dragged her away.

Grimacing, Eddie slowly pulled himself out between a row of bleachers with his crutches.

"Bobby?" Rachel called as she disappeared with Lucas into the line of spectators leaving the track area. "Bobby? Come over to my place later!"

"A damn shame," Eddie said, wiping at the front of his shirt. "Can't let some poor boy enjoy not one damn thing. Ain't that right, Sleepy Boy?"

"Yeah, you right," Sleepy Boy said. "Not one damn thing."

"I should've pounded his ass," Bobby grumbled, his fists still clenched.

Chapter Sixty-Eight

Bobby, Eddie, and Sleepy Boy sat in the back seat of a cab. The cab was finally moving. It had been stuck in traffic trying to leave the Fairgrounds for many minutes. Eddie was in the middle of the seat between them. Grinning, he held the bundle of cash he'd won in both arms against his chest like he was cradling a baby.

"Seeing that you're a man of limited means," Bobby said, studying him. "If you could do anything right now, what would it be?"

Eddie's face lit up. His grin grew wider.

"Shit! That's easy," he answered without hesitation. "I'd pass up on an all-night love affair with the most gorgeous hooker in New Orleans for an afternoon of fishin'."

"Fishing?" Bobby laughed.

"Damn straight!" Eddie nodded enthusiastically. "I's a young kid the last time I's outta this goddamn city."

"You know of a place to go?"

"Oh, I gots the place," Eddie continued to nod. "Isn't that right, Sleepy Boy?"

"Yeah, you right," Sleepy Boy nodded.

"Yessir. I gots the place!"

"Yeah?"

"Oh, yeah!"

"Is it close?"

"Real close. About an hour from here in a car."

"If I got us a car," Bobby asked, "will you take me there someday?"

"Yessir, my friend," Eddie grinned and continued to nod. "But seein' that we don't have a car right now, we'll have to settle for the next best thing tonight."

"What's that?" Bobby asked.

"Women!"

Chapter Sixty-Nine

The cab dropped the three off in front of Russell's Gentlemen Club on Bourbon Street. Sleepy Boy had no interest in going in. He took two $100 bills from Eddie and went on his way. Bobby also wasn't too interested in going to a strip club but could see how excited Eddie was, so he followed him into the club.

Leaning on his crutches, Eddie was initially stopped in the entrance way and prevented to come in until he flashed the young hostess at the door his tall stack of cash. Bobby kept close behind him. They finally made it inside, stopping to scan the club. It was excessively loud and packed beyond capacity.

Multiple nude and semi-nude women danced on different stages arranged throughout the main floor. Red and white spotlights illuminated the stages. Several crowded VIP booths were set up on the second level with a clear overhead view of the dance floor. Scores of waitresses with trays covered with cocktails and beers zigzagged their way through the busy club.

Bobby and Eddie worked their way to one of the many bars on the main floor and ordered drinks. It wasn't long before they were joined by a chesty brunette who had spied the money Eddie displayed. She immediately had her hands all over him and in and out of his pockets. He grinned and laughed, enjoying the attention. She whispered in his ear. He bought her and Bobby a drink. Before wandering off to one of the many private couches situated around the main dance floor, Eddie slid a whiskey drink and a few $20 bills to Bobby.

"Have fun," Bobby said as the brunette whisked Eddie away, carrying the drinks and helping him with his crutches.

"Yeah, you right," Eddie called out, smiling. "Don't worry 'bout that."

Bobby watched them. The stripper set the drinks on a table and eased Eddie back onto a couch. Eddie was grinning from ear to ear as she hopped into his lap, facing him. She slowly rocked her body on his and rubbed her abnormally large breasts back and forth across his face. As Bobby scanned the club again, he couldn't imagine anyone there having as good as time as Eddie, who giggled like a grade school kid at a tickle party.

Bobby turned back to the bar and stared to his drink. A couple of different dancers tried to engage him in small talk or even a private show, but he declined. He thought of Chuck. He worried Chuck was gone for good, maybe even dead. He wasn't much in the mood to be at the crowded club. He wanted to go back to Tommy Black's, but he knew he better hang around to make sure nothing happened to Eddie and his pile of money. After draining his drink and ordering another, he turned to check on Eddie. Holly stood behind, staring at him.

"Shouldn't you be looking for your brother?"

"What are you doing here?" he asked, appearing confused and checking the skimpy outfit she wore—a see-through negligee that covered the tight, red bikini.

"It's rather obvious, isn't it?"

"You work here?"

"Yes."

"Waitress?"

"I'm a stripper."

"You don't seem the type."

"You stood me up the other night."

"So, this is where you run off to every afternoon?"

"I took the day off to be you."

"What happened to your finger?" he asked, noticing the large bandage on her left pinky.

"You said you'd be at Tommy Black's every day," she went on, not answering his question. "Where were you?"

"I'll make it up to you."

"Do you know how hard it is for me to get a day off?"

"Let's meet later after you get out of here."

"I can't," she said, checking over her shoulder as her father watched from behind one of the many bars in the club.

"Let me buy a dance from you," he said, pulling the money Eddie had given him from his pocket. "Just to talk, in private. That's it. Just talk. That's all I want."

"I can't talk here," she said as Russell continued to watch her.

"Why?"

"My father owns the place. He keeps a close watch over me."

"Are you in trouble?"

"I have to go."

"Meet me later then."

"I can't."

"I'll wait at Tommy's for you. Please come later."

As she started to walk away, loud arguing could be heard. Eddie was being carried towards the front door of the club by two hulking bouncers, screaming and hollering.

"Hey!" Bobby yelled. "Put him down!"

"Bobby!" Eddie called out, violently squirming in the bouncers' arms. "Help, Bobby! They gots my money!"

Pushing himself away from the bar, Bobby rushed after them. Eddie's arms and legs flailed.

"Put him down!"

The bouncers kicked the front door open and heaved Eddie and his crutches out onto the busy Bourbon Street as curious tourists looked on. Just inside the door, Bobby patted on the shoulder of one of the bouncers from behind. Holly, who had been watching, called out: "Bobby! Don't!"

Todd, the club's main bouncer, turned.

"I want his money back!" Bobby demanded.

"What money?" Todd shrugged as he tried to step by Bobby.

"Gimme his goddamn money!" Bobby said, grabbing Todd's arm.

Unknown to Bobby, the other bouncer behind him had cocked his arm as if ready to throw a punch.

"Bobby!" Holly called out again, warning him. "Watch out! Behind you!"

Bobby turned, ducked the punch, and shoved the bouncer away from him. The bouncer crashed into the hostess stand at the entrance, knocking it down. Russell hopped over the bar he stood behind and rushed towards the commotion.

"Bobby, please!" Holly shouted. "Get out of here!"

Todd then lunged at Bobby who stepped out of his way. Bobby then nailed him with a hard right cross to the jaw, knocking him out cold on the floor.

"Aw, shit!" Bobby screamed out in pain, shaking his aching right hand.

"Get out of here!" Holly continued to warn him.

"I need my friend's money!" Bobby called to her as four large bouncers along with Russell sprinted towards him at the entrance.

"Bobby!" Eddie suddenly shouted from the doorway. "I gots us a cab!"

Bobby vaulted over Todd, who he had been knocked out, and raced through the door, grabbing Eddie on his way like a sack of groceries with his left arm. They hurried to the back of a waiting cab where Bobby tossed Eddie and his crutches before hopping in himself. As the cab pulled away, they glanced out the back window. Two of the club's bouncers futilely gave chase on foot as the cab quickly disappeared out of sight. Russell watched from the street in front of his club.

"What in the hell did you do back there?" Bobby asked, holding his swollen right hand against his chest.

"It's been a long time, Bobby."

"A long time for what?"

"Well, I... I..." Eddie stuttered. "I kinda whipped it out."

"Whipped what out?"

"Well, you know," Eddie half-grinned, zipping up his pants.

"Jesus Christ, Eddie!"

"I got a little excited, Bobby. I didn't get no chance to do nothin'! The next thing I know I's bein' carried out! Shit!"

"Dammit, Eddie!"

"They took my money, Bobby."

"All of it?"

"I'm nothin' but a broke down drunk again."

Realizing they were short on cash, Bobby leaned forward and tapped the cab driver on the shoulder. "You better let us off here."

Bobby and Eddie hobbled out of the cab and stood alone on a dark empty street of the French Quarter not far from Esplanade. Bobby held his busted right hand as the cab pulled away.

"I's sorry, Bobby. I didn't get you that steak."

"That's all right," Bobby said, trying to open his red and swollen hand. "I'm not hungry."

"How's your hand?" Eddie asked.

"It was getting better."

Chapter Seventy

At the desk in his office at the club, Russell sipped at a bourbon and counted large stacks of cash. There must have been over $100,000 on the desk. Todd stood beside him with his eye blackened and nose swollen. Another bouncer guarded the door to the office. Without warning, Holly barged in. The bouncer at the door tried to stop her.

"It's all right," Russell said, and the bouncer let her pass.

"You need to give me their money!" Holly shouted.

"What money?"

"You know what money I'm talking about."

"Why is that money so important to you?"

"Just give me the money."

"Who are those clowns anyway?"

"You won't even miss it."

"I don't set many rules in this place," Russell said, "but one of your new friends broke the most serious one. No indecent behavior on the floor of the club's main room."

"Come on! That stupid fucking rule is broken every night! I've seen enough small soft dicks in this place to last me several lifetimes."

"You've really been pissing me off lately."

"Give me the money!"

"They broke the rules." Russell shook his head.

Holly suddenly made a quick move for a stack of cash on the desk, but Todd grabbed her arm, twisted it behind her back, and directed her away from the desk, forcefully pressing her body against the wall.

"Who are those clowns?" Russell asked, leaving the desk and taking Holly's arm from the bouncer.

She didn't answer as he twisted her arm more and pushed it up her back. She grimaced in pain, refusing to answer.

"How bad do you want that money back?"

He released her arm with a hard shove. She quickly turned to face him. They stared. She stepped closer. Her face was red with rage.

"The club is full," he smirked. "I'll give you their money, but not until you earn the same amount back for me."

"How much was it?"

"Eighteen-hundred dollars."

"That's a lot of dances."

"You better get started then."

Chapter Seventy-One

Tommy Black's was dark and hazy. It was near daybreak. A thick cloud of cigarette smoke lingered in the air. The place was empty, except for Jack, who fiddled with his can of cheap beer, and Harry-O, who slept at the bar. Completely sober, Bobby stared into the light of the jukebox as his right hand soaked in a bucket of ice water. The Willie Nelson song, "Angel Flying Too Close to the Ground," played. Bobby turned to the open front door as Holly quietly slipped in, holding a paper sack. She limped slightly.

"This place lights up when you walk in."

She tossed him the bag, and he caught it against his chest with his left hand. They studied each other. Her eyes were red and puffy. Her hair was a mess. He turned back to the jukebox.

"I just put my last dollar in here," he said. "There's one song left. Your choice."

"It's all there," she said as he glanced to the bag.

He reached into and pulled out a large stack of cash in all denominations.

"How'd you get it back?" he asked, turning to her.

"You're pathetic. I was hoping you'd be the one."

"The one?"

"To save me."

They stared a moment as she wiped at her smeared mascara. She turned away and walked to the door. As she disappeared into the night, he glared at the exit.

"Everybody needs an angel," he mumbled as the Willie Nelson song ended.

Chapter Seventy-Two

Holding her red knee-high boots, Holly briskly hurried alone barefooted across the dark and quiet Royal Street. It had started to lightly rain. Bobby hustled after her. She cautiously checked over her shoulder. She sensed someone behind her and picked up the pace. Finally, Bobby called out.

"I'm not letting you walk away this time."

She kept walking and didn't turn; he continued to follow her.

"You shouldn't be walking alone this late at night," he called as she walked faster. "Holly! Come on! Wait for me!"

She stopped and let him catch up. They both breathed heavily. It rained harder. She wiped at the water that dripped from her curly blonde hair and streamed down her face.

"Leave me alone," she said. "Please!"

"Come on."

"Leave me alone."

"I can't."

"Please. Go away," she said as she turned from him and started walk away again.

"I'm walking you home," he said, chasing after her.

She abruptly stopped and turned.

"Go away!" she snapped. "You're trouble! I don't need any more trouble."

"If I'm trouble, you wouldn't have come back to the bar. You wouldn't have gotten the money back."

He handed her his leather jacket he had recovered from Tommy Black's earlier. She placed it over her head and started to walk away from him. She had slowed her pace considerably, though. He followed for many blocks but kept his distance. Finally, near Esplanade Avenue, she stopped at the door of her first-floor apartment. As she unlocked the front door, she glanced back before entering and saw him standing a block away in front of a club called The Checkpoint. The reflection of the orange neon light from the open sign of the all-night club glistened on the wet, empty sidewalk in front of him. She pulled the door open and hesitated a moment before entering.

The rain poured harder. Holding the soaked paper sack of cash in his busted right hand, Bobby watched as she kept the door open a crack. He glanced back in the direction of the French Quarter.

Chapter Seventy-Three

Chilled, Holly changed out of her wet clothes. She slipped on a pair of men's boxer shorts and a long-hooded sweatshirt that hung below her waist. Fluffing her wet hair with a towel, she walked into the small kitchen in bare feet and started a pot of coffee. As it brewed, she stepped to the open front door. Dripping wet, Bobby stood in the entranceway under the stoop. The bag of money was stuffed down the front of his shirt. She pushed the door open wider and turned for the kitchen.

She took two cups from the cupboard and filled them with coffee. Taking the cups, she returned to the front door. Bobby took note of the second cup of coffee.

"Cream or sugar?"

He shook his head as she handed him the cup of black coffee. He hesitated before following her inside. She directed him to sit on the small couch where she often slept. He took a seat and placed the sack of money on the table. He sipped hard on the hot coffee. She sat in a chair across from him. She crossed her bare legs and pulled them in tight against her chest, covering them with the bottom of the sweatshirt.

"How's the hand?" she asked, sipping her coffee. "You need to get it checked."

"You live by yourself?"

"The clinic opens at eight in the morning," she said as he continued to study the apartment.

"You're not from New Orleans, are you? Why do so many young people end up here?"

"I came here with my father. He needed a new start."

"And your mother?"

"She passed away when I was young. My dad was never the same after she died."

"How so?"

"He drank himself angry most nights."

"And you?"

"I'd dreamed about all the places I wanted to go and what I wanted to be when I grew up."

"Where did you dream about?"

"Not here."

"What did you want to be?"

"A ballerina."

"Ballerina?" he smiled, then grimaced as he slowly opened his busted hand. "Did you dream come true?"

"I dance with a local ballet group. The dream, it's still a work in progress."

"And your father?"

"Let's just say, we have a working relationship."

"And the stripper life?"

"It pays the bills."

He again glanced around her tidy but cramped apartment, sipping at the steaming cup of coffee.

"Do you like stripping?"

"Hate it."

"Why don't you quit?"

"I told you. It pays the bills."

"Come on, tell me the truth."

She stood, reached for Bobby's half-empty cup of coffee, and walked into the kitchen.

"It's complicated."

"What happened to your finger?" he called as she refilled his cup with hot coffee.

"Just a little clumsy."

"Clumsy?"

"Let's get that hand checked in the morning," she said as Bobby glanced at his swollen red hand then the sack of money. "I can take you."

"Why are you so worried about my hand?"

"I'm sure it's broken."

"It already was."

She returned and handed him the fresh coffee.

"You want anything to eat?"

"I'm good." He shook his head. "The pisser?"

"Through there," she pointed.

After he disappeared into the bedroom that led to the bathroom, she could hear him from the couch straining to urinate.

"Son-of-a-bitch. . ." he grumbled.

After a few minutes, he walked out with a pained expression.

"You all right?"

She got up from the chair and stepped towards him as he lifted his shirt, showing her the severe bruising on each of his sides and lower back.

"Don't let your babies grow up to be boxers."

She gently ran her warm fingers along the bruised and swollen areas of his sides, causing him to wince.

"Were you any good?" She lowered his shirt.

"I only lost once in fourteen bouts," he said as she directed him to the couch.

She sat next to him as he reached for the fresh coffee.

"Is that why you quit?"

"Nah, I beat a guy ranked tenth in the world last week," he proudly said. "As you saw from the bruises, he punched pretty hard."

"Tell me about the fight you lost."

"I got knocked out."

"When was that?"

"A couple years ago."

"Were you supposed to win?"

"He was a cupcake, hand-picked by my manager."

"What happened?"

"I beat him up pretty good for seven rounds, but. . ." He paused and glanced to her.

She studied him closely.

"I ran out of gas. By the last round, I was so tired I couldn't keep my arms up. He caught me with a clean left hook. I wasn't prepared for the fight. I partied instead of trained."

"How'd you do in the fight after that one?"

"I knocked the guy out in thirty-seven seconds."

"Was he any good?

"He was unbeaten and ranked eighth in the world."

"Lift up your shirt."

Pulling the bottom of his shirt up to his chest, he cringed as she delicately touched the bruised areas again.

"Beat up the body and the head will die. That's what Grainger believed."

"Grainger?"

"My last opponent."

"Was he right?" she asked, letting her warm hand rest on his damaged right side.

"All I ever wanted was to be champion of the world."

"And now?"

"I just want to find my brother."

She gently patted his side and pulled away from him, taking the coffee cups into the kitchen.

"Are you good there on the couch?"

"Sure, anything."

"I need to turn in," she said. "I didn't get any sleep last night."

Chapter Seventy-Four

Bobby rolled out of sleep. Holly's apartment was dark. He couldn't tell if the sun had come up. He slowly eased himself off the couch and crept into the kitchen to get a glass of water. His body was still sore from the boxing match days ago. He checked the clock on the stove. It wasn't quite seven yet. He drank the water and peered into Holly's room.

Tangled in a blanket and comforter, she soundly slept. Bobby stared at her. A small sliver of the light from the overcast morning spotlighted her pretty face. As she slept, she wore a contented smile. He couldn't look away, staring at her for several minutes.

Careful not to wake her, Bobby returned to the couch. He slipped on his shoes and grabbed the paper sack of money. He tiptoed to the door and was about to leave when Holly stepped into the room, stretching her arms over her head.

"Where you going?" She yawned.

"You don't have to be anywhere this morning, do you?"

"Are you coming back?"

"Yes. Wait for me."

"Where are you going?"

"To look for someone."

"Your brother?"

"Yes, and my friend, Eddie."

Under a black-and-gold New Orleans Saints umbrella that he found at Holly's apartment, Bobby spent much of the early morning walking the streets near Esplanade in the pouring rain in search of both Chuck and Eddie. He eventually found Eddie on the corner of Dauphine and St. Philip. Soaked, Eddie leaned on his crutches under a stoop of a busy convenience store. Bobby joined him and handed him the soggy bag of money.

"It's all there," Bobby said as Eddie pulled handfuls of five-, ten-, twenty-, and fifty-dollar bills from the bag.

"Shit, Bobby! What'd you do?"

"Fifteen-hundred dollars."

"We's becomin' good friends," Eddie grinned, staring at the cash in the bag. "Ain't that right, Bobby?"

"You need to get out of this rain."

"I gots nowhere to go."

"I got a room in a guest house in the Marigny for a few days," Bobby said, handing him a key. "I hope you don't mind. I borrowed three-hundred dollars of your money to pay for it."

"Borrowed? Shit, you can have it all if you want."

"Shower up. Get some sleep."

"My, my, my," Eddie smiled, staring at the key. "I have died and gone to heaven!"

Suddenly distracted, Bobby noticed a young man who resembled his brother dashing down the street and trying to get out of the rain.

"Hey, buddy!" Bobby called to the guy. "Wait! Hey!"

"Bobby, I needs to tell you something," Eddie said, as Bobby sprinted after the stranger. "It's important, Bobby! We need to talk! I done a mean trick to you. A real mean, awful trick."

"Hey! Hey!" Bobby yelled, waving his arms as he chased after the guy for several blocks towards North Rampart. "Hey! Chuck?"

Before Bobby could reach him, the stranger, who was unaware he was being followed, jumped into an idling car that waited for him.

"Chuck!" Bobby called one last time, standing in the pouring rain as the car pulled away.

Still under the stoop, Eddie studied the key Bobby had given him for a moment then reached down and picked up the umbrella Bobby had left behind. He popped open the umbrella, hopped out into rain, and headed for the guest house in the Marigny.

Chapter Seventy-Five

olly and Bobby sat in a tight booth of a popular diner and hamburger joint at the end of Bourbon Street. The place was loud and chaotic with excited regulars and animated servers barking back and forth at each other. A pair of frazzled fry cooks stood over a sizzling grill that was crowded with frying burgers, eggs, and potatoes. They continually glanced at the long row of order tickets clipped above the grill.

"Where did you go?" Holly asked over the noise of the busy eatery as she sipped a coffee and studied the menu. "I didn't think you were coming back."

"I got a room in a guest house near Washington Square on Elysian Fields," he said as she looked up. "I felt I was imposing."

"You weren't imposing."

"I used some of Eddie's money to pay for it. Then I found him and gave him the rest."

"Where was he?"

"Not far from here."

"I also gave him a key to the room. He needed to dry off and clean up. It was his money. I told him to get some rest, and I'd check on him later."

The distracted waiter suddenly appeared over them, holding his pen to a food check pad. He continually glanced over his shoulder to the completed orders the fry cooks were placing on a counter behind the diner's full bar. He then looked to Bobby who motioned to Holly.

"What'll be, hon'?"

"An order of scrambled eggs and some wheat toast," she said as the waiter looked to Bobby.

"And you, babe?"

"Two eggs over easy, an order of bacon, and a biscuit."

"Fantastic," the server grinned. "I'll be back with more coffee."

"When I was out looking for Eddie, I might have seen Chuck."

"You sure?"

"Pretty sure, but it was raining."

"Did he see you?"

"I called his name several times as I chased him down the street. The guy was trying to get out of the rain."

"Where did he go?"

"To a waiting car."

"Did he hear you?"

"I'm sure he heard me. He had to."

"But he didn't stop?

"No, he didn't stop."

"It may not have been him."

"It was him. I know it."

The waiter returned with a steaming pot of coffee and refilled their cups.

"What's he like?"

"Who?"

"Chuck. What was he like before he left Baltimore?"

"God, he was such a great kid, man," Bobby beamed. "So alive, always in charge of himself and everyone around him."

"Why'd he leave?"

"It was my fault."

"What happened?"

"I thought I was a big shit. I had just turned professional. I was training hard in the day and partying harder every night. I was hanging out with a rough crowd from the gym. I'd drag Chuck along with us. He was young, maybe seventeen. We'd get him drunk, get him laid." Bobby's voice suddenly trailed off, as he stared to the floor.

"You don't have to say anything else."

"You need to hear this," he said, pausing a moment before continuing. "I won my first big professional fight. I made a thousand dollars. I thought I was the richest man in the world. And for a couple weeks we celebrated like I was."

"I know where this is going."

"No one knows what those fights take out of me," he said, looking back at her.

"It's all right, Bobby."

"It's not," he said as she studied him. "I was drunk. Chuck and I were on a four-day binge, and I drove us into the back of a police car. The crash was so bad, you couldn't tell who was driving. I pointed to Chuck when the cops showed up."

"Because of your boxing career?"

"That's all I cared about," he nodded. "More than my younger brother."

"Bobb—"

"The cops arrested him for destruction of property, speeding, driving under the influence, et cetera, et cetera. My dad kicked him out of the house."

"And you never said anything?"

"I never said anything." He shook his head. "So, what do you think of me now?"

She studied him without answering.

"I have to find him," Bobby went on as the waiter delivered two plates of food to their table. "I pray he forgives me."

"I can help you look."

Chapter Seventy-Six

Bobby and Holly didn't say anything the next many minutes as they ate breakfast. They both were quite hungry, having not eaten much in the previous days. After eating most of her food, Holly glanced out the front window of the diner and noticed her father and Todd, his head goon, sitting in his parked Cadillac across Bourbon. She suddenly threw two $20 bills on the table.

"You all, right?" Bobby asked.

"Let's get that hand of yours checked."

"What did you mean that I may be the one to save you?"

Without answering, she pulled him up from his seat. He was still eating his breakfast. He tried to grab his coffee and take one last drink, but she yanked him out a side door of the diner that exited onto Dumaine. They disappeared down the street without her father seeing them.

Chapter Seventy-Seven

Bobby and Holly sat in the waiting room of a free clinic. The clinic was especially busy. They waited with young mothers and their bawling babies, as well as several elderly men and women. Bobby flipped through a boxing magazine he'd just purchased from a nearby newsstand.

"Woah," he mumbled as Holly looked over. "I'm currently the fifth-ranked light heavyweight in the world."

He reached the magazine over to her and showed her the list.

"Look," he pointed. "Right there, Bobby Raymond, number five. That's me."

"Number five?" she said. "In the world? That's pretty good, right?"

"Listen to this." He read the short write-up about himself as Holly leaned closer and slid her body into his. "Bobby Raymond, the tough street kid from Baltimore, is this week's surprise entry in the top five of the light heavyweight categories." He glanced up as she pressed against him. "With his impressive victory over highly regarded Alex Grainger in his last fight. Raymond may be next in line for a shot against Alberto Benitez, the world champion." He looked to Holly, who stared back. "Due to injuries and potential contract squabbles among the fighters ranked ahead of Raymond, handlers for Benitez and Raymond are working out the details for a possible fight in Atlantic City this June or July."

"A championship fight?" Holly asked.

"What details?" he asked, studying the article closer. "Nobody's talking to me."

He studied his busted hand as a nurse stepped into the waiting room: "Robert Raymond?"

He stood and looked to Holly.

"See you later?"

"Sure."

"Thanks."

"For what?"

"For everything. The place to stay. Bringing me here. Getting Eddie's money back. I owe you."

"You know where to find me."

"I don't know why you're doing all this for me."

Chapter Seventy-Eight

A drizzling rain fell. A dog barked as Bobby navigated an unfamiliar street in the somewhat secluded section of the Bywater neighborhood, located on the Mississippi River. The brightly painted homes sat close together, separated only by small patches of grass or narrow sidewalks. He studied a slip of paper he held in his recently casted right hand.

"Six ninety-three," he mumbled to himself, reading the numbers of the houses he passed. "And there's 694 across the street."

He suddenly stopped as the street ended and glanced around, searching for a house numbered 695. A teenager was riding a bike near him.

"Hey, kid, where in the hell is 695?"

"Six ninety-five?" The kid rode over to Bobby, braked, and straddled the bike. "This street ends here. There ain't no 695. You must be on the wrong street."

"No, I'm on the right street," Bobby said, after checking the slip of paper again. "Then, do you know a Tammany Parish?"

"Who?"

"Do you live around here?" Bobby asked, showing him the slip of paper.

"All my life."

"So, you know everyone who lives around here?"

"Just about," the kid nodded, studying the slip of paper more closely. "This says St. Tammany Parish. That ain't no person."

Bobby looked closer at the piece of paper, noticing the "St." denotation scribbled on it.

"That's one of Louisiana's parishes," the kid went on. "Parish?"

"Like a county. You're a long way from there."

Chapter Seventy-Nine

Eddie was stretched out on his stomach on the bed. He was completely nude. A trashy middle-aged hooker was on top, straddling him as she massaged his back. Her face was covered with red sores, and she was missing several teeth. Her hair had been dyed pink. They called her Skittles. Eddie cooed as her warm, fat breasts flopped on his back as she kneaded the cramped muscles of his scarred shoulders.

Without warning, Bobby busted into the room. Eddie flipped over and pulled the covers over Skittles and himself.

"Bobby?"

"Jesus Christ!"

"I didn't 'pect you back so soon."

"Get the hell out!" Bobby screamed at Skittles. He grabbed her clothes and shoes from the floor and slung them out the door. Half-dressed, she scrambled out of the room after them.

"Bobby, wait!"

"You mother fucker!" Bobby snapped, turning to Eddie.

"Now, now, Bobby, calm down!"

"Get the fuck out of here!" Bobby screamed, lunging at Eddie.

"I's just tryin' to have me some fun," Eddie said, rolling out of bed away from Bobby, dragging the sheets with him.

"I never want to see you again!"

"You gots to understand," Eddie said, reaching for his crutches. "I never get these kinds of opportunities, Bobby."

"I went looking for Tammany Parish, Saint Tammany Parish!"

"Bobby, I can explain!" Eddie pleaded; tears started to stream down his face. "Bobby, Bobby, please forgive me! At first, I was tryin' to scam you, make some cash, but you was so nice!"

"To think of all I did for you."

"I know, Bobby. You treat me like a real human being. You're a friend, Bobby, a real friend. I wanted to say somethin' sooner, but—"

"Get out!"

"Please, Bobby!" Eddie said, now crying. "I feels so bad!"

"Get your things! Get out!"

Wiping the tears from his eyes, Eddie hobbled around the room and gathered his belongings.

"We's still friends, right?" he asked, hopping on one leg out of the room, covering his privates with a handful of clothes as Bobby stepped towards him.

Eddie stopped outside the door and stared at Bobby, trying to grin. Bobby slammed the door shut.

Chapter Eighty

Appearing agitated after his encounter with Eddie, Bobby stepped in Tommy Black's in search of refuge and badly needing a drink. He did a quick scan of the bar, hoping Holly would be there. She wasn't. He took a seat on an empty barstool and plopped the heavy plaster cast covering his right hand onto the bar top.

"So, it is broken?" Butchie called out, holding up an icy bottle of Miller High Life.

Bobby nodded. "My last opponent had a very hard head."

"How bad is it?"

"It's broken in three places."

"Is that all?" a silky sweet voice whispered from behind him.

He turned, then glanced to the open door of the bar as if searching for someone. Rachel giggled behind him. She wore a short, flowered dress with cowboy boots and had her long brown hair braided into two ponytails.

"I knew I'd find you here."

"What'll it be, hon?" Butchie asked her.

"Vodka and cranberry." She looked back to Bobby. "What about your other bumps and bruises?"

"They're concerned about the bleeding in my kidneys. They're worried about clots."

"Are you worried?" she asked as Butchie slid her the tall drink he'd poured into a pint glass.

"They want to do more tests."

"Can I join you?" she asked. Bobby nodded to the empty stool beside him.

"I'll take a shot," Bobby called to Butchie.

"You okay?" she asked Bobby, studying his stressed look and fidgety posture.

Butchie filled three shot glasses. Bobby, Rachel, and Butchie each reached for one. They held the whiskeys up and saluted each other before swallowing them down. They all grimaced.

"Those are on me." Butchie stepped away to wait on a customer who'd just walked into the bar.

"Smile, Bobby," she said, sounding sincere. "What's the matter?"

"I don't want to talk about it."

"I'm worried about you."

"Don't. I'm fine."

"I've been everywhere searching for you," she said, placing her hand on his knee. "I can't stop thinking about you."

"I can't give you what you want."

"You don't know what I want."

"I'm tired. I'm beat up. I'm spent. You're none of that."

"I'll take care of you."

"I've been with you. I'll never be able to keep up. I just want to rest and heal."

"I'll make you better."

"It won't work," Bobby said, after glancing to the door as Tony Cannavaro, his manager, suddenly walked in. "Ah, hell. Can this day get any worse?"

"Give me a chance, Bobby," Rachel continued.

Distracted, Bobby dropped his head as if trying to hide his face. Tony slid the sunglasses he wore to the top of his head and scanned the dark bar. He spotted Bobby and grinned.

"Well, well, well," Tony called out loudly as he approached. "Mr. Bobby Raymond. The famous Bobby Raymond. I can't believe it, bumping into you like this."

"Yeah, imagine that."

Tony studied the cast on Bobby's right hand. He hopped onto an empty barstool on the other side of Rachel. He leaned in close to her and ogled her crossed bare legs. She slowly and seductively kicked one of her legs, the toe of her boot tapping against the back of Bobby's calf.

"Who's your friend, Bobby?" Tony asked, staring into Rachel's brown eyes and tossing a cell phone and credit card onto the bar.

"How'd you find me?"

"I arrive in a city, look for the most depressing dump I can find, and go there first," Tony said in front of Butchie.

"Hey, it's not that bad in here," Butchie said.

"Get me a gin and soda, and I'll get another round, whatever they want."

"Come on. How'd you find me?"

"You called Mary. You gave her the name of this place. This is where I came first."

"Mary?" Rachel asked as Butchie delivered another High Life for Bobby and a double vodka and cranberry for her. "Who's Mary?"

"It's never very hard to find you," Tony said, still gawking at Rachel. "Who's your friend, Bobby?"

"Who's Mary?" Rachel asked again.

"I'm Tony," he said, reaching his hand out to Rachel, who shook it.

"Rachel."

"I'm Bobby's manager."

"Former manager," Bobby said.

"Nice to meet you, Rachel," Tony said, still holding her hand. "What are you doing in this shithole with this bum?"

"Who's Mary?"

"Bobby's old flame. She tossed him out with the trash like all the others did before her. They were supposed to get married."

"Rachel?" Bobby fumed, glaring at Tony. "Can you give us a minute? I need to talk some business with Tony here."

"Stay, Rachel," Tony said, glaring back at him. "Bobby and I, we don't have any secrets."

"What are you doing here then?"

"What happened to your hand?"

"Take a wild guess."

"Who put the cast on?"

"Some intern at the free clinic."

"Bobby, Bobby," Tony shook his head and called out to Butchie. "Get us a round of whiskey shots. And one for you, too."

Butchie lined up the shot glasses and began to pour the whiskey.

"You don't let some green doc put a plaster cast on your million-dollar right hand," he said, reaching for one of the shot glasses and motioning for the others to grab one. "Here's to the next light heavyweight champion of the world!"

He knocked back the whiskey. Butchie and Rachel followed. Bobby stared at Tony.

"Million dollar?"

"Now, before I give you the details, promise me that you won't overreact," Tony said.

"What details?"

"I'm sticking around New Orleans for a couple of days, but you don't have to decide anything right away."

"I'm done fighting, if that's what you're getting at. I'm here to find Chuck. I'm not leaving until I find him."

"I'll be back here a few days after Christmas."

"What details?"

"You're ranked fifth in the world."

"I've already told you; I'm done."

"I know you, Bobby. This happens every time after a tough fight."

"Grainger beat me up bad."

"Once you get some rest, heal up, bang a few chicks," Tony said, glancing to Rachel, who had her hand in Bobby's lap. "And hide out in these dives for a while, feeling sorry for yours—"

"Not this time," Bobby interrupted, pushing Rachel's wandering hand away. "The fire's gone, Tony. I won fights that I shouldn't have with heart and guts. Without those, I'm done."

"I got you a shot at the championship." Tony hopped off the bar stool and slapped Bobby on the back.

Bobby lowered his head and closed his eyes.

"The world championship, buddy! You've dreamed about a championship ever since you first laced up the gloves."

"Why me?" Bobby asked, looking back to him. "What about the guys ranked ahead of me?"

"Castillo, the second ranked fighter, is not being offered enough guaranteed money. O'Bannon at three and Jackson at four have significant injuries."

"What about my injuries?" Bobby asked as Rachel returned her hand to his thigh.

"Don't you think it's amazing how all these circumstances have come together like this? It's as if fate wants you in that fight."

"Fate's full of shit," Bobby shook his head. "I'd be fighting with a broken hand and bad kidneys."

"So, you'll think about it?"

"I'm done, Tony. I've told you that."

"I've been negotiating for a June match. That's six months away. You've always been a fast healer."

"It's not enough time."

"So, you're thinking about it?"

"No, I'm out."

"Is five million fucking dollars enough money?" Tony asked as Bobby cringed. "I got them to guarantee the five million up front. We have until January first to sign the contract."

Suddenly, Holly cheerfully appeared in the doorway of the bar. She immediately spotted Bobby and excitedly stepped towards him, only to abruptly stop. She studied Tony before spying Rachel caressing Bobby's leg. She watched for a moment.

"I may need a tune-up fight," Bobby said to Tony.

"So, you really are thinking about it?" Tony shook his head. "But no tune-up. That'd be too risky, especially with the recent injuries."

"I can't, Tony. I can't do it. It was never about the money for me."

"What about all your debt?" he asked as Bobby glanced to Rachel who shrugged. "Your mom and Mary told me about your bills, your outstanding legal fees. You have no home. No car. Your folks are broke from your father's medical expenses."

There was a long pause as Bobby glared back at Tony. He broke off the staring match and looked to the door of the bar and noticed Holly for the first time. They stared at each other. He quickly glanced to Rachel and pushed her hand from his lap.

"When I come back here after Christmas," Tony continued. "We'll sign the contract, and I'll take you to Baltimore to see some real doctors and start training."

"I'm not leaving until I find my brother," Bobby said, hurriedly standing as Holly disappeared outside.

"I'll move to Baltimore with you," Rachel said.

"Sign the contract," Tony continued. "One fight. That's all. Your debt, your troubles, all gone. It's the world championship!"

"I'm not ready," Bobby mumbled, bumping into Tony as he scrambled out the door after Holly.

"You have six months to get ready! Heal up!" Tony called out, motioning to Rachel. "And stay out of trouble!"

Chapter Eighty-One

Holly was a half of block away on St. Peter, heading towards Royal Street. Bobby chased her.

"Holly!" he called out as she turned left onto Royal.

"This was a mistake!" she yelled back, rushing away from him. "I knew it the first time I saw you!"

"Wait."

"What was I thinking?"

"Holly, wait," he continued to call out as she suddenly stopped and turned to him.

"Who's the three-piece suit?"

"His name is Tony."

"Who is he?"

"He's my manager from Baltimore."

"Baltimore?"

"He handles my boxing career."

"What's he's doing here?"

"He's lined me up for a championship fight."

"Championship fight?"

"The light heavyweight world championship."

"Is that for a lot of money?"

"Five million dollars."

"Five million dollars?" she whispered in almost disbelief. "You'd be crazy to turn down that kind of money, right?"

"And I'd be crazier to fight the current world campion with one hand," he said, holding up his casted right hand. "I'd get murdered."

"Good luck," she said, turning and walking away from him again. "Seems you'll need it."

"Holly, wait!" he called, following her. "Wait!"

"Leave me alone," she said as she hurried away.

"Holly!"

She abruptly stopped and turned. "Who's the pigtails?"

"She's no one."

"Didn't look that way in the bar!"

"I'm not interested in her."

"Bullshit! Don't lie to me!"

"She thinks she can fix me."

"Fix you? In what way?"

"Let's just say, I'm not all the man I use to be."

"What does that mean?"

"After years in the ring, the love has been beaten out me. I haven't figured yet how to get it back."

"Can she?"

"Can she, what?"

"Fix you."

"She'll never get the chance."

"So long, Bobby," she said, stomping away.

"Holly." He chased after her and grabbed her arm. "Stop."

"Don't touch me!" she snapped, yanking her arm away.

"Please."

"Your friends are waiting!"

"I don't need to go back there. I want to be with you."

"I want to be left alone."

"They don't mean anything to me," Bobby pleaded, motioning back in the direction of Tommy Black's. "I don't want to fight again. I don't care about the money."

"And Pigtails?"

"She means nothing to me. I promise," he said. "Let me walk you home."

"Not tonight."

"How 'bout tomorrow? Can I see you tomorrow?"

"I don't know."

"Please. I won't let you down."

"I don't know if it's a good idea. Bobby, I ca—"

"Come on," he interrupted. "I'll stop by your place in the morning."

"I won't be home," she grumbled and stormed off.

Chapter Eighty-Two

After watching Holly disappear into the afternoon crowds, he waited for several minutes on the corner of the street, hoping she'd come back. She never did. With a faraway look in his eyes, he eventually returned to Tommy Black's like a wounded dog with its tail between its legs. He had nowhere else to go. Tony was gone. Rachel anxiously waited for him. She was thrilled he came back. He sat beside her. She rubbed his back.

"So, your angel flew away?" she said, nodding to Butchie who filled three shot glasses with whiskey. "Big deal."

"Where's Tony?"

"He left—said he'd look you up again before leaving town." She shrugged as Butchie pushed the whiskey shots towards them. "He wanted to wine and dine me tonight, and everything else in between."

"Why didn't you go with him?"

"I knew you'd come back. I want to be with you."

Along with Butchie, they swallowed the shots. Bobby and Rachel stared. He was vulnerable. She knew it, and he knew it. She was ready to pounce.

"I'm not ready for you to tell me goodbye for good," she said as he was unable to look away from her gaze. "At least, not tonight. I feel like it's coming though."

"But, Rachel, you—"

"Let's have a couple more drinks here," she interrupted. "I'll take you to dinner, to a nice place. My treat. We'll go listen to some local music after."

"Rachel, stop."

"It's supposed to be cold tonight, in the forties," she said, sounding more desperate. "I have plenty of blankets. We can spend the night at my place under the covers. Doesn't it sound fun to wrestle around with me, together, under the blankets? Let's keep each other warm."

"Why me?"

"Why not you?"

"I'm a mess."

"We're all a mess."

"It's because you can't have me. I'm a challenge."

"What does your angel have that I don't?"

"In my previous life, what seems like a hundred years ago, you wouldn't have been able to peel me off you."

"You just need your confidence back. I can help you with that."

"You're poison, Rachel. I take one drink of you, and I'm a dead man. And I wouldn't be your first victim."

"If this is goodbye," she said, reaching for his hand, "wouldn't it be so much more fun to say it in the morning after a night together. And I'd never come looking for you again. I promise."

She squeezed his hand tighter as he glanced away. She motioned to Butchie that they needed two more shots.

"And I swear to you," she said, leaning closer and practically blowing the words into his ear. "You will never forget me after tonight."

"Rachel, quit."

"And you never know, maybe something magical will happen. For both of us."

"But what you have to offer, I don't need anymore."

"What do you need?"

"I'm sorry."

Book Three

Let's Disappear Tonight

Chapter Eighty-Three

Holly was being followed through the streets at dawn. She had agreed to work a morning shift at the club for her father. It was usually the slowest shift of the day. She rarely worked it as it was normally reserved for the less experienced dancers or the new hires. She hurried across Esplanade and entered the Quarter via Royal Street. Mostly hidden on a side street, one of the bouncers from the club watched her from a running car. After she passed him, he turned onto Royal and slowly followed her from a few blocks away.

Holly eventually cut across St. Peter, then onto Bourbon, and ducked into her father's club. Although open, the place was dark, quiet, and empty except for one bartender who cleaned glasses behind the main bar. The club's lights and sound system were not turned on, likely because there were no customers present at that hour in the morning. Holly entered Russell's office and briskly walked by him without making eye contact. Holding a full glass of whiskey, he stared at her as she opened her locker in the dressing room in back and began to get ready.

"You're late."

"Not even 'good morning'?" she said, slowly starting to change into a dancing outfit.

"Where were you last night?"

"You tell me. Your goons followed me all night."

"Where in the fuck were you?"

"You gave me the night off."

"Hurry up then and get ready."

"There's no one here."

As she methodically changed out of her street clothes, Russell walked to his office door and stepped into the club. With his back turned as he hit a switch on the wall, she secretly pulled a butcher knife from her bag and placed it in her locker. All the lights inside the club came on. He hit another switch as she wrapped the knife in a towel, hiding it.

The intro to the heavy metal classic AC/DC song, "Hells Bells," started to play with the banging of bells. He found a knob and turned up the volume of the song to a very loud level. Holly stared at him as she pulled a one-piece silver and fringed bathing suit over her nude body. He watched her. After slipping on a pair of shiny, red knee-high boots, she checked her make-up in a mirror before slamming the locker door shut.

"Come on!" Russell yelled. "Hurry up!"

"Why?"

"You're late! You should've been out there by now!"

"The place is empty."

"Go dance," he said, dimming the lights in the club except for a spotlight that illuminated the main stage in the middle of the main floor.

"There's no one out there."

"I pay you to dance. Go fucking dance!"

"By myself?"

"Yes, goddammit! By your fucking self!"

"I'm going home," she said, angrily turning to her locker.

Russell threw the glass he held at her. It shattered on the wall above her head, showering her with ice, whiskey, and pieces of glass.

"Go dance!"

After a brief hesitation, she dashed by him into the club, shaking the whiskey from her arms and brushing at the broken pieces of glass in her hair. She glanced to the front entrance of the club. Two bouncers blocked it, glaring at her. She looked back to her father, who motioned to the empty, spotlit stage and turned up the volume even higher.

Chapter Eighty-Four

The guesthouse on Elysian where Bobby was staying was loud and lively. It was located next to a 24-hour bar. But the late-night revelry had nothing to do with keeping him awake. He was alone in the cold room. He didn't sleep. He couldn't stop thinking about both Holly and Rachel.

The night would have turned out differently if he'd left with Rachel. Though, he likely would've regretted that decision and hated himself for it. He surprised himself for not following her as that would have been the easy thing to do. Holly was the one he wanted to be with.

He arrived at Holly's place a little before ten o'clock the next morning, hoping she was still there. Because he couldn't sleep, he had spent the early morning looking for Chuck. Bobby wasn't about to give up the search, even though he was troubled about how Chuck may react if he ever did find him. He worried Chuck may be confrontational or even violent. But he had to find him. Both he and his folks needed closure. And he needed to apologize.

As he was about to knock on Holly's door, the front door slowly opened. He backed away from the door, expecting Holly. Instead, Emma Delore appeared. Surprised, he glanced around the front of Holly's apartment and to the houses on each side of the complex to make sure he was at the right place.

"I'm looking for Holly," he said as Emma, slightly hunched over, stepped out of the apartment and locked the front door behind her. "Is she home?"

Emma was neatly dressed, wearing a white hat and cheery, orange-and yellow-striped sundress that perfectly accented her caramel-colored skin. Her hands and face were wrinkled, but her brown eyes were alert and bright. She carried several empty shopping tote bags with her.

"Holly told me you might stop by," Emma said, extending her arm out to him as he looked confused. "I didn't want to leave without you."

"Where's Holly?"

"You and I are going for a little walk," she said, studying the cast that covered his wrist and most of his right arm.

"What?"

"It's market day for me," she said, still holding out her arm. "Holly usually takes me. But this morning, she's busy. She said you might be stopping by and would be happy to help me instead."

"Holly's not coming?"

"No, Holly's not coming," she shook her head. "Emma Delore."

"I'm Bobby Raymond."

"Mr. Raymond," she said, still extending her arm out, "now come here and walk next to me like the gentleman escort you should be."

Still confused, Bobby offered her his healthy left arm, and she took it. He looked back to the closed front door of Holly's apartment.

"No Holly?" he asked again as she dragged him down Esplanade towards the river.

"Hello, Ms. Delore," a man suddenly called from his porch as they passed.

"So, you and Holly are close?" Bobby asked. "How do you know Holly?"

"Good afternoon, Mr. Chaisson," she said to the neighbor with a slight nod, ignoring Bobby.

"Beautiful day, huh?" The neighbor grinned.

"Yessir, it is. It's always a beautiful day in New Orleans," she shouted back. "Especially in the mornings."

"Where are we going, Ms. Delore?" Bobby asked.

"Call me Emma."

"Where are we going, Emma?"

"Only a few quick stops today, Mr. Raymond," she said, nodding to an antique store owner as she walked with Bobby arm-in-arm towards Decatur Street. "I need some things from the market, then I thought we'd stop for a refreshment and a chat."

Chapter Eighty-Five

With no enthusiasm, Holly stiffly moved slowly to the rousing beat of the raucous Aerosmith tune, "Dude Looks Like a Lady." Her father leaned against the front of the stage, leering at her. She tried not to make eye contact.

"Take off your clothes!" he yelled. "How do expect any tips?"

Humiliated, she spun away from him, not even attempting to keep pace with the music and faced the back of the stage as she tried to hold back the tears.

"Turn around! Let's see some skin! Dance! Dance, goddammit! Dance like you mean it!"

Russell glanced first to the two bouncers at the entrance and then to the bartender. All three of them had looked away from the stage, feeling uncomfortable watching the awkward exchange between Holly and her father.

Russell motioned to the bartender to turn up the volume. The bartender adjusted a knob behind the bar as loud as it would go. By this time, Holly's body had crumbled to a heap at the back of the stage. She buried her face into her folded arms and tried not to sob.

"Take it off!" he yelled one last time, throwing a stack of cash at her and stomping into his office with the slam of the door.

Chapter Eighty-Six

The marketplace was busy that morning with mostly locals and a few curious tourists. The loud shouting of the barking vendors and the haggling customers echoed through the aisles of fresh produce stacked to the ceiling. Bobby and Emma strolled together through the crowd, who appeared to be fighting with each other for the apples, oranges, red peppers, green tomatoes, pecans, and peanuts. Emma reached a plastic shopping basket to Bobby.

"We'll only be a moment," she said, hustling him through the crowded aisles of the fruit and souvenir stands, heading to the far corner of the marketplace. "I've been coming here once a week for forty years. I have my favorite stand here in the back."

"Who's this, Ms. Delore?" said a short, thick, and tanned Latino man with a smile.

"A new friend who's helping me out today, Manny," she said as Bobby nodded hello.

"Where's Holly?" he asked as Emma filled the basket Bobby was holding with a head of lettuce and a bundle of bananas. "Will you be seein' Holly, Ms. Delore?"

"Probably later today," she said, reaching for a large purple onion and several cloves of garlic.

"I have a Christmas gift for her," he said, pulling out a necklace made with thick twine and bright orange and blue beads that looked like marbles. "I made it myself."

"It's beautiful, Manny," Emma smiled, taking the necklace from him and holding it up against her chest. "I'll make sure she gets it."

"Tell her Merry Christmas for me, please," he nodded. "Could you do that, Ms. Delore? Could you tell her Merry Christmas?"

"I most certainly will, Manny," she said, motioning for Bobby to give the basket full of fruits and vegetables to him.

"How much I do owe you?" Emma asked.

"Nine dollars," he said, placing the items in the tote bags and handing them to Bobby.

Emma gave Manny a twenty-dollar bill and waved off the change. "Thank you, Ms. Delore. Thank you so much. Merry Christmas."

"Merry Christmas, Manny," she said as Bobby nodded goodbye.

"Where to next, Emma?" Bobby asked. "A coffee?"

"Coffee?" she grinned, shaking her head. "My doctor tells me to avoid caffeine. I was thinking of something a little stiffer, like a cocktail."

"Do you have a place?"

"I have the perfect place, Mr. Raymond."

Chapter Eighty-Seven

And it was indeed the perfect place—a grand hotel from another time. After walking at a casual pace for a few blocks on St. Philip, they turned on Bourbon and stopped in front of a popular hotel that had been in business for over one hundred-twenty years. Two bellboys in red and yellow suits greeted Emma and Bobby at the glass front doors, holding them open as if Emma were royalty.

Bobby followed her inside, carrying the tote bags of produce with his left hand. He gazed at the vast and palatial lobby a moment as Emma walked ahead of him. The lobby was as large as a French Quarter block complete with cathedral-like ceilings, chandeliers of crystal and gold, and multiple white marble staircases that jutted off in multiple directions. Large murals of Andrew Jackson and Napoleon, faded from time, connected the walls.

Emma nodded hello to the concierge, to a young girl watering the numerous flower arrangements in the lobby, and to a bald man busy behind the front desk. They all smiled and warmly greeted her. A gentleman at a grand piano softly tapped the keys, playing a warm and sunny melody. He grinned and winked upon seeing Emma. She led Bobby through the lobby to a small, bright cafe filled with a variety of wild-growing ferns and yellow- and red-flowering hibiscus plants. They took a seat at a bistro table that was next to a bubbling stone fountain filled with pennies and blue water.

"Hello, Ms. Delore. The usual?" asked a young waiter.

"Yes, vodka and tonic with two limes."

"And you, sir?"

"A beer."

"Import or domestic?"

"Import."

"Is a Foster's fine?"

"Sounds good."

"Excellent."

"Everyone we pass in this town knows who you are," Bobby said as the waiter disappeared.

"Not everyone. I just walk the same streets and go to the same places. It does make one feel very popular and important now, doesn't it? But this is really the only day I get out anymore."

"Have you lived your entire life here?"

"All but ten years."

"Where else have you lived?"

"I was in Paris for a year and Barcelona the other nine."

"Yeah?"

"I was most fortunate to spend my formative years examining some of the finer pursuits this life has to offer."

"Such as?" Bobby asked as the waiter returned with the drinks. He poured the Foster's into a glass.

"Painting and drawing, literature, philosophy," she said and sipped from her vodka.

She chose her words carefully, speaking smoothly yet slowly. The words didn't exactly roll from her lips. They kind of hung there for a moment, until she was ready to give them away, as if lightly glued to her tongue.

"You were a student?"

"I traveled to Paris to study nineteenth century European literature. I lasted only a year. What teenager has any real interest in nineteenth century literature anyway?"

"What happened?"

"I fell in love with Barcelona after a weekend train ride to Spain with a classmate. What a gorgeous city. Spectacular. Barcelona was everything that Paris was but minus the pretension and conceit. The architect Gaudi had just started many of his projects. Have you heard of Gaudi?"

Bobby shook head.

"No one had ever seen work like his before. His unusual buildings and eccentric style were straight from another world. His works breathed. They were alive. They had come from the future. They blended in so well with the older architecture already in place. It was such an exciting time to be there."

"I can only imagine," Bobby said, sipping his beer. "So different from where I came from."

"I returned to Paris, packed my things as fast as I could, and moved to Barcelona the next day, without even taking the time to drop out of school. I rented a tiny apartment among the art and fashion shops and bohemian cafes in the Barrio Gothic district—the oldest section of the town. I fell in with other young artists living in the neighborhood at the time. We'd attend symphonies staged on the plaza behind the great Cathedral. We'd stay up all night drinking wine under the moonlight. It seemed the cafes never closed. And we'd sleep all day. I was even fortunate enough to have met Picasso while he was living there. I studied painting at the university."

"Were you any good?"

"I don't really know," she shrugged. "Some folks liked my work, but I didn't have the patience. I never was able to finish any of my paintings. It takes one who appreciates their solitude to paint. I enjoy the company of others too much."

"I understand that."

"I was so young. I was only eighteen when I arrived in Paris."

"You must've been scared to death."

"Not at all, Mr. Raymond. I was a mature kid. I had already seen far more than any young girl should've been allowed to see."

"Did your family have money?"

"Not exactly," she said, staring into the drink and playing with the straw. "But that was what everyone thought. It was quite the opposite. I was born in the attic of a one-time brothel over on Basin Street here in the city. I was what they called a trick baby. My momma was a prostitute in a section of the Quarter once called Storyville."

"I didn't mean to pry." Bobby shook his head, taking a drink of beer.

"No, no, Mr. Raymond, I'm proud of where I come from," she said, looking up and taking a big drink of the vodka. "That wasn't always the case though. For the first fourteen years of my life, I slept hidden behind a curtain in a parlor where my momma entertained her male friends, customers, johns—whatever you want to call them. When I couldn't sleep, I would peek through the curtain and watch a seemingly never-ending line of mostly disgusting, foul-mouthed strange men hop on top of my momma and ride her 'til she bled. Sometimes there would be more than one with her at the same time. Sometimes she would cry at the end of the evening, and I didn't know why. I would cry, too, but she never knew. I didn't want her to worry about me. She seemed to have enough to worry about."

"Jesus," Bobby mumbled.

"When I turned seven, the madam of the house, Auntie Millie, paid me a quarter every evening to carry a glass pitcher of beer from room to room to serve all the male visitors in the house. I just assumed I'd live my entire life in the house, working as my momma did when I was old enough."

"Were you close to your mother?"

"As close as would be expected. My momma wasn't proud of what she did. I think she tried to keep her distance from me. I know she didn't want me to end up there. I never really understood what she did for a living until I was older. My momma was black, but I never ever saw her with a black man. My father was white. I would look at my skin. I was somewhere in between. I never quite knew where I belonged. I wasn't accepted by the whites, and I was ignored by the blacks. I wasn't allowed to attend any of the schools here in the city. People knew who my momma was and what she did."

"How'd you get out of there?"

"Thank God for my father. He got me to Europe, which was as far away as possible. I was accepted there, especially in Barcelona. I blended in perfectly. My skin was dark, and I had black kinky hair like everyone else. They all thought I was Spanish, until they heard me speak anyway. My New Orleans accent was something I could not hide."

"So, you knew who your father was?"

"He was an international banker from France. A world traveler. A man of great wealth. He loved my momma."

"She must've been some lady."

"She was beautiful," Emma said, digging through her pocketbook and handing him a wrinkled black and white photograph that had yellowed with age.

"Yeah, she was," Bobby nodded, staring at the portrait of a beautiful young black woman in a flowing white dress sitting with her legs crossed on a bed.

"She didn't look like most of the girls back then. She was tall and lean. Her dark skin and unique appearance made her very popular in the house. She earned a lot of money for a lot of people. They oftentimes made her do some rather revolting things. But she always did what she was told."

"And your father?"

"When he visited New Orleans, he was allowed to take my momma out of the house because he paid so well. He'd buy her the nicest clothes, the finest jewelry, and the most expensive perfumes. He'd take her to the best restaurants, and they'd spend their nights in the most luxurious hotels in town. The other ladies in the house were jealous. He wanted to marry her, but he knew his family would never accept a black prostitute from America as his bride."

The waiter suddenly appeared with two more drinks.

"Thank you," Bobby said.

"Then my momma became pregnant," Emma continued. "He insisted he was the father, even though my momma never really knew for sure, and begged for her to leave the house." Emma paused to take a sip from her fresh vodka and tonic. "He offered her an apartment in one of the nicer neighborhoods and to pay her money to raise the child. But she turned him down. She couldn't leave the house. She was too loyal to Auntie Millie, who had taken care of her since she was a little girl. My momma asked him to instead take care of her unborn baby after the child turned fourteen."

"And that child?"

"I never knew what love really was until I was old enough to understand the sacrifice my momma made for me," Emma paused a moment. "She gave me everything that could've been hers."

Emma glanced away and didn't say anything for several minutes. The waiter returned.

"Everything all right?" he asked.

"We're fine," Emma smiled, trying her best to hide her teary eyes.

"Yes, we're good," Bobby agreed.

"So many people I met in Europe thought I was some spoiled rich girl from the States. No one knew my nights were spent crying— trapped behind a curtain, not allowed to make a sound, petrified of all the retched strangers who passed through my momma's bedroom each night. All the while I gagged on the stink of body odor, spilt beer, and all the cheap perfumes and colognes used to try and hide it. There were no sewers back then. My momma's customers would urinate right out the door of her room and into the street. I'll never ever forget how awful that house stunk, especially in the summer."

There wasn't anything Bobby could say. He just shook his head.

"My father rescued me from all that. The day I left for Europe my momma made me promise to never step foot in the Basin Street house again."

She paused to take a rather large sip of her drink.

"Adversity either destroys you or makes you stronger, Mr. Raymond. I benefited from what I saw, what I experienced as a child. I've tried to respect people and help those less fortunate. I eventually returned here and worked in different art galleries in the city for years and painted some. But something was missing in my life. My father then died, leaving me a rather large sum of money. Ever since that time, I've used it to look after orphans and runaways, mostly teenage girls, that end up in this city. I've looked after some two hundred kids in over thirty years. I find them a place to sleep, something to eat, and even some cash. But most importantly, I try to put them in the hands of the right people who'll get them the help they need."

Bobby took a drink from the beer and asked, "I happen to know one of these girls, right?"

"To answer your question I avoided earlier, Mr. Raymond, Holly and I are indeed very close," Emma said with a nod and a warm smile. "I don't see her as much as I used to, but she's an extraordinary young lady—so gentle, so full of love. She's made me laugh, and she's made me cry. No one had done that since I was young. We have a special bond, probably since we both lived through some hard times. But still, she needs a love I could never provide. She's never really had any friends here. She's afraid to get too close to anyone."

"I'll never forget the first time I saw her," Bobby said. "I was immediately drawn to her. There was something about her, something different."

"But I'm worried. I'm afraid she may do something reckless."

"How'd the two of you meet?"

"For another time, Mr. Raymond," she shrugged, taking the final drink of her second vodka drink. "If I was twenty years younger, I'd suggest we get another."

Emma waved the waiter over as Bobby reached for his wallet.

"Put your money away, Mr. Raymond. This was a pleasure," she said, setting a hundred-dollar bill on the table. "Now, come over here and help up me from my seat."

Bobby gently lifted Emma up and led her through the lobby of the hotel. She waved goodbye to everyone who noticed her leave. The two bellboys smiled and again opened the front glass doors. She generously tipped each of them as she walked out.

◆———▶•◉•◀•———◆

Chapter Eighty-Eight

Outside, the hot sun blazed. The humidity lingered heavy in the air. Slightly tipsy, Emma clung to Bobby's left arm as they turned off Bourbon, crossed Royal, and took Chartres Street to get her home. She was tired. They walked considerably slower than before. She still had plenty to say.

"I've entertained this crazy idea of moving back to Barcelona. I don't know how many years I've got left, but I still feel good. My greatest memories were there. The Spaniards have an energy and friendliness I miss. I know Barcelona has changed with time. It's been so long. But I'm hoping it hasn't. I know my old friends have moved on or even passed away, but I'm hoping they haven't. I know I'll never be able to retrieve that time again, but maybe there I'll find the youth I left behind. I have never stopped thinking about Spain, but. . ."

"But, what?" he asked.

"I know I'm not going anywhere." She sadly grinned after a short pause. "I'm sorry, Mr. Raymond. I spent this whole morning talking about myself. That wasn't polite, was it?"

"No. No. I enjoyed your stories very much."

"I hear you're looking for your brother."

"I'm nearly consumed with finding him. I did some rather awful things."

"Good luck in your search."

Bobby stopped walking and asked, "Have you ever been in love?"

"Now, what do you think?"

"Have you?"

"Once," she said as they started to walk again.

"Only once?"

"I was twenty-six, living in Barcelona. I had fallen in love with a young Italian writer, Paolo, who was traveling through Europe. Every weekend we'd take a trolley up to the highest mountain peak, the Tibidabo, which overlooked the city. There was an ancient church that looked like a castle up there along with an amusement park with electrical cars and trains and a Ferris wheel. I had never seen such things. From there, the city appeared to have been rolled out before us like a carpet, all the way out to the deep blue of the Mediterranean Sea. We felt so large standing up there as if the city belonged to us. It was ours."

"How'd it end?"

"End?"

"The love affair."

"My momma died from a blood infection. I traveled back to New Orleans for the funeral, leaving Paolo behind. I intended to return to Barcelona. I sent him a letter every day for weeks. They soon all returned unopened. I found out he had left Spain, and nobody knew where he had gone. I was devastated. I felt betrayed. I was furious. I decided to stay here. A year later, I received a letter from him. He wanted to meet me in Barcelona. I didn't respond. I threw the letter away. I couldn't forgive him. I wanted him to come find me! I wanted him to be prove his love to me! I wasn't chasing after no one!"

"Do you regret not going back to Barcelona?"

"Every day of my life, Mr. Raymond."

"And now, you're ready to go back?"

"I guess I'm finally over him."

"Did you ever marry?"

"Mr. Raymond, I don't just enjoy living here," she said, without answering him. "I absolutely love living here. It's taking me this long to finally get the courage to leave again. For me, New Orleans will always be sipping spicy Bloody Marys on the hottest Sunday morning you've ever known, laughing about the wonderful time you had the night before, and thinking about someone you once loved. I like all those things very much."

"I want to meet with you again," Bobby said as they reached Esplanade.

"That's a fine idea." She smiled as he helped her cross the street and up the steps to the front door of her house.

After reaching the top of the stairs, they looked below to the street. Holly suddenly appeared. Both Bobby and Emma studied her as she passively approached.

"She shouldn't be home this early today," Emma mumbled, loud enough for Bobby to hear.

Holly's body language spoke the truth. Her head was down. Her shoulders were slouched. She held her folded arms in tight against her chest. Her zombie-like gait was deliberate. Her make-up and curly blonde hair were messed. She had the look of someone who had been thoroughly defeated and was in retreat after giving up from a long battle.

Bobby glanced to Emma. She glared back with an expression that shouted, "You better rise up, boy!"

Bobby again looked below to Holly, who neared her apartment.

"She needs you," Emma whispered. "Keep an eye out for her. Don't let her do anything stupid. Please."

Chapter Eighty-Nine

Bobby hurried down the stairs and intercepted Holly before she reached the front door of the apartment. She immediately stopped upon seeing him, appearing to not recognize him at first in her trance-like state. They studied each other a moment until she desperately reached to him and collapsed into his arms. He took the apartment key from her trembling hand and unlocked the front door. He backed into the blacked-out apartment, dragging her with him.

"What happened?"

"I can't talk about it."

"Come on," he said, directing her to the couch. "Tell me. What happened?"

"Just hold me," she said as he gently eased her onto the couch, taking a seat with her.

"Do you need anything?"

"No."

"Can you tell what happened? It's all right."

She didn't answer as he gathered more of her body into his.

"Was it your father?"

She still didn't respond as he started to lift himself off the couch.

"Don't leave me," she said, grabbing for his waist.

"It's all right," he said, pulling away from her.

He walked into the kitchen and clicked on a small lamp. The muted glow of light instantly warmed the dark apartment. She couldn't hide a quick but forced grin that creased her lips as she watched him.

"Can you cover the windows?" she asked. He slid the blankets that hung from curtain rods completely over the windows of the place. "Make it look like I'm not here."

"Are you in trouble?" he asked, rejoining her on the couch.

Not answering, she rested her head against his chest. He softly caressed the top of her head and the back of her neck. Her body melted into his as they sat in silence for many minutes. He kept quiet until she was ready to talk.

"I can't go back," she whispered. "I can't go back there ever again. I may regret it."

He tightened his grip around her and remained quiet.

"Do you have anywhere to be?" she asked, craning her neck and searching for his eyes.

He shook his head and gently massaged her shoulder.

"Can you stay here with me?"

"I got you."

"Just hold me," she said, closing her eyes. "And please, don't let me go."

Chapter Ninety

Bobby struggled to open his eyes. Finally, he glanced around the room made cozy by the glimmer of white light from the lamp in the kitchen. On his back, he was locked in a tight embrace with Holly, most of her warm, blanket-covered body on him. The heavy cast on his right arm awkwardly rested on the top of the cushions at the back of the couch.

He searched for the clock on the wall. It was nearly nine. But with blankets over the windows, he couldn't tell if it was night or morning. He needed to continue his search for his brother. He was running out of time. It would soon be Christmas.

Holly began to stir. She shifted her body slightly. They faced each other. She still slept. Needing a more comfortable position, he repositioned his broken right arm and rested it across her chest. His arm methodically, and ever so easily, moved up and down with each quiet breath she took. He studied her contented face. She seemed to be smiling. They remained in that position for almost another hour until she awoke. During that time, he not once looked away.

"Are you all right?" He finally noticed her eyes were open.

She yawned and stretched her arms without responding. She intently watched him from the corner of her eyes. He tried to ease away from her on the couch to check outside. She tightly held him, leaning her face towards him, and wouldn't let go. They kissed, but only briefly. He pulled away and stared at her, looking for more. She slid most of her warm body off him and rolled from his arms, turning her back to him.

Having been mostly asleep for many hours, he was somewhat lightheaded as he staggered to one of the windows. He pushed a small corner of the blanket aside and peeked out. It was dark. Few people were on the streets.

"It's still night," he said. "We slept the day away."

"I'm starving," she said, speaking into the back cushions of the couch. "How 'bout you?"

Chapter Ninety-One

Bobby followed Holly to the front door of the apartment. She cautiously opened it and checked each side of the dark and quiet street, searching for her father's Cadillac. Not seeing it, she took Bobby's hand and led him out into the night.

"Where are we going?" he asked as she held his hand and leaned into him.

"The neighborhood's best place."

"Where is it?"

"A few blocks from here on Frenchmen," she said as they walked at a slowed pace.

"Is it any good?"

"Do you like Italian?"

"Everyone likes Italian."

"It's the best."

Holding his hand more tightly, Holly led Bobby to a non-descript red brick building on Frenchmen Street. An almost hidden, red-painted door with black and white letters that spelled "Alfonso's" greeted them. Popular with locals, Alfonso's was a hidden gem, a highly regarded Italian and seafood restaurant influenced by Cajun and Creole cooking. Bobby pulled the heavy door open for her and followed her up a set of dark and uneven stairs to the second floor.

They entered the restaurant. It was cozy, quaint, and dimly lit. The heavenly aroma of roasted garlic and melted butter pleasantly hung in the air. Wobbly spinning fans hanging from a high ceiling worked hard to keep the place cool. Bobby scanned the restaurant as they waited for a server. Numerous pieces of colorful, local folk art adorned the cluttered red walls.

Many tables, all covered with red-and-white checkered tablecloths, were crammed near each other to increase the seating capacity in the small dining room. There was only one other couple there. They were finishing their meal.

A server finally appeared, a young man who seemed to be in his late twenties. He smiled upon recognizing Holly and gave the length of her body a once over with roving eyes he couldn't disguise. She smiled back as he looked to Bobby.

"Holly, Holly, anywhere," the waiter said, motioning to the mostly empty room.

She led the waiter to a small table with two seats near a window with a view outside. Bobby followed them. The waiter pulled one of the seats out for Holly and directed her to sit. After the waiter dashed off to the kitchen, Bobby sat in the other seat.

"You come here a lot, huh?" Bobby asked, glancing to the server who poured waters at a small bar in the back.

"My favorite place."

"Our waiter seemed happy to see you," Bobby said before looking back to her. "But me, not so much."

"I think we caught him off guard. I'm always alone."

"What's good here?" Bobby asked, picking up the menu and scanning it.

"Everything."

"What's your favorite dish?"

"I either get the pasta with clams in white sauce or the pasta with shrimp and oysters."

The waiter returned with a basket of warm bread and glasses of ice water.

"Wine?" he asked Holly, who nodded. "Your usual red?"

She nodded again as he quickly disappeared to the bar in back.

"You've never come here with anyone else?" Bobby asked, pulling slices of bread from the loaf, still warm from the oven, and handing one to her.

"I've been here with Emma."

"No one else?"

"I don't think so."

"No other boys besides me?"

"Boys? I don't do boys."

"No other men besides me?"

"Nope."

"Why?"

"I don't know."

"Why no other men?"

"My life's complicated enough."

"How'd I get so lucky?"

"I guess you caught me off guard," she said as the waiter returned with a bottle of Chianti and two glasses. "Your timing was right. I was weak. You walked into the bar at exactly the right time."

The server opened the wine bottle and filled both glasses. "You two ready to order?"

"You eat seafood, right?" Holly asked Bobby.

"I'm from Baltimore," he said, holding his arms out and shrugging his shoulders. "The crab capital of the world."

"We're going to share two dinners," she said, looking back to the waiter. "One order of pasta with shrimp and oyster."

"Your favorite," he said, jotting the order on a small pad.

"And the cannoli combo."

"Lovely," the waiter nodded. "Which two cannoli?"

"The spinach and three-cheese one along with the corn and crabmeat one for the Maryland boy here."

"Great, great." The waiter rushed off to the kitchen.

Bobby reached for his glass of wine and held it up. Smiling, Holly did the same.

"And to think of all the stupid things I've done wrong," he said as if giving a toast, "and of all the bad choices I've made, and how my brother ended up here, and now you and I are here together."

"Let's not talk about any of this," she said, looking serious and pulling her glass back. "Not tonight. I'm not going backwards."

She lifted her glass again and pushed it towards him.

"I'm tired of constantly checking over my shoulder. I'm tired of running from my past, hiding from what happened last week, yesterday, or this morning."

"You won't tell me what happened this morning, will you?"

She shook her head. "From this point on, I'm only looking ahead, always moving forward."

They touched their glasses together, and each took big sips of the fruity wine.

"So, what happens next?" he asked.

"I have to perform in *The Nutcracker* tomorrow afternoon. After that, I'm not sure."

"Tomorrow?"

"Will you come watch me dance?

"I wouldn't miss it for anything."

Chapter Ninety-Two

After dinner, they had retreated to the couch of her apartment. Two containers of leftovers were next to them on a coffee table. Neither of them ate much. Both were quite tipsy. They passionately kissed, giggled, and playfully groped each other, their inhibitions lowered by the two bottles of wine they had consumed at dinner. Holly sat up, appearing more serious as she straddled Bobby who was on his back. She tugged at his belt with one hand and started to unbutton her blouse with the other.

"No," he mumbled, squirming under her.

"It's all right, Bobby," she whispered.

"Not yet," he said a little louder, clasping her hand with his as she tried to unbuckle his belt.

She stared back at him, disappointed, as a loud explosion sounded suddenly in the sky. They both glanced to the covered windows unable to see what was happening outside. Within seconds, a second blast exploded above the apartment.

"Let's go!" she exclaimed as they both slid off the couch and bounced onto the floor, their bodies tangled together.

"What's was that?" he asked as she helped him up when a third explosion rocked the neighborhood.

"Fireworks! Let's go!"

"Where?"

"Jackson Square," she said, yanking his body with her as they flew out the door.

"At this hour?"

"It's the city's official holiday season kickoff! Come on!"

Chapter Ninety-Three

Bobby chased Holly as she hurried towards the fireworks that exploded overhead. They reached Jackson Square in less than ten minutes. A large crowd had gathered there. On the steps of St. Louis Cathedral, a choir of teenaged black boys and girls in white gowns sang Christmas carols with as much passion as allowed in public. They swayed their bodies in perfect rhythm to the cheerful tunes they sang along with the firework show.

They danced and clapped their hands together, seemingly excited that the holidays had arrived, and they were still young enough to be optimistic about everything else.

As their jubilant voices rang out and filled the balmy midnight air, fireworks continued to explode over the Square, lighting up the clear black sky with flashes of blue and green, red and white, and showers of gold. The crowd oohed with each blast. Bobby glanced to Holly. Her grinning face shined under the brief but bright flashes of light from above.

"Why are you looking at me that way?" she asked.

"You're beaming. I've never seen you smile like that. It's nice."

"It's been a long time."

Bobby looked back to the sky, and he couldn't help but also think of Chuck. He could almost see his face in the clouds of smoke left behind after each quick blast of light and noise. It was as if Chuck had exploded into the world like a firecracker—a short blast of beautiful light in every color—but Bobby still had time to find him. He hoped he wasn't too late.

Chapter Ninety-Four

In the long shadows of the cathedral, Bobby held Holly tight against him until the last song was sung and the last firework was spent. They lingered in the Square for some time after the show, neither wanting the night to end. Holding hands, they strolled through the late but still lively streets of the French Quarter for many more hours, making small talk and occasionally stopping in different all-night joints for cheap beers, jukebox songs, and slow dances together.

It was as if they were afraid to return to her apartment. He didn't want to disappoint her, and she didn't want to come on too strong and spook him away. Finally, as the birds began to sing and the sun started to rise, they reached the front door of her place, nearly overcome with exhaustion but not wanting to sleep. Before quietly slipping inside, Holly glanced the early morning streets around her place to see if they had been followed. It didn't appear that they had. They collapsed entangled in each other's arms and slept that way through the morning and into the afternoon.

Chapter Ninety-Five

Bobby paced around her apartment as she got ready in the cramped bathroom before her performance later in *The Nutcracker*. He was nervous for her, even more nervous than he would be for one of his own fights. After a short wait, she awkwardly walked into the front room of the apartment, almost embarrassed of her made-up appearance. Her blonde curls were pulled tight into a bun on top of her head, and the make-up on her lips, cheeks, and eyes was perfect, highlighting the soft features of her pretty face. She had trouble making eye contact with him, continually checking her make-up in a mirror on the wall and brushing at her hair.

"You look amazing."

"I feel like a freak. I always do in these ballet get-ups," she said, turning to him but still avoiding eye contact. "Stop."

"Stop what?"

"Stop looking at me like that. I'm already self-conscious enough."

"You get made up like this every night for the strip club."

"Not like this," she said, looking back into the mirror.

"Here," he said, pulling a small, gold, heart-shaped necklace from his pocket.

"What's this?" she said, turning and reaching for it.

"Will you wear it?"

"It's for me?"

He undid the clasp of the necklace and stepped behind her. She helped him position it around her neck as he snapped the clasp closed.

"It's beautiful," she said, studying it more closely in the mirror on the wall.

"It belonged to my grandmother."

She turned, grinning. Her eyes were watery as she softly touched at them, trying not to mess her mascara.

"It's not worth much."

"It's worth everything to me."

"I would tape it to my ankle before fights for luck," he said, briefly before pausing. "I hope it brings you luck. I don't need it anymore."

Chapter Ninety-Six

Russell's top henchman, Todd, had been staking out the office of the local ballet company that Holly danced with. He watched from a black Cadillac parked across the street for an out-of-town visitor, the director of the San Francisco Ballet. Russell had got word that the San Francisco Ballet was trying to recruit Holly to join their company.

After waiting for several hours, a cab finally pulled in front of the office and a smallish, older man got out. Todd quickly checked a photograph he had downloaded from the internet to confirm the identity of the man he stalked. He dialed his phone and called Russell.

In only a few minutes, Russell arrived and motioned for Todd to join him as they hurried to the entrance of the ballet office. They entered a closed door without knocking. The office was neat and orderly. The guest from San Francisco was alone in the office. It appeared he was waiting for someone, sitting in a chair behind a desk.

Russell and Todd approached and towered over him. They looked like quite the pair. Russell was unbathed, unshaven, and intoxicated. Todd's face and right eye were still bruised from the punch he took from Bobby.

"Am I supposed to know you two?" the director asked, looking puzzled.

"That sure was a long way to come, buddy," Russell grumbled, "for nothin'."

"Excuse me?"

"You're not hiring the girl."

"Pardon?"

"You are not hiring Holly. She's staying here."

"What do you mean I can't hire Holly? We may offer her a position in our group. I brought the contract in case we like her performance," he said, holding up a several page document. "We've already interviewed her on the phone. She knows I'm coming."

"She's not signing any contract whether you like her or not,"

Russell said as Todd leaned forward and snatched the contract from the man's hand.

"Hey! What are you doing? Gimme that!"

"She's no longer interested," Russell said as Todd ripped the contract into pieces.

"But I don't understand. She seemed quite interested when I spoke to her."

"She works for me," Russell growled as Todd tossed the pieces of the contract on the director's head.

"Why are you doing this?" he snapped, swiping at the pieces of paper falling on his head and shoulders. "And who are you?"

"Holly's not leaving New Orleans. Not now. Not ever. Got it?"

"That's all well and good, but I think I should talk to her first."

Russell angrily slammed his fist on the table, startling the director.

"Now, what did I say?" Russell asked, motioning to Todd who roughly pulled the director from his seat and shoved him hard against a wall. "I want you to say it."

"Say what?" the frightened director asked.

"Holly's not going anywhere."

"I really should speak with her—"

"Say it!" Russell screamed, interrupting the cowering director, who had slumped against the wall and slid to the floor.

"Holly's not going anywhere," the director hurriedly mumbled, his voice cracking and his hands shaking in fear.

"Do you need us to call you a cab back to the airport?" Russell asked. "Your business here is done."

The director nervously nodded from his sitting position on the floor, curled like a ball against the wall.

Chapter Ninety-Seven

It was a raucous atmosphere for the matinee showing of *The Nutcracker* in the small theater. The place was filled with squealing grade schoolers overly excited to be out of school on a field trip and just as hyped for the fact that Christmas was only a few days away. Their constant chatter and giggles were nearly deafening. Teachers and chaperones paced the aisles, trying their best to keep the kids quiet and in their seats. Bobby had purchased one of the few remaining tickets.

He sat in the last row on an aisle not far from a door that led to the lobby. He was still feeling nervous for Holly. It felt as if his belly was filled with large fluttering butterflies. He never wanted anything more than for her to do well. She had told him that the director of the San Francisco Ballet was in town to watch her perform. This was the opportunity she'd always wanted. She needed to leave New Orleans, and she had to get away from her father. This was her chance.

The overhead theater lights blinked, letting everyone know that the show was about to start. A loud, high-pitched cheer rang out as the curtain rose, and the first characters of the ballet appeared. The stage was set with an enormous Christmas tree, beautifully decorated with sparkling candles and brightly colored glass bulbs. A hush suddenly descended over the young crowd. The kids sat on the edge of the seats, mesmerized by the ballet's holiday story. Finally, Holly stepped onto the stage, playing the young lead, Clara.

Bobby leaned forward in his seat. He barely recognized her. She shined like the brightest star in the nighttime sky as she effortlessly whirled across the stage with a confidence and youthful exuberance she had never shown him before. He couldn't help but smile. Goosebumps covered his arms. There was no doubt she was the main attraction. All the other dancers paled in comparison. He, and everyone else there, couldn't take their eyes off her. The spins; the leaps; her arm, head, and hip movements—they all were so natural and free.

After watching most of the first act, Bobby suddenly had an idea. He quietly stood, slipped out the back door into the lobby, and left the theater.

The evening air temperature was pleasant. The sky was clear as the sun started to set. Bobby deliberately walked through the Quarter, keeping an eye out for Chuck. He couldn't believe it was nearly Christmas Day. He had to find him.

The second-floor apartments that lined Chartres were decorated in lights—some all in white, others in combinations of red and green. Business seemed great. Royal and Decatur were packed with holiday shoppers. The jewelry, antique, and souvenir shops all were crowded. The restaurants and taverns were busy with parties and those out celebrating the season. Popular Christmas carols played from several of the businesses he passed. The mood in the city was lighter. The locals appeared happier and more friendly than they normally were. It was funny, Bobby had always wondered if the holidays came to tourist destinations like the French Quarter. It was nice to find out that they did.

In Jackson Square, he came upon a bearded local who was selling Christmas trees. The man spoke with a funny accent Bobby could barely understand and looked as if he had just stepped off a farm. He wore work boots caked with mud, a raggedy wool shirt, and bright orange suspenders. Bobby had noticed him days before selling trees and thought it would be a nice surprise to get one for Holly after seeing the large tree on *The Nutcracker* stage. He bought a perfectly shaped, six-foot tall Douglas Fir that surely would take up most of her apartment. Leaving a trail of pine needles behind him, Bobby dragged the bulky tree with his good left hand several blocks towards Esplanade and Holly's apartment.

Chapter Ninety-Eight

Enjoying the evening, Emma sat on the second-floor balcony of her house that faced Esplanade. She sipped at an icy lemonade and read a local newspaper. She leaned forward in her chair when she noticed Bobby dragging the Christmas tree across the street towards her. Grinning, she stood and braced herself on the railing of the porch. Bobby glanced up to her. She smiled back.

"Mr. Raymond, what'd you go and do?"

"Something for Holly."

"I thought you went to see her dance this afternoon."

"I did but left early. I wanted to surprise her with a tree. Isn't it a beauty?"

"Now, where you going to put it?"

"I planned to leave it on her porch until she got back."

"What about decorations?"

"I was going to the drug store next to pick up some lights."

"Hold on, now," she said. "I'll be down in a minute. Don't leave."

Emma disappeared inside the second floor of her house as Bobby dragged the tree onto the front porch of Holly's apartment. He lifted it up and leaned it next to the door. He waited for about ten minutes until Emma appeared. She had a key to Holly's apartment and carried two large paper shopping bags filled with Christmas lights and ornaments. She handed the bags to him and unlocked the door.

"Let's put the tree up and decorate it before Holly gets home," Emma said, glancing back to him as she pushed the door open.

"What about a stand for the tree?"

"I have one, but you'll need to get it. It's too heavy for me to carry," she said. "It's in the closet at the top the stairs."

"I hope this isn't a bad idea." He went to get the tree stand.

"It's a grand idea, Mr. Raymond."

Chapter Ninety-Nine

Bobby stood on one of two chairs that belonged to a small table from the kitchen. He draped multiple chains of white lights connected together on top of the Christmas tree and delicately wrapped them around it. Emma hung a variety of different ornaments, like shiny glass bulbs and plastic snowflakes, on the lower branches of the tree where she could reach. She handed others up to Bobby who hung them on the branches near the top. Darkness had started to fall over the Quarter as they hurriedly finished decorating the tree. Holly was expected to arrive home at any time. They planned to meet in her neighborhood for dinner after the performance.

"She tells me things I can't believe after having met you."

"I'm trying to change," he said, pausing from decorating the tree and glancing to the cast on his right hand. "It's hard. I have been the worst to the ones who cared about me the most."

"Your brother?"

"Yes," he nodded. "And others."

"You're the first fellow Holly's really spoken to me about."

"Why me?"

"At first, I think she wanted you to do some dirty work for her," Emma said, not looking at him as she continued to hang glass bulbs on the lower limbs of the tree. "Now, I'm not so sure."

"Dirty work? Does that have to do with her father?"

"I still worry she'll do something she'll come to regret," Emma nodded.

"But when it comes to me, you're not so sure."

"She seems to have fallen for you a little."

"I can't help but wonder what she could possibly see in me."

"There's an appeal to you—a vulnerability, an uncertainty. You look like a fighter, but you don't act like one."

"So, the cocktails with you the other morning were a job interview?"

"You could say that." She grinned.

"Did I get the job?"

"Holly feels safe around you. She grew up with the constant fear her father would explode and beat her to death one day. When you're around, she doesn't feel that way."

"So, I'm the bodyguard? The muscle?"

"That's part of it, but there's more."

"That's what scares me."

"What scares you?"

"All the other stuff. That I'll never be able to live up to what she needs in a friend, a lover, a partner. My problem has always been deciding between what is right and what is wrong. I always tended to do what was easy—which usually turned out to be wrong."

"Being able to admit that is growth. She's never been loved by anyone. Sure, she's had some short flings, but they never amounted to anything serious. She feels comfortable with you. And she's very cautious about who she lets into her life."

"But I'm a bum."

"Who could become a prince."

"I'm not pretty enough to be a prince."

"This isn't about looks, Mr. Raymond, or anything else on the surface."

"I'm afraid I'll let her down."

"Now, that is your problem, not hers. From what she has said, you've already let her down."

"I had doubts about seeing her again. Her life is messed up enough without me and all my baggage added to it."

"But here we are?" Emma said, motioning to the bloated and shining Christmas tree that filled Holly's tiny living room. "You wouldn't have gone to all this trouble if there wasn't something more between the two of you."

"Will you tell me now how you two met?"

"I was leaving a dinner social in the Quarter late one evening. It was one of those heavy Louisiana spring rains. The most beautiful young girl I had ever seen was standing in the pouring rain, asking people for change. She was soaked to the bone. She wore her blonde hair long then. Water dripped from it like a faucet. She was shivering, and I could tell she was frightened. She told me that she was hiding from her daddy. I offered to call the police, but she insisted that I not. Instead, she went home with me that night. She stayed for nearly a year until she reconciled with him."

"And she moved out?"

"I got her an apartment in the building next door."

"So, you keep an eye out for her?"

"I'm just here for support," Emma nodded. "But I didn't give her a dime. Sure, I bought her some things and took her out to dinner occasionally. She quickly found herself a job. She paid me rent when she lived in my house and chipped in for groceries. That was the deal she made, not me. I probably was a little too strict with her at first, but she never complained. She wanted my respect. She wanted to prove to me, herself, and eventually to her father, that she could support herself. She wanted to be independent. And she most definitely is, maybe too much."

"What do you think about her stripping?"

"She worked as a waitress first, but she wasn't making much money. She was always so concerned about her father. No matter what he had done to her, she felt she needed to help him. I was worried at first. I'm not a fan of those places, especially the men who run them. I've taken care of many girls who were obviously exploited and behaved recklessly in those clubs. But I thought Holly could handle it."

"Have you met her father?"

"Not face to face, but I've seen him around town. From what I know and from what Holly has told me, I could never like him."

"I know she's afraid of him."

"This is no life for her, living in fear and always checking her back. I'd like to get her out of here."

"We met by chance," Bobby said. "It was so random. It shouldn't have happened, but somehow, we found each other."

"You were the one meant to save her."

"And I was hoping she'd be the one who saved me."

Emma hung the last bulb she held and stepped back from the tree. Bobby climbed off the chair he had been standing on. He turned off the other lights in the apartment except for the ones on the tree. They both grinned like young children at a Christmas party, enthralled by the beautiful glowing tree that filled the small apartment.

"I better get out of here before Holly shows up," Emma said, gathering her things and heading for the door.

"Thank you, Emma. You make me feel better about myself."

"You've done good with this beautiful surprise, Mr. Raymond," she said, stepping out of the apartment. "You've done good."

Chapter One Hundred

obby had found a small radio in Holly's apartment. He tuned it to a local station that was playing only holiday carols. The white lights on the recently decorated tree shined, producing a warm glow over the room as the Dean Martin version of White Christmas played. Bobby paced the floor, trying to remain calm as he waited for Holly. Suddenly, he heard a noise outside the front door. He glanced around, anxiously searching for a place to sit or stand. He wanted to appear cool and calm. He awkwardly fidgeted beside the tree as the door opened.

Holly carried small grocery bags that contained two bottles of wine and assorted snacks. Surprised, Holly set the bags down and stared at the tree. She looked to Bobby who couldn't contain his excitement.

"What do you think?"

"Bobby? What in the world?"

"Merry Christmas!"

"What have you done?"

"I hope you like it."

"Like it?" she grinned, approaching the tree. "I'm in shock. I love it."

She reached for an old Polaroid camera on a counter in the kitchen.

"Here, come here." She waved for Bobby. "Let's get a picture."

Bobby joined her in front of the tree. They squeezed together. Bobby had never been as happy or as proud of himself for something he had done in his life before. He clumsily held his arms behind his back not knowing what to do with them. She nudged even closer into him. Neither of them could stop smiling as she snapped a selfie. A small square photo rolled out from the old camera. As Holly shook the photo to help it dry faster, they both turned at the same time and stared at the tree.

"This is the sweetest thing anyone has ever done for me."

Chapter One Hundred One

The strip club was mostly empty. There were only a handful of customers there that night. Several dancers and servers milled about the club with little to do. Russell paced behind the main bar near the inactive dance floor. He was angry about the slow night but seemed more upset about something else.

"Where the hell is she?" he barked at Todd, his primary bodyguard.

"Who?"

"Who? Holly! That's who!" he grumbled, knocking back a shot of whiskey. "Wasn't she supposed to work tonight?"

"You gave her the night off. She has ballet."

"Shit! I don't remember that."

"And she's off tomorrow. It's Christmas Eve."

"She's off on Christmas Eve? That's usually a big night for me. Is she here on Christmas Day?"

"Yeah, two shifts. You got her on both afternoon and night."

"Where is she now?"

"Home."

"Home?"

"The ballet's over. We followed her like you wanted."

"Is she alone?"

"She left the ballet alone and entered her apartment alone."

"And that new friend of hers?"

"We haven't seen him."

"Who the fuck is he?"

Chapter One Hundred Two

Sitting on a blanket on the floor next to the lit tree, Bobby and Holly sipped wine and shared small cuts of different types of cheese. She was nearly in his lap. They couldn't stop smiling.

"Do you know what Chuck and I did when we were kids after decorating the tree?"

"What?

"We'd crawl underneath it."

"Huh?"

"I don't know why we did it." He shook his head. "I remember climbing underneath, and jus' staring up into the branches and lights. It always gave me a warm, excited feeling."

Holly reached for some pillows on the floor next to the couch and tossed them under the tree. She spread out the blanket they were sitting on and pushed it underneath with the pillows. She took the wine Bobby held and set it on a nearby table. Laughing, Bobby pulled her tight against his body as they slid underneath the tree, facing each other.

"I'm no longer a kid. I'm much bigger now."

"This is silly," she giggled, "but we'll fit."

"I've never been more comfortable," he said with a serious gaze, "in a place, with a person."

"Me, too," she said as they studied each other.

"You look tired."

"I'm exhausted," she sighed. "Everything—the phone interview last week with the San Francisco group, the club, my father, the ballet, you."

"Me?"

"It's been a happy few days." She smiled, trying to keep her eyes open. "It's never been that way before."

"Please, sleep."

"I don't want to sleep now." She yawned as he brushed at the blonde curls that had fallen over her eyes. "I haven't heard back from the San Francisco Ballet. The director was supposed to be at the show to see me perform live. He was to meet me backstage. They liked my tapes. They might have a contract for me to sign, but he never got ahold of me.”

“I’m sure he was there.”

“But I never saw him.”

“That’s strange.”

“Did you stay for the whole ballet? I couldn’t see you in the back.”

“I left early. I wanted to get this tree up while you were busy.”

“What did you think?”

“About what?”

“My dancing.”

“You were amazing. Where’d you get those moves? You made it look so easy,” he said as she blushed and softly patted him on the chest. “If I had those moves, no one would have ever beaten me. I’d be champion of the world already. You are a butterfly.”

“Butterfly?”

“Willie, my first trainer, labeled boxers as either butchers or butterflies.”

“And you were?”

“A butcher can hit. I could out-punch anyone.”

“And a butterfly?”

“A butterfly can dance. They can move. They’re quick. They can stay out of trouble—not get trapped in the corners. I had none of that.”

“What if someone were both a butcher and a butterfly?”

“There’s has only been one fighter who was both.”

“Who?”

“Muhammad Ali,” he said, imitating the great boxing champion’s unique voice. “The greatest of all-time.”

“Maybe I can teach you to dance sometime then,” she grinned as her eyes started to close.

“Go to sleep, Holly.”

“No, no, no, let’s keep talking.”

“Tell me about your favorite Christmas.”

“I don’t really remember. . .”

“Come on,” he nudged her. “Every kid had at least one special holiday memory.”

“We quit celebrating Christmas after my mother died. My dad stopped putting up a tree.”

"You must have one nice memory," he said as she closed her eyes and grinned.

He nudged her again with his elbow.

"I know you have one. Let me hear it."

"I loved horses when I was a kid. I so badly wanted one," she said, glancing away. "It was a rainy Christmas morning. I recall a long drive with my mom. We finally get to a stable. My dad was waiting for us, standing in a foot of mud. The most beautiful little pony was next to him."

"Do you remember what the pony looked like?"

"He was reddish-brown," she said, looking back to him. "They called him Randy. He was so gentle."

"You think about that day a lot, don't you?"

"My father stood in the rain with us for hours. He trotted me and the pony around in the mud. And when they tried to get me down, I cried. We were all soaked and freezing. I cried all the way home. I thought the pony was mine, but the pony ride was the gift."

They studied each other a moment. She glanced away, appearing almost embarrassed about telling the story.

"You first wanted to be a world champion," she said, looking back to him. "Now you want to find your brother. What will you want after that?"

"It'd be nice to truly love someone."

"Will you come with me to San Francisco?"

"I will follow you anywhere."

"What about your brother?"

"I still have time. I have to find him."

Chapter One Hundred Three

Bobby awoke to Holly shaking him. The sun had just come up. Small slivers of light filtered through the cracks between the blankets that hung over the windows. Their bodies were still partially under the decorated Christmas tree where they had fallen asleep the night before. Bobby had pine needles stuck to the side of his face and in his disheveled hair. He strained to open his eyes as Holly grinned next to him, tugging at his body. He tried to roll over, away from her.

"Come on," she said, continuing to shake him. "Get up."

"Why so early?"

"Wake up. It's Christmas Eve."

"Gimme another hour."

"Come on," she said, playfully slapping him with a pillow. She struggled to pull him out from under the tree.

"We don't have to be anywhere for hours."

"We have a party to go to," she said, tugging at him with more force.

"What party?"

"At Tommy Black's."

"It doesn't start 'til noon."

"I want to get there early."

"What for?"

"I have a surprise for you."

"Surprise?" he asked, leaning up after sliding out from under the decorated tree.

Chapter One Hundred Four

After some coffee and quickly cleaning themselves up, Holly and Bobby hurried to Tommy Black's on foot. He had trouble keeping pace as he chased after her down Royal Street. He'd never seen her so excited for something before. She'd occasionally stop to allow for him to catch up before dashing off again.

"Come on," she called as he lagged behind.

"What's the rush?"

"We don't have much time!"

"Much time for what?"

He continued to sprint after her as she turned onto St. Peter. She stopped in front of Tommy Black's. Butchie had been waiting there for them. Nearly out of breath, Bobby finally caught up to her. Butchie handed Holly what looked to be a set of keys.

"One of those is for my cousin's place," he said, motioning to the keys. "You can stay there if you like. No one will be there tonight."

"Thanks, but we plan to get back sometime this evening."

"This evening?" Bobby shrugged.

"We're going to the beach." She smiled, tossing the keys to Bobby. "Butchie is loaning us his car."

"Beach?"

"Biloxi," she said as Bobby looked puzzled. "Mississippi."

"The tank is full," Butchie said, pointing to a 1990s model Buick that was parked in front of the bar. It was a boat of car that appeared to be in fairly good shape.

"Have fun," he said.

Bobby studied the keys in his hands; Holly was beaming.

"You have to drive. I lost my driver's license years ago."

"I can't drive. I've never gotten a license."

"You never got a driver's license?"

"I grew up in New Orleans. I didn't need one. I could bike or walk anywhere I had to go."

"Come on," she said, grabbing his hand and leading him to the car.

“I don’t have a swimsuit.”
“I got you one. It’s in the car.”

Chapter One Hundred Five

After getting behind some initial slow-moving traffic in central downtown, Bobby pulled Butchie's Buick onto Interstate 10 and headed east for the 90-minute trip. Holly bounced around in the passenger seat, excited for a day at the beach, but more importantly, thrilled to get out of the tight and sometimes suffocating confines of the French Quarter. But her father and the strip club were not far from her thoughts as she escaped from the city for the first time in years.

"I really shouldn't be driving," Bobby said, glancing over to her before checking the speedometer. "If I get pulled over, your new boyfriend will be spending the holidays in jail."

"My new boyfriend?" she grinned. "Oh, is that what you are?"

"Why aren't we staying the night, like Butchie offered? We should stay through the New Year."

"I have to work at the club tomorrow."

"I thought you weren't going back."

"That's why I wanted to get an early start, so we'd have a whole day at the beach."

"On Christmas Day? Doesn't your dad ever close that place?"

"It'll be my last day there."

"Don't go back. You can't. Emma's really worried that. . ."

"Just two more shifts," she interrupted.

Chapter One Hundred Six

As they continued the daytrip, there wasn't much to see. A thick fog obscured much of the view from the interstate as the Buick raced through bayous and wildlife refuge areas as they traversed the Twin Span Bridge that crossed a small portion of Lake Pontchartrain.

The old Buick, many years past its prime, handled well as it barreled through the swamps of southeastern Louisiana to cross the Pearl River into Mississippi. Continually aware he possessed no license, Bobby turned onto a lesser travelled, cut-off road that led to U.S. Route 90 towards Bay St. Louis, Pass Christian, and Biloxi.

On 90, the speed of the Buick slowed, but the scenery improved. The fog began to lift, replaced by a golden morning sky filled with high hanging clouds in the distance. Bobby drove for several miles along low-lying, white sandy beaches with breathtaking views of the estuaries, bays, and rivers that formed the southwestern coast of Mississippi and the northern part of the Gulf of Mexico.

Ancient oak trees that once lined the road or marked the different properties had been reduced to stumps, obvious reminders of the high winds and ocean surge caused by different hurricanes throughout the years. Along each side of the scenic highway, they also passed family steak and seafood restaurants, waffle and pancake houses, and an occasional resort or beach motel, many painted in art deco blues and pinks. Bobby desperately needed a coffee. He craved a large southern breakfast. But Holly wouldn't let him stop.

She sat up straight in her seat and rolled down the window to lean out for a better view. The deep blue ocean waves were calm and light. The beaches were mostly empty except for a few early morning hikers. The cigarette stale air of the old car was immediately replaced by the cool but salty morning air from the nearby Gulf. Bobby wanted to stop and walk the first beach they saw. He couldn't wait to wade in the cool Gulf coast waters. Holly directed him onward as they headed east to Biloxi.

After a quick stop at a convenience store where Bobby and Holly filled a Styrofoam cooler with ice, beer, soft drinks, and snacks, they parked in a lot at a public beach in Biloxi. The lot was mostly vacant, likely due to the early hour and the fact that it also was the day before Christmas. They were separated from the Gulf of Mexico by only a hundred yards of flat, groomed white sand. For several minutes, they gazed as if hypnotized by the slow rolling waves of the clear Gulf water.

Bobby reached for the door handle to get out of the car, but Holly stopped him. She tossed him a pair of swim trunks.

"Whose were these?" he asked, inspecting the trunks. "An old boyfriend? I hope they fit."

"Just put them on," she said, sliding down low in the front seat and pulling her shirt over her head.

"What are you doing?"

"Changing."

"Here?"

"No one will see us," she said, unsnapping her frilly black bra as Bobby stared at her naked chest.

She quickly slipped on the bikini top of the bathing suit she had brought with her.

"You going to put on yours?" she asked, shimmying out of the shorts and panties she wore.

Bobby continued to gawk as she slid her slender body lower in the seat, naked from the waist down.

"What are you staring at? You've seen me naked before."

"I know, but. . ." he started to say, continuing to ogle her.

"Why's this different?"

"I'm not sure. It jus' seems naughtier. Like we're doing something we shouldn't be."

"Do you like what you see?"

She reached for the heavy cast on his right hand and pulled it towards her. He offered no resistance as she rested it on the silky bare skin of her warm thigh. They both watched as he started to softly caress it with his exposed fingers, looking into each other's eyes. She quietly sighed as she took a deep breath.

"Put your swim trunks on," she said, not allowing him to look away from her eyes.

She continued to hold her hand on his fingers that stuck out the end of the cast, not letting him move them away.

"I'm sensing things I haven't felt in a long time," he confessed with a whisper as if embarrassed to admit. "I'm not ready to get out of the car yet."

He eased his hand closer to her naked groin area. At first, she allowed it, but a car suddenly pulled into the lot and parked near them, disrupting the mood. She pushed his hand away.

"Put your suit on. Let's get to the beach."

Chapter One Hundred Seven

Holly had spread a large blanket and several beach towels out onto the sand. Warmed by the early morning sun and not far from where the rolling waves stopped, she had pulled the heavy cooler onto the blankets and towels so they wouldn't blow away. She and Bobby lounged there with the steady breeze coming off the water most of the day, sipping beers and staring at the cloudless sky that framed the clear but busy waters of the Gulf.

They gazed at numerous boats trawling for shrimp not far offshore. They studied a lone lighthouse in the distance. They watched the many great blue herons in flight. They shooed away the persistent seagulls who badgered them for handouts. The beach had been mostly quiet except for a few small families and groups of teenagers.

They didn't say much at first. Bobby had trouble keeping his eyes off Holly. He spied her from behind a pair of dark sunglasses. She wore a skimpy red and white bikini that was candy-striped. Her long and thin legs glistened in the bright sun, as did her oiled belly and arms. Bobby had never seen her so relaxed. The ever-present worried look she struggled to disguise daily in New Orleans was briefly gone. He didn't want to disrupt her. She had checked out to a better place.

The day slipped by. A scattering of clouds had rolled in over them, cooling the afternoon. Holly slid her sunglasses to the top of her head. There were circles deep beneath her eyes. Now, she again appeared exhausted. Her thoughts had returned to New Orleans, the club, and her father. The full day at the beach hadn't completely rejuvenated her. Bobby was feeling a little buzzed from the several cans of beer he had consumed. He knew they needed to get something substantial to eat before heading back to the city.

"Are you hungry?" he asked. "Soon the restaurants will open up."

"I want to lay here a little longer."

"You must be dying of thirst," he said, reaching for an ice-cold bottle of water from the cooler and holding it out to her.

She shook her head, not looking at him. "I'm good."

"And it seems the bars have lit their lights," he said, motioning beyond the main road to a strip of small taverns and seafood joints. "A cold and fruity drink awaits us, if you like."

"Let's stay here on the beach until the sun goes down. I don't get to see it much. I'm like a cockroach. I sleep most of my days and live my life at night."

"Why do you do that to yourself?"

"I can't live like that anymore. It's like I'm wasting away."

"Why'd you go work for your dad?"

"I didn't want to let him down. I thought I needed to support him. He's the only family I have."

"What happened to him?"

"I don't know." She shook her head, still gazing to the calming water of the Gulf. "It all changed after the club had some success. He started drinking too much. Taking drugs. He began dating some of the girls at the club. And he never got over the death of my mother."

She lowered the sunglasses over her eyes and turned to Bobby.

"He had become someone else. Someone I think he hated."

"And he took it all out on you?"

"Yes," she said, looking back to the water. "He took it all out on me."

"What if we didn't go back to New Orleans tonight? Let's stay at Butchie's cousin's place. We have a key."

"We need to return his car."

"What if we disappeared tonight?"

"I must work my two shifts tomorrow."

"I don't want to go back. Let's get some drinks. Have a nice meal. Come on, let's stay the night. I'll get you back to New Orleans early in the morning."

"We can't."

"We can do whatever we want."

"He'll come looking for me. I can't take the chance."

"All right but promise me. After we return Butchie's car, you'll work your shifts, and then we'll run away. Okay?"

"What about your brother?"

He looked away and didn't answer.

Chapter One Hundred Eight

Bobby and Holly stayed on the beach until dark. To pass the time as the sun slowly set, she sat by the water's edge, her sunbaked body covered in an oversized, hooded sweatshirt. Her cheeks and forehead were red from the sun. The light but constant breeze tossed her blonde curls in her face. She had pulled her bare legs under the sweatshirt and up against her body to warm them.

Bobby entertained her by frolicking in the surf of the cool sixty-five-degree December Gulf water, trying to keep the plaster cast on his right hand from getting wet. She giggled and laughed at his goofy underwater antics. He splashed her with water with his left hand. He rolled across the wet sand and buried himself in it with the cast on his right arm sticking out. He even plucked an unsuspecting starfish from beneath the waves.

After the sun had dropped, they loaded the Buick in the dark with their things, before scurrying across the road and disappearing into a half-century old seafood joint. Among a rowdy, full house of local fishermen, they shared pitchers of beer, baskets of French fries, bowls of oyster chowder, and pots filled with six-inch jumbo shrimp boiled in spicy Cajun seasonings. They loaded the jukebox with twenty-dollar bills. They sang and danced together for hours to songs by the Rolling Stones, The Clash, Tom Petty, and The Who. They both laughed so much their bellies ached.

At last call, Bobby and Holly did one final shot of high-end bourbon. She paid their tab and led him outside onto the wooden deck at the front of the place. The clear night sky was bright with stars and a near full moon that reflected over the calm Gulf water. Under the orange neon glow of a 'Fresh Seafood' sign, she tightly held onto him.

She studied him with a serious look he'd never seen from her before. It initially frightened him. He fidgeted in her arms. She tightened her embrace around him. Finally, he leaned his face forward. They kissed. The taste of her warm lips, salty from the ocean air, took his breath away. She quickly pulled back and looked away.

“I don’t want tonight to end,” he nervously whispered.

“We have to go back,” she said, taking his hand and directing him towards the parked Buick. “I need to take care of something at the club before we can disappear.”

Chapter One Hundred Nine

It took them nearly two hours to get back to New Orleans. Bobby cautiously navigated the dark and mostly empty highway, being careful to maintain the posted speed limits. Holly sat in the middle of the front seat and leaned her body against his. After merging onto Interstate 10, he draped his right casted arm over her and pulled her closer.

They didn't say a word for most of the drive. He continually glanced to her, checking to see if she had fallen asleep. She never did. She stared ahead in silence with little expression to the roadway that rushed under them. Finally, she sighed. The bright lights of the New Orleans skyline had appeared in the distance.

Chapter One Hundred Ten

Bobby dropped Holly off at her place before heading to Tommy Black's to return Butchie's car. He found a spot a few blocks away and hustled to the bar. He peered inside. Strings of blinking, colored Christmas lights lit the crowded and boisterous bar. The jukebox blared. Jack, Broadmore, and Harry-O had their arms draped over each other's shoulders and drunkenly sang the Cheap Trick song, "Surrender." Bobby entered as a loud cheer rang out.

"Hey, Bobby?" Broadmore yelled, wildly waving his arm. "Come join us! The jukebox's free tonight! It's loaded with all your favorites!"

Bobby grinned and nodded to them as if he'd be over in a moment. Butchie was quick to fill a shot glass with whiskey and pushed it to Bobby as he took a seat at the bar.

"Where's Holly?"

"I dropped her off at her apartment."

"Is everything all right?"

"Yes," Bobby nodded, swallowing the whiskey.

"Did you guys have a good time?"

"The best. We owe you."

"You want a beer? They're on the house tonight for the party."

"No, no thanks. I need get back to her," he said, shaking his head. "I do need a favor though."

"Sure, anything."

"Can I keep your car for another day?"

"Yeah, absolutely." Butchie nodded, motioning to the rowdy bar. "Where am I gonna go? These knuckleheads will be here all night."

"Thanks."

"You guys goin' somewhere else?"

"Nah, I have to close out some business here."

"Nothin' illegal, is it?"

"Nah, nah. I'll get the car back to you tomorrow night."

"You sure everything's all right?"

"Holly and I," Bobby said, standing up from the stool, "we're getting out of town."

"She needs it."

"Thanks for letting us use your car."

"Anything for Holly."

"I'll see you tomorrow."

Butchie nodded and Bobby turned for the door. The opening line of the Bruce Springsteen song, "Thunder Road," came blaring out of the jukebox. Jack, Broadmore, and Harry-O loudly sang along: *The screen door slams, Mary's dress waves.*

Jack noticed that Bobby was leaving.

"Hey, Bobby!" he yelled over the music. "Where you going? We still have songs left! Don't leave!"

Chapter One Hundred Eleven

Christmas morning came quietly. Bobby dressed in the dark. The sun had yet to rise. He was quiet so as not to wake Holly, but she watched from under the covers of the bed. They didn't go to sleep until well after two in the morning. She didn't know where he was going and was hesitant to ask, but did anyway: "What are you doing?"

"I have some business to wrap up here this morning," he said.

"When will you be back?"

"Hopefully, before nightfall."

"Nightfall?" she asked, sitting up in bed. "Can I ask where you're going?"

"I have to find Eddie."

"And not Chuck?"

"I need to apologize to Eddie. I know I can find him. But Chuck. I need to keep looking." Holly was amazing, and everything seemed perfect, but he was beginning to wonder if he shouldn't have spent less time with her and more time looking for Chuck.

"I don't want you to leave me alone."

"Don't you have to dance at the club today?"

"Unfortunately."

"Don't go. Wait for me here?"

"I don't know, Bobby. I have to go."

They stared a moment before he turned for the door.

"Have your things packed," he said, not looking at her.

"Bobby, I love you," she called as he stopped before leaving. "I've never said that to anyone before. Not to my mother. Not to my father. No one."

"Just be ready," he said not turning to her.

He stepped out the door but stopped before leaving and leaned inside.

"I love you, too, Holly."

Chapter One Hundred Twelve

It was an overcast Christmas morning. Bobby cruised the quiet New Orleans streets in Butchie's Buick, searching for both Eddie and Chuck. After several passes through the French Quarter, he finally spotted Eddie. He sat under a porch stoop on a deserted street not far from Canal. Bobby slowly pulled up to him. Unsure who it was, Eddie leaned forward on his crutches as if ready to hop away if needed. He squinted at the windshield of the approaching Buick, trying to see who it was.

"What the hell?" he mumbled to himself as the driver's side window lowered. "Bobby? Is that you?"

"I wanted to apologize."

"No. No. I'm the one who needs to be apologizin'. I's just tryin' to survive, Bobby. It's been like all my life. I know some things I do just ain't right. But I ain't got much, and…"

"It's okay, Eddie."

"I've been sick ever since I seen you last. Please find it in your heart to forgive me."

"Are you free right now?"

"Some call it free. I call it bored. No one's as bored as me right now."

"Can you show me how to get to that fishing hole you talked about?"

"You's jokin', right?" Eddie asked with a serious look.

Chapter One Hundred Thirteen

Holly briskly walked through the French Quarter to the club. She was late for her first shift. She knew she should've already been there but got a late start after agonizing most of the morning over whether she should even show up at all. She was afraid her father would come looking for her if she didn't.

Also, she worried he may have found the knife she hid in the locker. Days before, in her desperate state she hadn't even considered that he may search through it. As she rushed to the club, it was no longer about finding the strength to actually use the knife against him but about getting to it before he did.

As she neared the club, she had convinced herself that she was walking into a trap. She talked out loud to herself, "What if he did find it? I'm finished."

Chapter One Hundred Fourteen

Russell's strip club was slower than he expected it to be and had been that way the last week or so, likely because of the holidays. Bored, drunk, and coked up, Russell anxiously paced the main floor of the club. He had been on a 72-hour booze-and-drug bender. Agitated, he walked about the roomful of inactive dancers and servers who had but only a few customers to wait on. Several of his dancers sat at one of the club's bars gossiping and enjoying their complimentary shift drinks to pass the time.

"Where the fuck is everyone?" Russell moaned, staggering behind the main bar where some of the dancers were sitting. "And who said you all could get a drink?"

To the disappointment of the ladies, he gathered their drinks and started to dump them out.

"Hey!" they all yelled.

"If you ain't dancing, you ain't drinking!" he hollered back.

"Then what are we all doing here?" one of the young ladies asked. "The place is empty. Let us go home. It's Christmas."

"We'll get busy," he barked. "I promise. Later. After Christmas dinner. They'll come here. With their Christmas money."

"Then get us our drinks," another young lady said.

"You all are paying for 'em."

"Come on, Russell," Todd, his bodyguard, spoke up. "Let 'em have their drinks. Where's the Christmas spirit?"

"Give 'em their drinks then! Fuck! I don't care! But keep track, it's coming out of their tips!"

The bartender started to pour drinks for the ladies at the bar.

"And where in the hell is Holly?" Russell screamed, scanning the club.

"I don't know," Todd shrugged.

"She's supposed to work a double!"

"You don't need her," Todd said. "Leave her be."

Chapter One Hundred Fifteen

B utchie's old Buick bounced on worn shocks down a muddy rural road. On either side clung swampy marshes of black water filled with moss-draped cypress trees. Bobby was driving, with Eddie smiling away in the passenger seat as zydeco music blasted on WWOZ. They passed a cemetery with crumbling, above-ground tombs and camps of Cajuns and their shacks and boats.

They studied a ragged group of bearded men on a wooden dock skinning an alligator that hung from a tree, likely in preparation for Christmas dinner. Bobby laughed as Eddie told stories about the times he used to visit the area as a kid.

Finally, they reached a mostly hidden dirt path that veered away from the main road and led directly to a clearing alongside a river. It didn't appear as if anyone had used the road in quite some time. The low-riding Buick had trouble navigating the dirt road because the grass had grown high between two muddy tire tracks that extended the length of the path all the way to the river's bank.

Bobby parked by a dilapidated dock that was held together with rotting wooden planks.

Eddie struggled out of the car and hopped to the edge of the river unable to contain his excitement. He stared into the shallow, murky water for a few minutes as Bobby collected rented fishing gear from the trunk.

"It's amazin' how things change with time," Eddie said as Bobby joined him. "This fishin' spot don't look at all the same as it did when I's a kid. But it still smells the same. The smells I's a smellin' right now makes me feel ten years old again."

"Come on," Bobby said, helping Eddie onto the dock and leading him to a spot that seemed secure.

They sat on the edge of the rickety dock, and Bobby helped Eddie, his fingers gnarled from arthritis, bait a fishing line, then baited his own. Eddie excitedly casted his line into the river first as Bobby smiled and watched. He soon followed, tossing his line several feet past Eddie's line. Neither said a word for many minutes as they watched the slacked lines bob on top of the water.

Bobby broke the silence: "How'd you lose your leg?"

"Ah, Bobby," Eddie said, staring at the fishing pole he held, "I never thinks of that day. That's when I has a job. I have me a wife."

"You had a wife?"

"A very sweet lady she was."

"Where is she now?"

"I'm sure a better place than where I'm at. I don't know."

"Any kids?"

"No kids. I fucked it up before we has the chance to have any."

"What'd you do?"

"I was deliverin' seafood from a local fishery to the restaurants in the city," he said with a shake of his head. "But every mornin' I'd wake with a thirst for alcohol too big for me to control."

Eddie paused for a moment as he reeled in his line.

"And I always blow my money, Bobby. There's spenders and savers in this world. I'm a spender. If I gots the money, I spends it all 'til it's gone, never thinkin' 'bout the next day."

"So, what happened with the leg?"

"The drinkin' catched up with me real fast." Eddie pulled out a flask, took a big sip, and wiped his mouth as whiskey dripped down the front of his shirt. He swatted at the flies that buzzed around his head. He extended the flask to Bobby who reached for it and took a small hit.

"I passed out next to a dumpster behind a bar," he said, grabbing the flask for another sip. "I didn't even hear the damn garbage truck. It picks up the dumpster, empties it, and lets it drops down on my leg. It sliced it clean off right below the knee like a guillotine. Shit. . ."

"Jesus!"

"They put me in the hospital for a month. My first day out, I drinks me a whole fifth of Old Crow, and I was back to where I started. It's been exactly the same ever since."

"I'm sorry, man," Bobby said, reeling in his line.

"Ain't nothin' for you to be sorry 'bout, but you know, it ain't so bad, anyway."

"Why's that?"

"My life. It's simple, not complicated at all. I can't complain about much, really. It doesn't take a lot to make me feel good. Not too many damn fools can say that. They need everything to be happy—money, new cars, big house, vacations."

"Five million dollars," Bobby mumbled.

"I hardly needs nothin'. Maybe a cup of coffee that's hot. A slice of bread with a little butter on it. A stick of gum flavored with cinnamon. A friend," he glanced to Bobby. "You've been a good friend. I hate myself for takin' your money."

A fish suddenly struck Eddie's line, causing his pole to sharply bend. Eddie's body violently jerked forward.

"Woah, baby! Bobby, I think we gots us a big one! Help me! Help me, Bobby!"

Standing, Bobby dropped his pole and joined Eddie, wrapping his arms around him. They leaned back together and braced themselves against one of the dock's pilings, tugging hard on the pole as Eddie struggled to reel in the line.

"We got 'em, Bobby! We got 'em!"

With a splash, a large, reddish fish thrashed its body on the surface of the water as they fought to pull it up onto the dock.

"What is it?" Bobby asked, reaching for a large net.

"That's a red drum," Eddie said, straining to hold onto his fishing rod as Bobby scooped at the jerking fish. "The rich folks eat 'em in the fancy restaurants. They like 'em blackened in a grill."

"He's a monster!" Bobby hooted, finally getting the fish into the net and pulling it out of the water.

They dragged the squirming fish to the middle of the dock. Bobby dumped it out of the net as Eddie stood with the help of his crutches and pulled the slimy, fighting fish off the hook. He studied it a moment before holding it out in front of him. His grin widened as he awkwardly hopped to the edge of the water on one crutch with the fish under his arm like a football.

"You letting it go?"

"I have no business takin' the life away from this old fish or any other creature." Eddie tossed the fish so it splashed back into the river. "Swim on, my friend. Swim on."

They watched the fish a moment as it darted around in circles, dove deeper into the water and disappeared.

"It makes me sad bein' way out here, thinkin' 'bout when I was young, when I still had a chance," Eddie said, staring at the water. "Let's get out of here, Bobby. I wants to get back to the city. That's where I belong."

Chapter One Hundred Sixteen

Holly was a block from the club. She stood on the corner of St. Peter and Bourbon. She was paralyzed by fear—afraid it would be her last night alive. She couldn't risk confronting her father at that point. She was already late and knew he'd be intoxicated and out of his mind angry.

After staring at the blinking white lights of the entrance to her father's club for many minutes almost hypnotized, she instead turned and frantically dashed towards her apartment. She hoped Bobby would be there when she got back. She knew she needed to get out of town as soon as possible.

Chapter One Hundred Seventeen

Irritable and restless, Russell paced the club. He was sweating profusely. His heart pounded like it was about to burst through his chest. He had sucked down numerous shots of whiskey for most of the day, trying calm the fires in his head.

He eventually was right about business. As the day turned to night, the club had gotten significantly busier and livelier. All the stages were occupied with dancers, and the stools around them were filled with attentive and deep-pocketed customers. Unlike earlier in the day, his servers were actively delivering beer and cocktail orders throughout the expansive club. But he couldn't appreciate any of it. All he could focus on was the fact that Holly hadn't shown up.

"Where the fuck is she?"

"Don't worry about it," Todd said. "We've got it covered."

"She needs to fuckin' be here, goddammit!"

"Go home, man. We got it under control. Try to get some sleep."

"I'm going to get her."

"That's a mistake."

"Give me my fuckin' keys!"

"Don't, Russell. Go home. You need to sleep it off."

"Fuck you! Give me my keys!"

"You want us to go instead?" Todd asked, knowing that Russell wasn't in any condition to drive or visit Holly. He worried Russell might do something he'd come to regret.

"Give me my goddamn keys!"

"Russell? Don't do this."

Russell suddenly reached behind the bar and brandished the large butcher knife that Holly had hidden in her locker.

"Look what I found," he said, gritting his teeth and tightly clenching the knife's handle.

Chapter One Hundred Eighteen

The sun had started to set. It took longer than Eddie thought it would to get in and out of the swamps and back country. They finally reached the French Quarter. Bobby pulled onto Dauphine. The streets were quiet.

"Where am I taking you?" Bobby asked.

"Don't matter to me none. I gots nowhere to be."

"What are you doing tonight for Christmas?"

"The same thing I do every night. I sits and waits for a miracle. How 'bout you?"

"Run away from five million dollars."

"I'm goin' to miss you, Bobby."

"Take care of yourself, Eddie."

"Don't you worry about me."

"I'll never forget you."

"Nobody ever forgets me," Eddie smiled. He pulled himself out of the Buick with the help of his crutches. "No sir, not me."

Bobby laughed as Eddie shut the passenger door and leaned into the open window. Eddie's expression had suddenly turned serious.

"You, okay?" Bobby asked.

"I didn't want to tell you this, Bobby, but. . ." He nervously squirmed as they studied each other.

"Tell me what?"

"Bobby, your bro—bro…brother..." he stuttered.

"My brother what?"

"Your brother's dead."

"Chuck is dead?"

Chuck's unidentified body had rested in the morgue for weeks after he went missing. A city cop who occasionally drank at Delia's finally identified him. Ned was devastated. Arthur and Ben were let go. During the time Chuck was gone, Elizabeth would stop at the bar every day to see if there was any news about him. Immediately upon hearing of his death, she went to her apartment, quickly packed, and boarded a train home for San Diego.

"He got hit by a streetcar somewhere down by the river," Eddie continued.

"Are you sure?"

"Yeah, I'm sure."

"When?"

"Recently."

"Recently?" Bobby asked as Eddie nodded. "I was too late?"

"I's sorry, Bobby."

"An accident?"

"The fellow who told me says he jumped in front of it."

"Jumped in front of it?"

"That's what they think."

"Oh, God."

"I's so sorry."

"When'd you find out?"

"I just found out. I wasn't goin' to tell you." He grimaced. "I thought if you didn't know, you'd still have hope, and he'd live forever somehow that way. But you should know. Your family should know."

"Shit, Eddie," Bobby mumbled.

"I's sorry, Bobby. I hated to hear it."

"Are you sure about this?"

"He worked at a little dive in Mid-City. His picture's on the wall. His ashes are on a shelf behind the bar. The owner paid the cremation fee. No one knew where he came from or how to find his family."

"What's the name of the place?"

"Delia's."

"You're sure about all this."

"I'm sorry, Bobby."

"Thanks, Eddie. You've been a good friend."

"I did some mean things to you."

"Don't worry about it."

Bobby shook his head as Eddie reached his crippled hand into the window of the car.

"And I'm sorry about your brother, Bobby," Eddie said, wiping tears from his eyes as Bobby grabbed his hand and squeezed it. "Please stay in touch."

"I will. I will," Bobby said, releasing Eddie's hand. "Don't you ever die, Eddie. Don't you die on me."

"No, Bobby. Not me. I'm goin' live forever."

With a slight nod and an easy grin, Eddie hopped away on his crutches, quietly disappearing into the night. Bobby slumped forward and rested his head against the steering wheel of the car, too numb to cry.

Chapter One Hundred Nineteen

The sun had set. Darkness covered the French Quarter. Bobby was late. Holly anxiously paced about her apartment. Her packed bag leaned against the wall next to the front door. She walked into the kitchen and started to pour herself a glass of water.

She stopped and reached for an open bottle of red wine, pouring it instead. Taking a sip, she went to the window and peered into the darkness. She stepped out her front door for a better look and checked Esplanade in both directions. The street was empty and quiet.

Chapter One Hundred Twenty

lthough it was Christmas, Delia's was open, but no one was there. Bobby decided to make a brief stop before heading back to Holly's apartment. He quickly scanned the place and took a seat behind the many beer tap handles at the bar. The walls of the place were covered with beer ads and paraphernalia, numerous colorful posters, and several wall-size oil paintings.

The place was lit only by the blue and white neon of several beer signs located throughout the cramped and cluttered tavern. As Eddie had indicated, Bobby spotted what appeared to be a recent 14x18 inch, black and white, framed photograph of Chuck, prominently hanging on the wall behind the bar. At first, Bobby didn't recognize him in the photo because of his much chubbier face and longer hair.

Chuck obviously was happy when the photo was taken. He wore a wide expressive smile—the kind of smile one wears before breaking into an uncontrollable belly laugh. Bobby stared up to the photo for many minutes, unable to look away. He couldn't help but laugh out loud. It seemed as if Chuck had been waiting there for him and glaring down with a mocking, ornery look that asked, "Where have you been, asshole? I've been waiting for you."

Ned, the owner who was working the bar, approached Bobby.

"You need something?"

"A High Life and whiskey," Bobby answered, not taking his eyes from the photograph.

Ned quickly returned with the drinks.

"And can you tell me who's in that picture up there?" Bobby asked, pointing to the photo.

"That's Chuck. He used to work here. Great kid. A troublemaker and jokester. But a great kid."

"Work here?"

"Yeah, he'd been a bartender here."

"Where'd he go?"

"Sadly, he's no longer with us. Rest his soul. He was the best."

"What happened?"

"Died in a tragic accident," Ned said, studying Bobby who continued to stare at the photo. "You know him?"

Bobby shook his head, not sure how he should answer the question. He wasn't ready to let Ned know that Chuck was his brother. He hadn't quite fully processed his death yet.

"We didn't know nothin' about his past, like where he came from or if he had any family. I think he was from up north somewhere, or the east coast maybe. We tried to find his relatives but had no luck."

"What was he like?" Bobby asked, knocking back the shot of whiskey.

"Come on!" Ned enthusiastically grinned. "Are you kidding me? He's the only one who's ever worked here and got their picture on the wall. And we've been open for over sixty-five years. Like I said, he was the best! What a character, though. He brought the fun to this place. Everyone loved 'em. You should've been here for his wake! It was a hoot! He would've loved it!"

Ned stared at the photo of Chuck. He thought back to the night of the wake as Bobby drank his beer.

Delia's was crammed with people who had come to celebrate Chuck's life. The occupant capacity for the bar as set by the state's liquor commission had been exceeded by over three times what was allowed. It had been like that all day and into the evening. Feeling guilty about Chuck's death, Ned had decided to make all the draft beer in the place free during the wake. At one point in the afternoon, a beer delivery truck was summoned to replace all the kegs of beer that already had been consumed. The truck remained parked outside throughout the night as the beer continued to flow.

Chuck had made a lot of friends during his short time in New Orleans. And they were all at Delia's that day—drunk. There was loud singing. The jukebox continually played the James Brown songs he loved. There was much crying and hugging and toasts. The shots of whiskey and tequila flowed non-stop. There also was joke-telling, as many of the regulars made their best effort to remember all the stupid jokes Chuck liked to tell—always butchering them. He was loved by so many. And he likely didn't realize or appreciate it when alive.

At the end of the night while most of the folks were still there, Ned got out a ladder and climbed it behind the bar. He motioned to one of the bartenders to turn off the jukebox. The place went silent. He then unwrapped a framed picture. It was a black and white photograph of Chuck, smiling. Unable to hold back tears, Ned reached the photo into the air. The crowd at the bar roared in applause before starting unprompted into the Ewan MacColl song made popular by The Pogues, "Dirty Old Town." Ned turned and hung the photo on the wall as everyone sang the song loudly—for Chuck.

The homeless young man who often sold Chuck cue balls staggered in. With a heavy pack on his back, he fought his way through the crowd. His dog waited for him outside. The kid motioned to a bartender.

"Can I help you?"

"Is Chuck here?" the kid asked, pulling out two shiny white cue balls.

The bartender studied the kid a moment, then the balls, and glanced to the photo of Chuck that hung on the wall.

"Chuck's gone, kid."

"For good?" the kid asked, staring up to the photograph.

"Yeah, for good."

The kid briefly hesitated, then extended the two balls towards the bartender who shook his head.

"Sorry, buddy."

The bartender then walked away. The kid stood at the bar for a short time before putting the cue balls back into his pack and walking out of the place.

"Can I have another?" Bobby asked, bringing Ned back to reality. Bobby pushed the empty shot glass forward, before taking a large drink of beer.

"You from around here?" Ned asked, filling the shot glass.

"Nah, nah, jus' passing through."

"What brought you here on Christmas Day?"

"I was feeling a little homesick," Bobby said, downing the second shot. "Thought a beer and couple shots would help."

"I'm glad I could help someone," Ned said, closely studying Bobby who threw a twenty-dollar bill on the bar and stood to leave, finishing the beer. "It's been dead in here all day."

"About the kid's accident," Bobby said, motioning to Chuck's photo on the wall. "How'd he die?"

"Got hit by a streetcar. The driver claimed he didn't see 'em on the tracks."

"Was it an accident or did the kid—"

"Accident," Ned interrupted without hesitating as if there were more to story, staring into Bobby's eyes and not looking away.

"Accident?" Bobby asked again.

"Yeah, accident," Ned nodded, still not looking away.

"Okay, thanks for the beer and shots," Bobby nodded to him. "Merry Christmas."

"Merry Christmas." Ned watched Bobby leave, before studying the photograph of Chuck.

Chapter One Hundred Twenty-One

There was a gentle tapping at the door of Holly's apartment. Looking relieved, Holly rushed to open it, thinking it was Bobby. Instead, it was her father. Unsteady on his feet, he barged past her and marched around the small living room. His face was flushed, his pupils dilated. He reeked of alcohol. Holly immediately backed away and tried to keep her distance from him. He studied the lit Christmas tree.

"Where'd the tree come from?"

"What do you want?"

"I came by to wish my daughter a Merry Christmas."

"You need to leave."

"I'm not going anywhere," he said, nearly stumbling over the coffee table as he stalked her around the room. "You didn't show up for work today. I was short."

"I'm done."

"Done? Done with what?"

"I'm not dancing at the club anymore."

"You're not done 'til I say you're done."

"I'm leaving town."

"Where you goin'? You can't do nothin'. Strippin' is all you know."

"I'm joining a ballet."

"A ballet? What ballet? The San Francisco ballet?"

"How do you know about that?"

"Have you heard from them lately?"

"What are you saying?" She paused. "You didn't?"

"I did!" he smirked, clumsily tracking her around the room. "I sent them back home with their fuckin' tails between their goddamn legs! You still answer to me, my darling."

"You bastard!" she screamed, wildly swinging her right arm at him as he ducked out of the way.

"So, you better get that sweet candy ass of yours to the club as soon as possible. The place is bumpin'. And it will be that way until New Year's Day."

"No! I'm done!"

"Come on," he slurred, reaching for her. "Let's go. You got nothin' else, babe."

She slapped him across the face. He touched his cheek where it had started to bleed.

"Get out!" she yelled. "Get out!"

Angry, he grabbed both her arms, pushing her hard into a wall.

"I found the butcher knife in your locker!"

He pushed her again against the wall but harder. Crying, she scanned for an escape. The faint sound of a siren could be heard.

"So, you actually thought you would kill me, huh?"

"Beat your own daughter! Make her strip and entertain your disgusting friends so you can make a living!"

He pinned her against the wall; she spit in his face.

"You fuckin' little whore!" he hollered, violently pulling her from the wall and throwing her into the Christmas tree.

Holly and the tree awkwardly crashed to the ground. Glass bulbs and ornaments broke after hitting the floor. She was partially buried beneath the tree and tangled in a string of lights. Russell angrily kicked over the coffee table that separated them and stood over her. Blood ran down his cheek. The sound of multiple sirens was somewhat louder.

"Stop it!" she cried, trying to push the tree off her and crawl away from him. "Stop it! Get out!"

"Merry fuckin' Christmas!" he mumbled, grabbing her legs as she tried to get away and pulling her towards him.

She screamed for help. The door opened. Neither of them heard it in the commotion. The sirens were louder.

"You ready for your last strike, bitch?" Russell maniacally groaned, cocking his right arm.

It was Emma who had entered the apartment. She yelled, trying to distract Russell as she reached for a small lamp that had fallen on the floor during the scuffle. As she hurriedly approached behind Russell's back, she raised the wooden lamp with both hands over her right shoulder. But before she could club him, he hurled his thick right fist towards Holly.

"Strike three!"

The forceful punch landed hard on the side of Holly's face, knocking her unconscious. With all her strength, Emma slugged Russell across the back of the head with the lamp. Dazed, he slumped over onto his side and rolled onto the floor. The sirens blared louder.

Hyperventilating, Emma took several deep breaths to calm herself. Holly laid motionless on the floor. Russell rubbed at his head and moaned beside her. Nearly out of strength, Emma fell back onto the couch, still grasping the lamp tightly. Russell eventually lifted himself up, still rubbing his head and trying to shake it clear. Finally on his feet, he stepped towards Emma and stood over her. Holly began to stir. Emma noticed Holly moving. The sirens from approaching police cars were very loud.

"Run!" Emma yelled, trying to distract Russell. "Run, Holly!"

Dazed from the punch, Holly glanced around the messy apartment, looking confused. Her jaw was swollen. Her right eye had already started to blacken. Blood gushed from her nose. She clumsily pushed herself onto her hands and knees. Her vision blurred, she spotted her father, then Emma. Russell quickly turned to Holly who tried to crawl to the door.

"Run, Holly!" Emma yelled again.

With her last bit of strength, Emma yanked on the rug under Russell's feet, knocking him off balance just enough to let Holly scramble by him. At the open door, Holly paused as her drunk father staggered into a wall and fell to the ground.

"Go! Holly! Go! He'll kill you!"

"I can't leave you!" Holly screamed, squinting at Emma with blurred vision and her head pounding.

"Go! I called the police! They're on their way!" Emma continued to yell, nearly breathless. "Please, go!"

With a cloudy head, Holly glanced outside the apartment as Emma, hyperventilating, suddenly passed out. Russell's Cadillac driven by Todd, the head goon from the club, squealed to a stop across the street. Holly staggered back into the apartment and tried to gather Emma, but she was unresponsive. Russell grabbed one of Holly's ankles. She frantically kicked her foot free and forcefully booted him in the throat, knocking him back into the wall. She turned as Todd appeared at the door, blocking it. In a full sprint, she ran at him.

"Stop her!" Russell yelled from the floor, holding his neck.

Todd didn't react quick enough as Holly bull-rushed into him, forcing him out of the way. She sprinted in a stumbling gait over the uneven sidewalks of Esplanade, wiping at her bloody nose and crying. She ran into the hazy night and tried to disappear into the maze of the dark French Quarter streets. The sound of multiple sirens wailed behind her. Even in her compromised state of mind, she felt like a coward for leaving Emma behind.

"Get her!" Russell hollered. "Don't let her get away! Bring her back to me!"

Todd gave chase. Holly desperately checked over her shoulder. A couple of blocks ahead of him, she cut down an unlit driveway, before throwing herself onto the ground and rolling her body under a dumpster. She panted uncontrollably; her chest heaved in and out. She tried to compose herself. Todd trotted by and passed the driveway. She wiped at the blood on her face, trying to stay calm. She sighed, thinking for a moment she was safe. She then heard footsteps. Todd had backtracked and appeared at the entrance of the driveway. She spread her arms and legs out flat over the ground, as if trying to melt into the pavement. Todd slowly approached the dumpster. She held her breath.

Chapter One Hundred Twenty-Two

Bobby had returned the Buick to Tommy Black's, parking it on the street in front. He rushed inside. Butchie held up an icy bottle of Miller High Life. Bobby shook his head and tossed him the keys and hurried to the pay phone near the restroom.

Lighting a cigarette, he checked his watch and dialed the phone. The line on the other end rang several times before it was finally answered. Sounding weak, his father's voice came over the line and accepted the charges.

"Pops, how are you?"

"They're sendin' me home."

"Sending you home?"

"Yeah, from the hospital. They're tellin' me there isn't much more they can do for me here."

"How you feeling?"

"Bad. I can hardly eat anything anymore. I've lost so much weight."

"And the pain?"

"Real bad. I have trouble sleepin' most nights now."

"I love you, Pops."

"I love you, too, son. How's the hand?"

"Broken. They put a cast on it. It's supposed to stay on for a couple months."

"When you fightin' again?"

"Who knows? It depends if the hand heals up right."

"When you comin' home?"

"I found Chuck," Bobby said after a short pause.

"What?"

"I found Chuck. Can you believe it?"

"You found Chuck?"

"Is mom there with you?"

"She went home for the night. You need to call and tell her. She prays every night for him. How is he?"

"Great! Great!"

"Is he workin'?"

"Yeah, yeah! He tends bar at a hip little place in the middle of New Orleans."

"Is he good? Is he lookin' good?"

"He's great! He's very popular down here. You should see it. He found his home."

"How does he look?"

"Good, good. Happy. He looks very happy."

"You two comin' back here for New Year's?"

"I don't think he can get off. New Orleans is jumping this time of year," Bobby's trailed off. "But I'll see what I can do."

"You need to call your mother and tell her the news."

"I will. I will."

"Can I talk to him?"

"He's at the bar right now."

"Have him call me in the morning."

"Hang in there, Pops." Bobby paused for a long time as he listened to his father's raspy breathing. "I need to tell you something. It's been bothering me for years."

"What is it?"

"I was the one driving our car on the night Chuck and I wrecked," he said, again pausing. "But you knew that?"

"Your mother and I both knew."

"Why didn't you say anything? Why'd you kick him out of the house? Why'd you let him run away?"

"I thought it was something you two should work out. Part of growin' up, you know. Your mother didn't agree."

"I really screwed up, Pops. You don't have any idea how bad I messed up. I will hate myself forever. I wish I could go back and do it all differently."

"Me, too, Bobby. But we can't. Your mother was right. She's always right."

Dropping his head, Bobby gripped the phone receiver more tightly and started to feel nauseous. He tried not to cry. He glanced up. Butchie watched him from behind the bar.

"Hey?" his dad mumbled into the phone, sounding nearly out of breath. "Give my love to Chuck next time you see him. Tell him to call me and your mom in the morning."

"I will, Pops. I will."

"Knowin' he's out there. . ." his dad started to say but stopped. "Thanks for going all that way and lookin' for him. Your mother will be overjoyed."

"Merry Christmas, Pops. I'll see you soon."

Chapter One Hundred Twenty-Three

Bobby dashed on foot to Holly's apartment, knowing he was late. It took him less than ten minutes to reach Esplanade. He was not prepared for the scene that awaited him.

Red, blue, and white lights flashed repeatedly from multiple emergency responder vehicles. Three police squad cars, one unmarked detective's car, two ambulances, and one fire truck were parked in each direction outside Holly's apartment. Bobby stood, paralyzed in shock, afraid to get closer. A large pit grew in his gut. A sharp pain shot through his chest. He struggled to catch his breath. He expected the worst. As he watched two paramedics rush a stretcher inside the apartment, he dashed across the street.

"Holly!" he screamed. "Holly! Holly!"

As he reached the sidewalk in front of her place, he was immediately intercepted by two policemen. He struggled to get by them.

"Holly! Holly!"

He fought with the two cops until Russell was led out of the apartment in handcuffs with his head bowed. Upon recognizing Russell and noticing his battered appearance, Bobby wrestled more violently with the cops, trying to free himself. He thrashed his arms and kicked his legs, wanting to confront Russell who was marched by the pair of detectives to a squad car.

"Asshole!" Bobby hollered. "What'd you do to Holly? You asshole!"

Russell briefly glanced to Bobby without much of an expression before the detectives forcefully lowered his head and shoved him into the back seat of the police car. Bobby continued to struggle with the cops holding him, trying to free himself.

"Settle down," one of the cops said. "Settle down, buddy."

"What happened to the girl?" Bobby cried out, hysterically. "Tell me! What happened to the girl? I need to know! She can't disappear without me! What happened to the girl?"

Chapter One Hundred Twenty-Four

Bobby had been training for the light heavyweight championship of the world for over four months, mostly in New Orleans. The fight was scheduled to be in Atlantic City later that summer. He wanted it to be close to Baltimore so his family and friends could easily attend. Sadly, his father had died a week after Christmas and wouldn't be around to see him fight for the world championship later that summer.

Bobby had returned home to Baltimore during that time only once. It was for a few days for his dad's funeral. It was then he told his mother about Chuck's death. It was quite a blow she wasn't prepared for and could never fully accept. She didn't understand at first why Bobby had lied until she appreciated how prepared for death her husband was after hearing that Bobby had supposedly found Chuck alive.

Bobby was in the best shape of his life. His hand and other injuries seemed to have healed, at least enough to agree to fight Benitez, the champion. He had quit smoking and had cut back on the drinking, though he regularly frequented both Tommy Black's and Delia's, having gotten an apartment near the latter in Mid-City in New Orleans. But he hadn't seen nor heard from Holly since Christmas morning.

On the nights after her nasty confrontation with her father, Bobby had searched the Quarter for her non-stop, with little sleep or food. It had been almost four months since. He repeatedly called the San Francisco Ballet and checked their website. No one knew of Holly, and she wasn't listed on their roster of dancers. She had disappeared.

He hoped she was okay and prayed she was still alive. He didn't know if she had run away or gotten kidnapped by one of her father's henchmen. She would've contacted him, he believed, if she had gotten away. He also frequently visited Emma, who fortunately had recovered from her scuffle with Russell. She had not heard from Holly either. Bobby thought of her always, along with Chuck. It was good that he'd agreed to the championship fight. It gave him something to focus on other than Holly's disappearance and Chuck's death.

Chapter One Hundred Twenty-Five

It was the middle of July. Over twenty people filled the chaotic and noisy locker room in an Atlantic City casino, including Bobby's handlers, trainers, and Tony, his agent, as well as numerous staff from the arena and boxing promotion company. Two doctors had given Bobby a quick physical and collected a small sample of blood for drug testing.

The locker room was surprisingly small and quite hot. Bobby tried his best to keep calm, constantly wiping sweat that poured from his head, back, and shoulders. He sipped at water from a clear plastic bottle, trying to stay hydrated.

In a long silky gold and black robe, he sat in an open locker. The Polaroid of he and Holly standing in front of the Christmas tree was taped to the locker door over his shoulder. He stared at his taped hands as if in a trance. He flexed his right hand several times, hoping it would stay together for twelve rounds. His strategy for the fight was simple. His only chance, he thought, was to go for an early knockout.

Suddenly, there was pounding on the door. Tony and one of the fight promoters looked at each other and shrugged. The pounding continued. The fight promoter went to the door and slowly opened it. A security guard whispered to the promoter.

"It's a young woman," he said, after turning to Tony. "Wants to see Mr. Raymond."

"What's she want?" Tony asked.

"Says it's urgent."

"It'll have to wait," Tony said, glancing to Bobby who was at his locker taking deep breaths with his head bowed.

"She says it can't."

"How much time do we have?"

"Five, maybe ten minutes, at the most."

"Tell the guards to bring her to the door," Tony said, after a short pause. "I'll get Bobby."

Chapter One Hundred Twenty-Six

Still wiping at the sweat on his head and face, Bobby stepped out of the locker room. Holly waited there, flanked by the two security guards. She looked great, appearing somewhat older and more sophisticated. She had grown her curly blonde hair longer and wore a stylish black leather jacket and designer jeans. It had been a long time since she and Bobby had been together. His heart seemed to jump out of rhythm upon seeing her. Neither showed any expression at first. They studied each other a moment. Finally, she smiled and held out his grandmother's gold necklace he had given her.

"I figured you might need this tonight," she said as he took it and squeezed it against his chest.

"I thought the worst."

"Emma saved me."

"Where'd you go?"

"I ran away."

"Where?"

"I took a bus to California."

"Why didn't you let me know you were all right?"

"I wanted to make sure my father was going to prison. I didn't want anyone to know where I was."

"Mr. Raymond," the promoter broke in. "It's time to go."

"Including me?"

"I'm here now."

"Mr. Raymond, let's go," the promoter said, tugging at his robe.

"I start with the ballet in San Francisco next month."

"Your dream came true," Bobby said as the promoter pulled at him.

"Now do yours."

"It's time, Mr. Raymond! Let's go!"

"Where will you be?" Bobby called to Holly as the promoters and his trainers started to whisk him away.

"Waiting for you."

Chapter One Hundred Twenty-Seven

248

The crowd noise was nearly deafening, even in the locker room. Looking determined and sweating profusely, Bobby pulled the hood of his boxing robe over his head. He was surrounded by his trainers and handlers who massaged his shoulders and rubbed his arms. Before leaving the locker room, Tony motioned Bobby over and shouted into his ear over the commotion.

"This is it, brother! Like I said, fate has set this up."

"Fate is a rather cruel beast."

"Don't do anything stupid," Tony advised. "Take a dive if you need to. Remember, the money's guaranteed."

"I didn't show up here to lose."

About the Author

Jim Antonini is an award-winning author from West Virginia who has had three novels published by Pump Fake Press: Bullets for Silverware, a gritty, murder-mystery thriller set in the backwoods of West Virginia and a finalist for the Appalachia 2020 Best Appalachian Book of the Year; Like Falling from an Airplane, a romantic, urban drama set on the downtown streets and back alleys of San Francisco; Wild Bill Rides Again, about a socially awkward middle-aged family man who steals one million dollars and goes on an unforgettable joyride across the country.

Jim also co-wrote *The Hot Dog Diaries*, a book about Gene's Beer Garden – Morgantown, West Virginia's oldest and most beloved neighborhood bar. All four books are available online at https://www.jimantonini.com